My LITTLE SECRET

ALSO BY L.A. CASEY:

Slater Brothers series

Dominic
Bronagh
Alec
Keela
Kane
Aideen
Ryder
Branna
Damien
Alannah
Brothers
The Man Bible

Maji series

Out of the Ashes

Standalone novels

Frozen
Until Harry
Her Lifeline

My LITTLE SECRET

L.A. CASEY

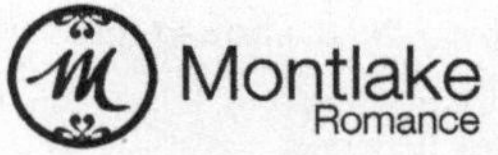

This is a work of fiction. Names, characters, organizations, places, events, and incidents are either products of the author's imagination or are used fictitiously. Any resemblance to actual persons, living or dead, or actual events is purely coincidental.

Published by Montlake Romance Publishing, Seattle

www.apub.com

ISBN-13: 9781477809563
ISBN-10: 1477809562

Cover design by @blacksheep-uk.com

Cover photography by Wander Aguiar Photography

Printed in the United States of America

My
LITTLE
SECRET

CHAPTER ONE
RYAN

"Ye' look like you're about to cry, princess."

That gruff voice destroyed the only inkling of peace I had managed to feel in the year since my entire life was turned upside down. But then why should I feel any semblance of peace, when my beloved father had none? Prison made inmates feel a lot of things, but I doubted that peace was one of them . . . especially when you were innocent.

"Ay, princess, I'm talkin' to ye'."

I opened my eyes, and focused my vision on the blurred trees that passed by at a rapid pace, and listened to the steady rumble of the engine instead of the godawful music that poured from the car radio. Taylor Swift wanted people to look at what they'd made her do, and I didn't want to. I didn't want to do anything.

"I don't wanna talk," I replied to my cousin Eddi. "I just wanna sit 'ere and think, okay?"

I glanced at her hand as she shifted up a gear. I hadn't had much interaction with her in eight years. Before my da went to prison, I only saw her at Christmastime, and maybe Easter if we showed up randomly at her house for a drop-in visit. Since my da wasn't around anymore, my auntie and Eddi were more active in my life, but just because they were the only family I had. I figured my auntie felt responsible for me, since she was the only adult I had left to turn to.

My only cousin, Eddi Stone, was nineteen years old, and from what I'd heard from my da she was a lovely girl, but from her sullen expression when she picked me up an hour ago, I knew she hadn't willingly offered to drive the two hours into the Kildare countryside to collect me and haul me all the way to Dublin. My auntie Andrea, Eddi's mother and my mother's sister, would have volunteered her, and unfortunately I was the recipient of the mood swing it created.

Just what I need, another headache.

"Look, princess," Eddi grunted, "we can play the quiet game as soon as we get home, and never speak a word to each other for all I care, but for now I want to talk. If ye' don't, I can pull over and ye' can walk your arse the rest of the way to Dublin. How's that for an ultimatum?"

I wanted to correct her on two things. Her home was *not* my home, and would never be my home for an abundance of reasons; and two, my name was *not* fucking "princess".

"Fine," I relented, and my fingers flexed. "Talk."

Eddi didn't waste a millisecond.

"Did ye' know what your da had done *before* he got arrested?"

The muscles in my jaw rolled side to side as tension filled my body. If there was one topic on the face of the Earth that I didn't want to discuss, it was this one.

"No," I answered through gritted teeth. "I didn't know, because nothin' he's been charged with is the truth. He's *innocent*, Eddi, we've already talked about this durin' his court appearance last year, *and* after he got sentenced. Ye' asked me the same question then, and I told ye' the same answer. I had no fuckin' clue about anythin'. I *still* don't know how it all went down."

"Bullshit," Eddi countered. "He openly *admitted* to concealin' evidence in a homicide case. They literally have his confession on tape. The news people said so."

I balled my hands into fists.

"He said what he did for reasons I don't understand yet, but what I *do* understand is me da, and he would *never* hurt another person, much less help someone who did. He seeks justice and sends the monsters who do those appallin' acts to prison; he doesn't help them get free."

Silence stretched out in the beat-up Ford Focus we rode in, but only for a couple of seconds.

"I think you're in denial, princess," my cousin said with a complete lack of compassion. "Your da was sentenced to seven years behind bars, and from what Ciara said to me ma durin' his trial, he'll most likely get between one or two years suspended for good behaviour, *if* he keeps his head down, but that's still a long time. He's already been locked up a year, and nothin' has changed about his case. He's servin' his time because he committed a crime."

My lip curled upwards into a snarl, and I managed to contain the outburst that was dying to be released, though barely. My hands trembled, and clasping them together only helped a little.

"Don't give me lessons on the law, cousin," I said, my tone clipped. "The law has been a constant factor in me life, or have ye' already forgotten what me da's profession is?"

Or was.

In a mumble she said, "A lot of good bein' a barrister has done for 'im."

I bit my tongue at the jab and didn't respond.

"I'm sorry," she sighed a moment later. "That wasn't funny."

"No," I agreed. "It wasn't."

I had found out early on in my life that Eddi was not a particularly jocular person – not from my past encounters with her, anyway – and so far, it looked like things hadn't changed. She was what my da would call a "free spirit", which I think was a polite way of saying she was a hyped-up female dog.

"Bitch."

The car swerved a little, and caused me to latch on to the handle of the passenger door with both hands.

"*Excuse* me?" Eddi blurted out. "What'd ye' just call me?"

I widened my eyes, shocked when I realised that I'd said what I was thinking out loud.

"Nothin'," I said, keeping my gaze on the passenger-side window. "I wasn't talkin' about you."

"Yeah, right," she huffed. "Ye' were talkin' about someone else who just insulted ye' then?"

I leaned my head back against the headrest and let go of the door handle.

"I'm not doin' this, Eddi," I said, hearing defeat in my tone. "I'm not emotionally stable enough to entertain a fight with ye', so do me a favour and leave it out."

She scoffed.

"And ye' think an argument with *you* will give me some sort of sadistic pleasure?" she sneered. "*Please.* The last thing I wanna do is talk to ye', let alone fight with ye'. I just wanted to get to the bottom of whether ye' knew what was goin' on with your da."

"And I already told ye' that I had no idea."

"But how? Surely ye' noticed *somethin*?"

I looked at her, and instead of snapping at her like I had prepared to do, I paused – because from her side profile, she looked exactly like my mother. From a particular picture that I had seen of her, anyway. She had the same-shaped nose, the same long eyelashes, the exact same plump red lips, and of course, the fiery auburn hair . . . features that I most definitely did *not* inherit.

Eddi looked more like my mother than I did.

I didn't have any memories of my mother, or none that I could recall very well at least. I only knew of her through dozens of pictures, video recordings, and tales that my da had told me. He portrayed my ma like a beautiful princess, but unfortunately one who did not receive a happily ever after. I rarely got sad when I thought of my mother because I never really knew her, but I sometimes mourned the relationship that could have been. She died from kidney failure when I was four.

"Princess," Eddi hissed, pulling me from my thoughts. "Ye' aren't even *listenin'* to me."

"I'm not ignorin' ye'." I blinked, turning my gaze forward. "I just have a lot on me mind. Don't take it personally. I think more than I talk, I always have."

I tensed when the engine made a suspicious sound, but relaxed when I looked at Eddi and saw she wasn't alarmed.

I swallowed. "D'ye reckon we should've just taken *my* car instead of leavin' it in the garage at me house?"

"No, I don't." Eddi snickered and patted the dashboard. "Don't mind 'er, Betsy."

"Betsy?"

"Have ye' got a problem with the name Betsy?"

I raised an eyebrow. "No, but I question your mental state for namin' your car in the first place. I didn't think people actually *did* that."

Eddi glanced at me but didn't comment further, not even when the car made the same chugging sound.

"Okay, we *really* should've taken my car."

"Relax, princess," my cousin pressed. "This Ford will get us anywhere your Beemer would."

"Alive?"

"Smart-arse."

"I'm not bein' smart," I stated. "I'm just—"

"Panickin' over nothin'," Eddi interrupted. "Relax, we'll be grand."

"Famous last words," I mumbled under my breath.

"Besides," my cousin continued as if I hadn't spoken, "there isn't a chance in hell you're rollin' up to me house in a virtually brand-new Beemer, and have people thinkin' me and me ma suddenly came into money. We've done well not havin' the house broken into the last few years, and your car isn't messin' that up."

I stared at my cousin, waiting for her to laugh, to smile . . . to *something*, but she didn't. I was already second-guessing moving out of the only home I'd ever known and into the house of a relative I barely knew, and to boot I had to worry about my security? *Forget that.*

"Get CCTV cameras, an alarm system, or a dog that's trained to—"

"We're savin' up for the first two," Eddi interjected. "We don't all have money to burn like you or your da."

I didn't respond.

"And while we're on the subject of money, don't let on that ye' come from it."

I furrowed my brow. "What?"

"We don't live in a pretty little village in the countryside with acres of empty land surroundin' us. Me and me ma live in a council estate, and not a particularly safe one at that as of late, so do *not* let on to anyone that ye' talk to that ye' come from a rich background, okay?"

I'd known she lived in a council estate; I could remember playing in her house when we were children. It hadn't seemed at all scary then, but if things had got worse over the years, I'd have to take Eddi's word for it.

I swallowed. "Okay."

"No one knows that we're related to your da either," Eddi continued, "so no one is goin' to know anythin' about ye'. So for the love of God, do *not* let anyone know—"

"I don't wanna talk about me da to *you*, Eddi," I snapped, "so there isn't a chance in hell that I'm goin' to strike up conversation about 'im with strangers."

Silence.

Eddi cleared her throat. "Right, that's good."

I folded my hands and put them on my lap.

"How long are ye' plannin' on stayin'?"

The question caught me off guard.

"I don't know," I answered honestly. "Me da didn't want me livin' on me own in the house now that Johanna's moved out. She's taken ill and can't work for us anymore. He doesn't want to hire someone new because they'll have to live with me, and I'm not comfortable around strangers."

Eddi nodded. "Right, I forgot ye' had a housekeeper."

She said it in a condescending tone, which told me what she thought of my family having a housekeeper. I didn't address it or acknowledge it in any way. I remained silent and hoped that our lengthy conversation had been enough talking for Eddi.

"Have ye' got a fella?"

Guess not.

I looked at my cousin like she'd grown a second head.

"A what?"

"A fella," she repeated. "Have ye' got one?"

I continued the bemused stare.

"I don't know why that would be a factor," I said with a slight shake of my head. "Is this girl talk? Is that what's happenin' 'ere?"

My cousin laughed, and from her tone I knew the joke was somehow on me.

"Eejit," she giggled to herself.

When she said nothing further, I pressed and asked, "*Well?*"

"I asked if ye' had a fella so me and me ma would be aware of 'im if he came round to see ye'. I didn't ask out of genuine interest in your love life."

That made much more sense than girl talk.

"Oh, right." I cleared my throat. "No, I don't have a fella. D'you?"

Eddi side-glanced at me. "Is *this* girl talk?"

My lips almost twitched. Almost.

"No," I answered. "It's just need-to-know information if I'm goin' to be livin' in a house where a lad comes and goes. I'd like a heads-up if that's the case. Like I said, I'm not very comfortable around strangers."

"It's not the case." Eddi yawned, loudly. "I don't have time for a fella. Me only relationship is with me job, and before ye' say it, I know that it's pathetic."

I didn't think it was pathetic, but I knew if I said that it wasn't, Eddi wouldn't believe me. A comfortable silence settled over us for a minute or two, but when my cousin took in a breath, I knew she was going to keep on talking and I began to feel mentally drained. I wasn't a very sociable person – I rarely left my house – so my conversation with Eddi was the most exercise my vocal cords had gotten since Johanna moved out of the house last week.

"Are ye' mentally prepared for this?"

"For what?"

"For the change in your life that movin' to Dublin will cause."

I laughed humourlessly. "Nothin' has been more life-changin' or has damaged me more than me da bein' arrested, then admittin' to the charges before bein' shipped off to prison. Livin' in Dublin will be a walk in the park."

"If ye' were livin' in a townhouse or a penthouse maybe, but ye'll be livin' in Tallaght, princess. Ye'll be roughin' it compared to what you're used to. Ye'll be livin' in a three-bedroom house that isn't big enough to swing a cat around in, and ye'll be surrounded by thousands of other people breathin' down your neck to boot. Not to mention the crime with gangs that's been makin' the news lately."

I wasn't sure if she was purposely trying to scare me, but either way, it was working.

I gritted my teeth. "I can deal."

"Ye' better," Eddi said, "because the last thing I need is to baby ye' after ye' have a mental breakdown."

I wasn't sure what I'd done to warrant her acting so cold towards me, but I wasn't about to let her know that her attitude hurt my feelings.

"I appreciate the love, cousin."

I practically felt her rolling her eyes. "Whatever."

I had been in Eddi's presence just one hour, and already it was enough to last me a lifetime. I didn't know how to feel about that, because Eddi . . . she was my only cousin. She was my family, my blood, but we didn't get on. Being around her reminded me why we never spoke. I used to tell myself it was because we lived two hours away from one another, but in reality it was because we lived a world away from one another. We went out of our way not to be involved in the other's life. Eddi looked down on me because she thought I was materialistic, and I looked down on Eddi because she made me feel inadequate for being born into a life of privilege.

"Don't worry, cousin." I grinned, slyly. "Ye' won't notice I'm there. Promise."

"I doubt that," Eddi grumbled. "I could smell ye' from a mile away. What in God's name kind of perfume *is* that?"

"Victoria Beckham," I huffed as I inched closer to the passenger door. "I only used two sprays of it."

"Two sprays too much."

I scowled. "You're unbearable."

"Says the young one who smells like a hoor's handbag."

I clamped my lips firmly together to stop myself from saying something I couldn't take back in the future.

"Are ye' done talkin'?" I hissed. "'Cause I am."

Eddi grinned as she drove, but much to my delight, she spoke no more. I tried my best to relax in my seat in the midst of the newfound silence, but I couldn't. I was agitated, and my cousin was entirely to blame. I thought about my situation – and my da's – constantly, but that was usually when my emotions were stuck on sadness. Thinking about it while being frustrated was almost worse. I had all this pent-up energy that I couldn't release, and it made me want to cry.

Being on the verge of a breakdown, I thought, *is the story of me life.*

One year ago, shortly before my eighteenth birthday, I had lived an entirely different life. I was effervescent, and often joked that my purpose on Earth was world domination. While I knew that I didn't have the brains for world domination, or the social skills, I did have the passion to put my entire being into something that interested me. But apart from that drive, I was blissfully mundane. When it came down to things, I was pretty ordinary in every area of my life, and I was okay with that.

I was what one would call spoiled, but without the "brat" that usually accompanied that word . . . or so I liked to think. My entire life had always consisted of two very important things, things that had been constant in my nearly perfect existence: love and money. Both of which were supplied generously by my da – Joe Mahony, one of the top criminal barristers in the Republic of Ireland.

My da was very well-respected in his line of work. He had a 93 per cent success rate, and considering he was up against the worst of the worst, day in and day out, in the Criminal Courts of Justice, that alone showed how good he was at his job. Though he worked a lot, and sometimes would be holed up in his office for hours, if not days on end, he never failed to make time for me, even when he didn't have any to spare. He never made me feel second-best to his job; he made me feel like everything he did was for me. I was his entire world, and I knew it.

I was, without shame, a daddy's girl. It was a bond that had been formed at birth, and grew in strength after my mother died.

That bond was why everything hurt so bad. The man I had known my entire life couldn't have done what he was accused of, because despite what people said he'd done – what *he* said he'd done – I refused to believe it. I knew my da, I knew his heart and I knew what lengths he would go to in order to protect people. He had been seeking justice on behalf of those who couldn't seek it for themselves for as long as I could remember.

He didn't do what he said he'd done.

I *knew* he'd done nothing wrong, even if the rest of the world didn't believe him.

CHAPTER TWO
RYAN

"Princess," Eddi called, pulling me from my thoughts. "We're 'ere."

I rapidly blinked, and looked from my left to my right, noticing we were now parked on a small driveway.

"We are?"

"Yeah," my cousin grumbled. "Ye' zoned out."

I felt heat stain my cheeks.

"I do that sometimes."

Getting lost amongst my thoughts was something I had been scolded about more than a few times while growing up. People would think I was being rude, and ignoring what was going on around me, but in reality, I was thinking. My da said I had tunnel vision, and I could tune the world out and forget about everything if I wanted to. I used to believe him until he was arrested, because when I tried to block that out, I failed.

"Look," Eddi said, focusing on me as we unbuckled our seat belts. "Me ma is chuffed that you're comin' to stay with us. She's been cleanin' like a mad woman this entire week, and she even got some new decor to pretty the place up for ye'. She thinks that you movin' in with us is goin' to change everythin', and that we'll finally become a real family."

I watched my cousin carefully, waiting for the catch.

"Okay."

"What I'm sayin' is," Eddi said with an unblinking stare, "don't disappoint 'er."

I didn't have a chance to reply as she climbed out of the car and forcefully closed the door behind her. I sat in silence for a moment, my eyes lingering on the now-vacant driver's seat. My mind was stuck on Eddi's words. *Don't disappoint her*. What the hell did she mean by that? How could I disappoint her ma?

It wasn't *my* fault that my da and her ma fell out after my ma died. My auntie had wanted us to move to Dublin to be closer to her and Eddi, but my da couldn't leave our house. It was his, and my mother's, dream home. He couldn't part with it, and he didn't want to raise me anywhere else but there. It caused an argument that turned into a feud for years, and it only dissolved when my da went to prison and both he and my auntie decided that being a family was more important than holding on to grudges. Though everyone was now on speaking terms, it was obvious that our "real family" was still a work in progress.

With a frustrated grunt, I exited the car, slung the strap of my bag over my shoulder and closed the passenger door behind me. I glanced at my surroundings, and blew out a deep breath.

Everywhere I turned, something was downgraded from what I was used to, and I hated that I noticed it. I was grateful that I had somewhere to go, I truly was, but I hated the situation I was in. In my head, I knew how snotty and uptight that came across, but I couldn't help that I felt that way. Moving to Dublin was not something I'd wanted to do, but when Johanna took ill and my da instructed me to go and stay with my auntie and cousin, I was left with no choice. Of course, I pleaded my case to my da that at eighteen, almost nineteen, I was old enough to live in our house on my own, but he wouldn't hear of it, so . . .

"Here I am," I sighed, finishing my thought aloud.

I turned to my cousin, who was standing at the boot of her car, leering at me with a sadistic grin. She was watching me observe the world she lived in, and it appeared she could read my thoughts that I wasn't impressed with what I saw – and that amused her.

"Are ye' goin' to cry *now*, princess?"

"I bet ye'd love that, wouldn't ye', peasant?"

Eddi's smile slowly slid from her face, and her eyes narrowed to slits as she glared at me, so I glared right back at her. If she wanted to poke fun at me and call me princess, I'd throw "peasant" right back in her face as quick as a heartbeat. I refused to let her think she could walk all over me just because we were different people.

"Whatever," she said with a shake of her head. "*You* get the box room."

As I'd been to Eddi's house a few times before when I was a kid, and in recent years at Christmas, I knew exactly what room she was talking about. Her house had three bedrooms; two of them were ridiculously misnamed "double" size and the other was *supposed* to be single size, but according to Eddi the room was dubbed the box room by the residents in the area because it was "as spacious as a coffin". All of the houses in the estate had the same layout, so the nickname caught on pretty quick, apparently.

Small room or not, I would thank my auntie profusely when I had the chance, because while I wasn't jumping for joy that I had to live in her house, I was extremely grateful that she'd taken me in when my da asked. From my memories of her, Andrea was possibly the coolest woman on Earth, which is why I didn't understand why her offspring was the Devil.

"Aren't ye' goin' to help me with me stuff?" I asked Eddi as she began to walk around her car and towards the house. "I've a fair bit with me."

She paused, turned, and mocked me by bowing. "Of course, princess."

"Forget it," I snapped, hiking the strap of my bag further up my shoulder. "If you're goin' to be a bitch, I'll do it me bloody self."

Eddi shrugged. "So do it yourself, I won't lose sleep over it."

She turned and walked into the house without giving me a backward glance. I glared at her back until she was out of sight. I quickly focused on getting my belongings out of her car, and after struggling with the catch for a moment, I finally got it open. The simple action caused me a pang of regret. For my eighteenth birthday, nearly one year ago, my da had bought me a brand-new BMW as a present. Now, staring down into Eddi's boot, I had never missed my car more. I never had to physically open it, I just pressed a button.

I shook my head, knowing I had to suck it up and learn to accept that my new life involved a *lot* less than what I was used to.

"Nice bag," a voice said from behind me. "Is it *Gucci*?"

I looked over my shoulder at the man who was speaking to me. He looked to be in his early twenties. He was leaning against my auntie's garden wall with his arms folded on top of the bricks and his chin resting on them. From what I could see he was tall, had jet-black hair and a thick pink scar on his face that ran in a jagged pattern from under his left eye down to his neck, disappearing beneath his jacket. He had slightly crooked, white teeth that seemed to gleam when he smiled, too. I didn't know why, but the vibe I got from him told me he was trouble.

"Thanks," I said curtly. "And yeah, it's Gucci."

"Is it yours?"

"Is what mine?"

"The bag."

"Is the bag that's over me shoulder mine . . . what would make ye' think that?"

The words were out of my mouth before I could stop them, and my body instantly tensed as I waited for the fella's reply. I was relieved when he snorted and seemed unbothered by my sarcastic answer to his question.

He ran his eyes the length of my body. "You're not from around 'ere."

"How d'ye know that?"

"Because I know everyone in this estate," he answered, tilting his head to the side. "I'd definitely remember a pretty face like yours."

I tensed. "I'm just visitin'."

He looked at all of my bags in the boot of Eddi's car. "Seems like you'll be visitin' a long while."

I felt so uncomfortable that I didn't know what to do with myself. I adjusted the strap of my bag once more just to give myself something to do; the man's eyes locked on it again.

"Ye' look very put together, if ye' don't mind me sayin', love. Ye' look . . . expensive."

My heart pounded in my chest, and I blurted out, "The bag's a knockoff, it's not real."

That seemed to surprise him, but before he could say something, he looked over my shoulder and with a wicked grin he said, "Heya, Andie. How are ye' on this fine night?"

"Clear off, Anto," my auntie demanded as she approached me. "I won't have ye' hangin' around me property and botherin' me niece."

"I was just sayin' hello to your *niece*," Anto said, his eyes moving back to mine. "Ye' know me, I'm basically the street's welcomin' committee. I didn't want to leave the poor young one without a fair greetin'. What kinda man would I be if I didn't say 'ello?"

He sounded innocent enough, but my gut told me he was anything but.

"I don't care, Anto. Now clear off."

Anto grinned, flicked his bright blue eyes to me and winked. "See ye' around, good-lookin'."

He turned and walked over to a bunch of young fellas sitting on the wall of someone's garden opposite my auntie's house, who were all wearing a lot of dark-coloured clothing. They all looked in my direction after Anto spoke to them, so I spun around and busied myself with my bags. My auntie came to my side and helped me, so it only took one trip to get everything into the house. The second the door was closed and locked shut, she twirled to face me, and her face lit up with what I can only describe as pure joy.

"Ryan! Honey, *look* at ye'. You're beautiful."

I felt my cheeks heat up as I smiled. "Thanks, Andrea. It's so good to see ye'. It's been a while."

Nearly a year to the day since I last saw her. I'd refused to see her, or Eddi, after my da went to prison. I retreated into myself and the only person I spoke to was Johanna.

"That it has, honey."

When she stepped forward and wrapped her arms around me in an embrace that would rival a boa constrictor, I found that I didn't have to put effort into returning her affection, it just came naturally. I was genuinely happy to see her, and it was in that moment I had never been happier to be in family's presence. Even if we weren't the most functional family, we were still family.

"I've missed ye' somethin' terrible, hon," she said when we separated. "You *and* that father of yours."

I forced a smile. "You and me both."

"I'll be visitin' 'im soon," she assured me. "Gettin' the weekend off work lately has been a nightmare."

My auntie seemed to sense my mood change at the mention of my da, because she shouted for Eddi.

"Yeah, Ma?" my cousin answered as she walked out of the sitting room, sipping from a can of Diet Coke. "What's up?"

"Help Ryan upstairs with 'er bags."

Eddi looked down at my bags, then back up to her ma. I knew she wanted to make some sort of snotty comment, but with her ma being present she seemed to hold her tongue, which amused me greatly. She didn't speak, only nodded as she placed her can on an end table in the hallway, turned and grabbed two of my duffel bags, then without a word, hauled them upstairs. I didn't want to stir things up any more than they already were with her, so I grabbed my remaining two bags, fixed my handbag over my shoulder again, and after giving my auntie a quick reassuring smile, I followed Eddi up the stairs.

When I was in my new room, I made sure to keep my displeasure to myself so as not to upset Eddi, who was watching me intently as I glanced around. When she left me alone, I looked around once more and sighed. It was even smaller than I remembered – a *lot* smaller.

Eddi had informed me earlier that her mother had got me a new single bed, as well as a new mattress, and that they'd moved in Eddi's old chest of drawers so I'd have some storage space. She'd hung a rack on the back of the door so I'd have somewhere to hang my coat, and put a few other things up, but that was it.

The decor was simple, but pretty. Bright, colourful wallpaper with sparkly silver paint splashes that gave the illusion the room was bigger than it was, but only just. I noticed my bed was made up with silver duvet covers too, and I momentarily wondered if it was my auntie or cousin's idea to keep with the theme. With a shake of my head to clear it, I got to work. Unpacking my bags and placing my clothes into the chest of drawers took my mind off my situation. It took half an hour, but after I pushed my now-empty duffel bags under the bed, I placed my hands on my hips and looked around the room.

My room, I mentally corrected in the hope that I would get used to that fact soon.

My portable prized possessions, besides my car back at my actual home, were my MacBook, iPhone, iPad, and iPod, and they were neatly spaced out on my bed. I didn't realise how many Apple products I owned until they were lined up next to one another, and these weren't including my spares. My make-up and make-up brushes were lined up in order of use, and I knew I had to be careful with them so they would last for my time here, as I couldn't afford any replacement make-up, not until I got a job somewhere. I had access to my da's money, but now that he wasn't around, it felt wrong to spend it. I wanted to get a job so

I wasn't a burden to my auntie, but I didn't even know where to apply for one because I had no work experience.

A soft knock on my door got my attention.

"Come in," I called.

The door opened, and my cousin stepped inside.

"Me ma wanted me to tell ye' that dinner is— Oh my God, is that the new Beauty Blender foundation?"

I looked at the bottle of foundation Eddi was talking about, then back to her and nodded. I had a few bottles of that one, then others in lighter shades for the winter months when my skin became fairer.

"Oh shite, *look* at all of that. You've high-end, brand-name *everythin'*."

Eddi came to my side, and her eyes roamed over the make-up like it was a gold mine. To any make-up lover, it *was* a gold mine, so I guess I couldn't be surprised at her reaction to my collection. It *was* pretty amazing, and what I'd brought with me was only my travel make-up; it was nothing compared to my stash at home in my glam room.

"I've more in the duffel bag under me bed. I didn't have enough room for it in the drawers."

Eddi whistled. "You're lucky. I'd kill for make-up like this."

I glanced at her, and didn't see a stitch of make-up on her face. She was naturally pretty, so she probably only wore the bare minimum. There were days when I only put on lip balm, then other days where I went full glam for no other reason than I enjoyed the careful process of applying it all.

"Ye' can use it whenever ye' want; we're the same tone so me shade range will match ye' nicely. I have new sponges and clean brushes ye' can use too."

My cousin looked at me, and blinked, surprise evident on her features.

"Why would ye' make that offer?"

"Despite what ye' think of me, I'm *not* greedy."

I just wasn't used to sharing my things, because I had no one to share them with.

Eddi didn't respond to my statement, but said, "I can only apply basic foundation. I'm shit at contourin' and blendin' so it'd be a waste to use any of it."

"I can do it for ye' sometime, or ye' can watch me and see how I do it, if ye' want? Ye' can copy from me then and see how ye' get on."

She danced around my question and instead asked, "Did ye' learn from your da's missus?"

I bristled at the mention of Ciara Kelly, my da's fiancée.

"No," I told her. "Ciara and I don't get on all that well. I learned from YouTube tutorials and practice."

"Why don't ye' get on with Ciara?"

"We just butt heads, and always have."

Eddi said nothing further on the matter. "Dinner's ready."

"Be right down."

At the mention of my soon-to-be stepmother, I flexed my fingers in annoyance. I hadn't heard from Ciara in a long time, and I knew she hadn't been to visit my da in prison either. I never missed a visiting day, while she had missed the last eight months of them. He didn't want to talk much about her whenever I brought her up, but I knew he was worried about her and so I'd assured him she was alive and well. I'd had to call the firm my da owned to find out, because Ciara worked there, and the receptionist had confirmed she was okay. But it didn't make a difference knowing that she was okay, because she still stayed away from my da. Ciara had stopped visiting him, the man she was supposed to marry, and I wanted to know why.

I inhaled a deep breath, exhaled it, then headed to the bathroom where I washed up. After I walked downstairs, I paused for a moment when I entered the kitchen. My auntie and cousin were sat at the table waiting for me. The sight of them made me feel a pang of something that hurt my chest. I always sat at the table when I ate dinner, but this was the first time in a year that I'd have company.

"Sorry," I said as I took my seat. "I was washin' me hands."

"No worries." My auntie smiled. "It needed to cool anyway."

She reached for my hand, so instinctively I gave it to her. I watched as she took Eddi's hand, and almost flinched when my cousin reached for my other one. She did it with a bit of an attitude, but when our hands connected, she didn't squeeze my fingers to the point of pain, so I took it as a sign that maybe we could learn to be civil. I switched my gaze back to my auntie as she began to pray, then quickly closed my eyes and rid my mind of thoughts so I could silently echo her prayer.

"Amen," the three of us said in unison when Andrea finished speaking.

I kept my composure, but I was really freaked out. I had never, in my entire life, prayed before I ate. It was kind of nice, showing appreciation to God for enabling us to have food when many went without it. It made me think just how different things would be for me here, and about what else I might learn and how I might adjust. By the time my visit here came to an end, I could be a totally different person, and I wasn't sure if that was a bad or a good thing.

"Dig in," Andrea chirped as she began to serve herself from the assorted plates on the table.

I mimicked her and Eddi until my plate had cuts of meat, a scoop of mashed potatoes, a scoop of veggies, some roast potatoes and gravy. My mouth watered. I hadn't had a home-cooked roast since the last time I was in this very house, which was over two years ago . . . before everything with my da went to hell. Johanna had attempted it many times, but she never could get it quite right to suit my taste buds. As I ate my meal, I savoured each bite as if it were my last.

"You're a really good cook," I told my auntie. "This is delicious."

She smiled. "Thanks, hon."

"We can take turns cookin' throughout the week, if ye' want? I'm handy around the kitchen."

"*You* know how to cook?" Eddi said, and I wasn't sure if it was sarcasm or shock in her tone. I didn't care enough to ask.

"Eddi!" My auntie scowled.

"It's fine," I said, and looked at my cousin. "I learned a few months ago when Johanna started to feel sick and couldn't come to work as often. I hated gettin' takeout when she wasn't there, so I learned how to cook for meself. I watched loads of cookin' shows, and read cook books. I practised a lot, even though I burnt many dinners. I like it. It . . . relaxes me."

Eddi said nothing further, she just blinked as she digested what I'd said, then went back to eating her food. My auntie cleared her throat.

"I'd love ye' to help with the cookin', Ryan. It'll be nice to come home from work and not have to do it."

To me, that sounded like she was the one who did all of the cooking, and from the look on Eddi's face she'd just realised that as well, and she didn't seem very happy about it.

"I'll pitch in more with the cookin', Ma," she said. "Between the three of us we'll be grand."

Andrea was pleased to hear her daughter say this; I watched as her face lit up at the offer.

"That sounds good to me," I added. "Three pairs of hands are better than two. It gets the job done quicker."

"Speakin' of jobs," Andrea said after a few minutes of silent eating, "I put in a good word for ye' at the SuperValu where Eddi works, and ye' have an interview there on Friday. When I spoke to your da on the phone last week he said ye' wanted to get a job. I know ye've not settled in yet, so if ye' don't want—"

"No, Andrea," I interrupted with a smile. "I definitely want to. I didn't have a clue where to even begin to apply for a job, so thank you."

"Ye'll get the job," she said with confidence. "If you're anywhere near as hard-workin' as my Eddi 'ere, they'll never let ye' go."

I chuckled along with her, but lost my smile when her expression suddenly turned worrisome.

"I don't want to upset ye', Ryan," she said, gnawing at her lower lip. "But we need to have a serious talk."

My stomach churned with nerves.

"Okay." I swallowed and set down my knife and fork.

"Things around 'ere aren't like they are in the countryside," Andrea said with a sigh. "I know there are bad apples everywhere, but you've lived in a private house and were home-schooled all your life. We don't have anythin' like what you're used to around 'ere, and I want to make ye' aware of that."

I *was* aware of it; it was why the place freaked me out so much. It was miles away from what I was used to, and everyone knew it.

"I understand," I said tentatively. "Eddi already filled me in on what not to say to people about me background."

"Good." My auntie nodded. "But ye' also need to be filled in on who ye' should, and *shouldn't*, talk to."

"Okay."

I wasn't sure where she was going with this, but from the look on her face and her tone when speaking, I wasn't optimistic about it being something fun.

"Ma," Eddi suddenly cut in. "Let's not talk 'bout this. I'll fill Ryan in about everythin' later . . . let's just eat dinner for now. Okay?"

Andrea looked at me, then back at her daughter, and nodded. After that, we ate dinner and talked about a lot of things in general. I wasn't the best person to hold a conversation with, but I was thinking of it as practice. I was more of a listener than an active talker.

I'd been home-schooled my entire life, so I wasn't the most talkative person. Our house was pretty isolated, and coming into regular contact with other children wasn't a common affair. My ma had died around the time that I was due to start pre-school, and while I know my da had told me it was easier to home-school me because of the long commute, I'd realised over the years that he kept me at home with him because he needed me close. It made grieving my ma easier.

His overprotectiveness was also the reason why he never encouraged me to go and make friends, which resulted in me being somewhat of an introvert. When his career started taking up more of his time, he couldn't teach me anymore so he'd hired a tutor to come to our house and continue my education. My tutor had a daughter around my age whom she brought to work on some days, and I'd considered her my only real friend. Unsurprisingly, she cut off contact after my da was arrested and sent to prison.

My plan had always been to go to college and study nursing. When my mother was ill in the hospital, the nurses had seemed like angels who took care of her when she was in pain. That always stuck with me as I grew up. I wanted to be the person that could help someone else, even if only minimally.

However, when I finished my schooling, the thought of going straight on to college, and being surrounded by thousands of people, freaked me out. My da had just gone to prison, and I simply didn't have the mindset for it. Taking a gap year seemed like the most logical thing to do.

While I was in Dublin, though, I needed to work, to earn money but also to do something to rid myself of all the pent-up energy I had. To give me something to distract myself from my problems. I had the drive, and the belief to make a great career for myself in helping others, but for now I'd settle with nailing this supermarket interview and landing the job.

After dinner, we all cleaned up, then moved into the sitting room and watched some television. When it hit ten o'clock, I was ready for bed. I bid my auntie and cousin goodnight, climbed the stairs and went into my new bedroom. After I changed into my pyjamas and settled under the bed covers, the gears in my mind started to turn like clockwork.

As usual, my thoughts were of my da, and the reason he was where he was.

From the moment I'd learned of his arrest, and what he'd been charged with fourteen long months ago, I had been a mess of confusion. What he was charged with, what he'd *admitted* to, simply couldn't be real. Not him, not my da. The two months after his initial arrest flew by. He had multiple court appearances, and then suddenly there was a sentencing and he was taken away to prison. He'd been in prison for a year already, and I was no closer to accepting it. During his time away, the only anchor I'd had was Johanna, because she lived with me, and I managed to cope with her around. When she moved in with her family so they could take care of her, that was another blow to me.

It was a chilling nightmare – one I could not awaken from.

Nothing about it made sense. Arthur Hopkins had been a man who was heavily involved in the gangland crime that littered the country, but mainly County Dublin. As far as the Irish people were concerned, he wouldn't be missed, but in the eyes of the law he was a civilian who'd had his life unlawfully taken from him. Da had been the barrister hired to put the man who'd killed him in prison.

It was just like every other case my da took on, but this time, something happened. Something went so terribly wrong that Da was arrested and charged with concealing evidence in a homicide case. He had somehow come into possession of a CCTV recording of the murder, and without that evidence, John McCarty – the accused murderer – could have very well got away with the crime because the only eyewitness account had been recanted very early on in the trial. I wasn't sure why my da didn't reveal the tape's existence – without it a murderer could have walked free – and I couldn't get him to tell me why during my visits with him.

All I could get out of him was: "I had no other choice, I had to protect my family."

I had no idea who he was protecting us from, or why there was a need to protect us, but I desperately wanted to find out. I wasn't sure *how* I was going to find out. In fact, I had no bloody clue. But I had to do something.

Anything.

"Me ma wanted me to see if you're settled in."

I jumped with fright, and nearly fell off of my bed. Placing a hand on my chest, I turned my head and glared daggers at my cousin.

"Jaysus, Eddi!" I exhaled. "Ye' scared me half to death!"

She choked on a laugh. "Sorry."

I had never seen a person more *not* sorry for something in my entire life.

"Make some noise in future," I suggested. "Footsteps, a cough . . . anythin' instead of silent ninja movements."

My cousin grinned lazily. "Ye' seem settled enough to me."

With that said, she entered my room and closed the door behind her. "Can I chat to ye' for a second?"

I didn't seem to have a choice in the matter, but I nodded anyway.

"I want to talk to ye' about what me ma was discussin' at dinner."

I gnawed on my lower lip. "Okay."

Eddi leaned her shoulder against the wall and folded her arms over her chest. Her eyes were locked on mine, and her demeanour was the picture of seriousness. I knew the following conversation was *not* going to be about my make-up collection this time.

"Okay, so, we have gang issues round 'ere."

I couldn't speak, only stare. She'd said that sentence with such calm, I wondered if I'd heard her correctly. I leaned forward and waited for her to continue.

"There's one particular crew that claims the entirety of Tallaght as their territory. Basically, if ye' want drugs, they supply it. If some shite is kickin' off, they're usually involved in it."

"They?" I quizzed. "What's their name?"

"They don't have a gang name." Eddi shrugged. "We aren't in America, where they name shite like that."

I snorted, and my cousin assumed I was laughing at her.

"Ye' know what, ye' can find out what they're like for yourself if you're goin' to—"

"Give it a rest." I cut my cousin off with a frustrated shake of my head. "I'm not bein' a bitch and laughin' at ye'. I was laughin' at what ye' said 'cause it was *funny*."

My cousin couldn't hide her surprise, and that caused me to chuckle.

"Ye' need to stop jumpin' to conclusions, Ed," I said softly. "I know ye' think the worst of me, but I'm not as bad as ye' think. I'm not 'ere to bother anyone, I'm *here* because me da wanted me to be."

Eddi didn't look like she believed me, but she didn't threaten me again. I was taking it as a step towards progress.

"So," I pressed, "who're this gang of people I need to be wary of?"

"I don't know all of them, I don't get involved with the Disciples if I can help it."

"The Disciples? I thought ye' said they didn't have a name?"

"They don't," Eddi said before scratching her neck. "Not a gang name like Bloods or Crips, anyway. When people refer to them, they say the word 'Disciples' because that's what they are and it's caught on. Even *they* use the term now. They follow their leader, whoever he is, like the disciples followed Christ. Without question or hesitation. It's always been that way with them."

So, technically, they *did* have a gang name. I wanted to point that out, but seeing as I was already on thin ice with Eddi, I kept my mouth shut and nodded in understanding.

"So, about the Disciples, all I know is to tell ye' to stay out of their way. They're horrible people who do horrible things. Ye'll know them when ye' see them. They have a certain look about them, a different atmosphere almost. They're trouble, and not a crowd ye' want to be mixed up in."

I continued to nod because I didn't know what to say.

"It'll be fine," Eddi said after a prolonged silence. "I've lived here all me life and they've never bothered me. Except Anto Lynch, that is. Whenever he sees me he feels the need to get on me case, but other than that, they've not bothered me."

I made a mental note to remind myself of that just in case I was freaked out when I eventually saw one of them.

"Earlier, when I was bringin' in me bags, a bloke named Anto introduced 'imself to me."

Eddi grunted. "I know. Me ma told me about it. That's Anto Lynch, he's a big-mouthed dickhead, and yes, he's a Disciple. Ignore 'im if he speaks to ye' in the future. That's what I do."

I bobbed my head, terrified I had already come into contact with one of the people Eddi had warned me to steer clear of.

"So yeah," she continued, "they have sleepers everywhere, so watch out for them too."

"What's a sleeper?"

"A person who doesn't stand out as a member of their crew. Ma is convinced Mr Joe who owns the shop across the road is one of them, so watch your mouth around 'im."

"Okay." I widened my eyes. "But how am I supposed to spot them if they look normal?"

"That's the point, you're not supposed to. Just do what I do, and don't talk shite on the Disciples to *anyone*, okay? Ventin' to me is cool, but *only* when we're at home. They have ears everywhere, and startin' some shit with them is not worth it. Trust me."

Jesus Christ, this is too much.

"I got it."

"D'ye?" Eddi pressed. "Because we aren't in your castle anymore, princess. This here is real life, not some fairy tale."

I gritted my teeth. "I said I *got it.*"

"Good."

I waited until I relaxed some before I spoke again.

"Do any of them live 'round this area?"

Eddi nodded. "A few."

Oh God.

"Anyone in particular?"

"Ash Dunne."

"Ash?"

"It's short for Ashley."

I nodded. "So I've to steer clear of this Ash?"

"At all costs," Eddi said firmly. "Don't look or speak in Ash's direction. Ever."

"Oookay. Anyone else, apart from Anto Lynch?"

"Sean Dunne, Ash's brother. He's only a kid and he isn't bothersome, but Ash is raisin' 'im so—"

"Where are their parents?"

"Their ma died of kidney failure about two years ago, and I've never seen their da. It was always just Chloe, that was their ma's name, Ash and Sean."

My heart stopped for a moment. I knew exactly what the Dunne siblings were going through, because my mother had died of the same thing. I felt for the Dunne family in that moment. This Ash person shouldered the weight of her mother's passing, all the while taking over raising her younger brother. That was admirable in my books, gang member or not.

I couldn't begin to think how hard their lives had been. At least when my ma died, I had my father to turn to for comfort. Who did they turn to apart from each other?

"How old is Ashley?" I asked. "She can't be that bad if she's raisin'—"

"He."

I blinked at Eddi's one-word cut-off.

"I beg your pardon?"

"He," she repeated. "Ashley is a he, and he's twenty-three."

I didn't mean to laugh but I did, and it earned me a roll of her eyes from my cousin.

"You're laughin' at a lad with a name that's more common for a girl when *we* have the manliest names goin'?"

I scratched my neck.

"It's a contradiction, I know," I said before folding my arms across my chest. "When ye' think about it, though, I only have a lad's name because of *you*. At least ye' can spell yours so it looks different. I can't."

Eddi grinned. "Me ma and da were bein' cute when they named me. They only wanted one child, and wanted to call the baby after Granda in memory of 'im, so 'ere I am. Your ma and da lost the plot when they named you."

"Oh, right." I threw my hands up in the air. "We both know me name was picked because me ma didn't want *you* to have to suffer alone with a lad's name in life. Our mas were pregnant at the same time when they decided this. They saddled me horse to yours, so if *you* were goin' down, then I was goin' down with ye'."

Both Eddi and I laughed, thinking of our parents, but after a few moments, the sound stopped and the smiles slipped away. Our names had a sweet story, but the reality was that, apart from having male names, we had nothing in common. We weren't close, not even remotely, and I knew how sad that was without anyone having to tell me.

"So." I cleared my throat. "Ash Dunne is bad news?"

"Yeah, he's one of the big shots within the Disciples unit. If ye' see blue lights flashin' up the road, it's usually the guards, or paramedics, makin' a call at his house."

"Ye' say that like it's the norm."

"It is." Eddi shrugged. "His house gets raided a lot, and sometimes a member of his crew gets hurt there and someone off the street calls an ambulance."

"How d'ye know it's someone off the street?" I quizzed.

"Because," Eddi answered with a chortle, "the Disciples don't *willingly* go to the hospital when they're hurt. They've got a private doctor to take care of them, under the radar. Everyone knows that."

I was sure there was a reason for that, but I really didn't want to know it.

"I'm goin' to get some sleep," Eddi suddenly said, and pushed away from the wall. "Remember what I've said. G'night."

"Night."

She left my room and closed the door behind her. I stared at the closed door, and for the millionth time I wondered why I'd agreed to move here. I knew there were bad souls everywhere, but living in close proximity to the very people who contributed to the gangland troubles that rocked the county was not a comforting feeling.

I did my best to force all thoughts from my mind, but as usual my subconscious drifted to my da, and I wondered how he was doing. Was he in his cell? Was he okay? Had anyone hurt him? Was he scared? The latter was the worst to come to terms with. I didn't want him to feel fear, not where he was.

I lay back, rested my head on my pillow, and just like every other night since he'd gone to prison, I cried myself to sleep.

CHAPTER THREE
ASHLEY

"Are ye' goin' to cry, princess?"

I held back a sigh filled with despair, because no one would ever know, or understand, how much I wanted to fucking cry. I couldn't show that kind of weakness though, which is why my emotions turned to rage whenever something went wrong in my life. I turned my murderous gaze onto my too-cheerful best friend, Anto Lynch, and all but snarled at him.

I wanted to punch him for his taunting, even if it was playful, but I didn't. I turned away from him and didn't waste a second longer on focusing my energy on him, because he was not the cause of my anger. No, the source of my problem was the piece of shite who'd broken into my house and ransacked the place. It looked like whoever did it was in a hurry, because the only room that was turned upside down was the sitting room. From what I could see, anything of value was broken beyond repair, but that wasn't what made me furious.

Someone had been in my home when I wasn't there, and the feeling that brought was sickening.

"Don't start with me," I warned my mate. "I'm seein' red right now."

"I'm leggin' it then, 'cause I'm not about to be your punchin' bag."

"Shut the fuck up," I snapped at Anto's teasing. "Help me clean this shite up before Sean gets home from school. I don't want 'im to see any of this."

"Look at the place," Anto said, gesturing to the room with his hands. "The two of us won't be able to clean all this up, not by the time he gets home from after-school club anyway."

"So call some of the lads," I griped. "And warn them, if they flake, I'm goin' to shove me fist down their throats."

"I'm sure they'll be more than happy to help us once I relay those words of encouragement."

I ignored his tone as he got out his phone – a brand-new phone that I had never seen before – and began tapping on the screen.

"Where did ye' get that?" I asked, nodding towards the new Android.

He grinned. "It fell off the back of a lorry."

It was stolen, then.

"How much to get me one?" I questioned. "Me iPhone is on its last legs, and I'm not due an upgrade for another year."

"No money." Anto waved a hand. "I've a shiteload of them, I'll grab one for ye' later."

"Nice one."

"I would have brought one over with me if I knew ye' wanted an Android. You're normally an Apple hoor, so I figured ye' didn't want one."

Even though I was seething with anger, I managed a chuckle.

"I'm not a picky man," I said with a forced grin. "I like different brands . . . all shapes and sizes too."

"Are we still talkin' 'bout phones?"

"Nah."

"I know, that's right," he chortled, still tapping on the screen of his phone. "Ye' fuck more slags than I do, and *that*'s sayin' somethin'."

I lost my grin.

"Ye' can't be nice to women's faces then call them slags behind their backs *after* they have sex with ye', man. That's tasteless, even for you."

"Sure I can," Anto countered with a one-shoulder shrug. "They love when I'm an arsehole and insult them, though I really don't understand why they find it so attractive. I wouldn't put up with that kind of disrespect. Not a hope in hell."

At that, I laughed.

"You're a thick."

"I'm aware," he said, then clapped his hand against my arm. "While we're speakin' of birds, did I tell ye' about the beaut that just moved in down the road?"

That perked my interest. "No?"

"*Mate!*" He purred, or tried to, as he jokingly pumped his hips back and forth. "She is *unreal.* She's Eddi's cousin."

"Eddi Stone?" I questioned. "I didn't think she had family other than 'er ma."

"Me either, but she has, and she's a proper ride if I've ever seen one," Anto said, waggling his brows. "I think she's stayin' with them for a while. I saw them carry a lot of bags into their house for 'er last night. 'Er arse is edible."

"What's 'er name?"

He thought about that for a moment, then cringed. "I didn't get that far. Andie ran me off before she'd had the chance to tell me."

Amusement filled me. "That woman has as much bite as she does bark."

"I know," Anto hummed. "I always wonder if Eddi has that fire, but she practically runs in the opposite direction whenever I'm close to 'er, so I guess not."

"Ye' know good and well that 'er ma warned 'er off comin' near any of us," I chuckled. "No one wants their daughter ruined by a Disciple."

"True." My friend grinned. "But that's never stopped us. Those good girls always want to set a Disciple on a righteous path, and they think theirs is the fanny to do it. Who am I to deter them from their goal of makin' us bad lads good?"

With a shake of my head, I turned from Anto and stared down at my smashed-up sixty-inch plasma TV. I had only bought it a week ago, and already it was ruined. I lost any trace of humour and gritted my teeth.

"Who would have the neck to do this to me?" I thought out loud. "This is too ballsy."

Anto tucked his phone back into his jeans pocket.

"Someone with a death wish," he answered. "Who would run the risk of messin' with one of us? Everyone knows they'd get broken up for a hell of a lot less. We're Disciples, *no one* fucks with us."

I ran my fingers through my hair in frustration.

"Today, someone did. No one comes to mind about who it could be though, and I don't like that."

"Me either," Anto agreed. "This was personal though . . . they stabbed holes in your pictures for fuck's sake. In your face, and Sean's."

Rage flowed through my veins at the thought of someone threatening my little brother. The ruined photos were the first thing I'd noticed when I entered the room, and they made me sick.

"Bin all the pictures, and the frames too. I'll get new ones."

"I'm sorry about the photos, man. I know ye' loved the ones of your ma—"

"They were copies." I cut Anto off, not wanting him to talk about her. "I have the originals in me floor safe upstairs, and I have extra copies backed up on a memory stick. I'll get them printed out again, don't worry 'bout it."

Anto seemed to relax. "Thank fuck for that at least."

I nodded in agreement. We got started on the cleaning while we waited for some of our lads to show up, and it didn't take them long. There was a knock on the front door ten minutes later, which I was glad to hear. I opened the door and slapped my hands against my mates' as they filed into my house one by one.

"Who the fuck did this?" Deco Lane demanded when he observed the scene.

Deco was a six-foot-five mountain of muscle, but he didn't have the heart of stone to match it. We had grown up together, been mates all throughout school and still kept our friendship going when we became Disciples. He had a similar temperament to me, and right now he looked as feral as I felt.

"No clue yet," I said. "But don't worry . . . I'll find out."

"And when ye' do," Deco continued, "let me get a few hits in. I could be gettin' me hole instead of bein' 'ere cleanin' up this prick's mess."

Amused, I patted him on the shoulder.

"I appreciate the sacrifice, man. I'm sure Beanie is gutted he isn't gettin' pounded by ye' right about now as well."

Deco shook his head, grinning as he moved over to Josh Doyle, aka Doyler, who was holding a roll of black bin liners. I caught it when he threw it my way, pulled off a bag of my own and got to work binning everything that I deemed worthless. I shook my head when I heard Anto on the phone asking someone to get a skip to my house within the hour. I knew he'd get one too; no one could ever seem to say no to Anto. The charming bastard that he was.

Between the four of us, we managed to get the entire house clean and tidy two hours before Sean normally got home from after-school. The rubbish was taken away in Anto's mate's skip, so there was no evidence of what had happened. What was even better was that Anto's current girl went shopping for me when she stopped by to help us. Out of the money I gave her, she got me new lamps, new picture frames, the same photos as before reprinted, new cushions for the settee, new curtains, and some random decor stuff that she said I *had* to have. She bought me a duplicate television from Argos, too. While we cleaned and put the television up on the wall, she placed the items around the room, and when I stopped to look around, I had to admit she'd done a good job.

"Thanks, gorgeous," I said as I bent down and gave her a lengthy kiss, suggestively hugging her body to mine. The girl's hand wasted no time in finding its way to my cock. She palmed it until I had a pretty decent semi going. I grinned into her kiss, and just as I was about to pull her outside where there was *some* privacy, I leaned away and winced as a slap was delivered to the back of my head.

"Hands off, dickface."

I slung my arm over the girl's shoulders. "Don't be jealous."

"I've nothin' to be jealous about," Anto deadpanned. "Tell me 'er name."

I drew a blank, and everyone laughed, even the girl.

"It's Kara," she said, winking up at me.

I grinned at her, then looked at Anto.

"Can I have five minutes alone with *Kara*?"

"Five minutes is embarrassin', mate," Deco said as he sat on the settee, tapping on the screen of his phone. "Say fifteen to save face, at least."

My lips twitched at his jibe, but my eyes were on Anto. He knew me, and when I was angry and couldn't take it out on the source of that anger, sex was the best outlet. Anto rolled his eyes, which I knew meant yes to my question. Without a word, I pulled Kara out into the hall and shut the sitting-room door behind us.

"I don't fuck girls that Anto fucks," I told her, moving her down into the kitchen, where I closed the door and pressed my back against the wood.

She laughed. "Bro code?"

"Precisely." I licked my lips. "We share, but only to a certain extent."

"Fine," she said as she reached for the hem of her dress and pulled it over her body. "I'll suck ye' off, and you—"

"I'll finger ye'," I interrupted, staring at her lacy black bra and barely-there thong. "I don't do oral sex on women I don't have an established relationship with, d'ye understand?"

Kara plastered herself against me. "But that's not fair, Ash."

"I'll make ye' come, don't worry."

With that promise, she dropped to her knees before me, undid my trousers, pulled my briefs down to my mid-thigh and took my semi-hard cock in her hand. I placed my hand on her head as she attempted to lick the head. She looked up at me and I exhaled. She looked like sin on her knees before me, and the sight caused my cock to harden in her hand.

"I have to put a condom on," I told her. "It's in me back pocket."

She rolled her pretty blue eyes, reached into said back pocket, and pulled out the packet. As she focused on that, I flicked my eyes up to the clock, remembering the time so I could hold back from coming too soon. Deco was right – anything under five minutes was embarrassing.

"I'm goin' to start doin' this in future," Kara told me as she opened the packet and rolled it on with her fingers, drawing my eyes down to said fingers. "I need to protect meself from STIs."

"Good girl," I said, smoothing stray hairs away from her face. "Your safety should always be your first priority, and if some chap doesn't like it, he can lump it."

"For sayin' that," she said as she leaned in and swirled her tongue around the head of my cock, making it as hard as can be, "I'm going to make your knees weak."

I sucked in a breath and flattened my palms against the door behind me as she took my length to the base of her throat and swallowed.

"Christ," I exhaled, lifting one hand to her head to tangle it in her hair. "*Fuck!*"

Kara spent her time slowly, painstakingly, deep-throating me until my eyes threatened to stay crossed for the rest of my days. She spent so much time doing this, I wondered how long she'd had me in her mouth but I didn't want to look to find out. Each time the head of my cock hit the back of her throat, she swallowed, and the muscles of her throat contracted around me, squeezing me like a vice. I'd never experienced that before, and I knew that I never wanted another blow job again, unless it involved that particular detail.

"Kara," I hissed as a shudder ran through me. "Yes, baby."

She hummed and it sent vibrations to my balls, and the sensation caused my hips to involuntarily buck forward, sending my cock straight to the back of Kara's throat once more. She didn't gag, she didn't complain, she didn't stop; instead she encouraged me to do it *again*. She gripped my bare arse, dug her fingers into my flesh and pulled my hips forward, repeating the action.

I growled as I placed a second hand on her head, steadied my feet and began to fuck her mouth at an even pace. I looked at the clock and noted she'd been giving me head for exactly nine minutes. I needed to stretch that out, so I kept my pace slow and even, and thought of everything other than how good my cock felt.

"Fuck, Kara," I grunted. "Your mouth . . . *uh* . . ."

She hummed again, so I sunk my teeth into my lower lip, and having reached my breaking point, I picked up my pace and fucked her mouth with no remorse. Without warning, my balls drew up tight, and the contractions started and my hips began to jerk.

"*Yes*," I groaned as the pressure released itself in the first spurt of cum.

I held on to Kara's head for dear life as the pressure built again and released quicker. This followed three more times before I was spent, and my body sagged back against the kitchen door. My heart was still pounding, and my hands fell from Kara's head. I hadn't realised my eyes were closed until I heard a giggle, and I barely lifted one lid and looked down. Kara's smug face came into view, and all I could do was lazily grin.

"Enjoyed that, did ye'?" she asked with a shit-eating grin on her face. "Looks like ye' did."

Now that I had my bearings, I binned the condom, pulled up my briefs, righted my trousers and focused on her. As I approached her, she began to quickly back up, which made me laugh as I shot forward, grabbed her and hiked her up onto the counter. I parted her thighs, stepped between them, then caught Kara off guard by kissing her. I faintly tasted cherry, and reminded myself that was most likely the flavour of the condom she'd had in her mouth. My fingers brushed the fabric of her thong, and the material was coated in her desire. I hummed into our kiss as I ran my finger up and down, feeling her pussy beneath it.

This was the part where selfishness became me. I loved sex. I loved performing and receiving sexual acts, but since I never emotionally cared about any of the women that I fucked, once I wasn't feeling pleasure I zoned out completely while I pleasured them. While I fingered Kara, I was vaguely aware of how wet she was, how much noise she made and how hard her fingers dug into my shoulder. But I returned my focus to her only when her body sagged against me and her hips jerked away from my touch, indicating she'd come.

"Enjoyed that, did ye'?" I asked, repeating her earlier words. "Looks like ye' did."

She smiled at me, her eyes closed, and it made me laugh.

"Ash," she mumbled when she opened her eyes. "When me and Anto stop playin' . . . you and me are startin', d'ye hear?"

"Loud and clear, babe."

Loud and fucking clear.

I helped Kara down from the counter, and thanked her when she grabbed some disinfectant spray and washed the area down. It saved me from doing it later. Before we left the room, she tugged her dress back on and ruffled her hair. When we entered the sitting room, the lads were watching television. Deco paused what he was doing, looked up and said, "Five minutes, me arse."

My lips twitched.

I looked to my left just before Anto shoved my body away from Kara's, which made me laugh. She wasn't his girlfriend – he never had a girlfriend, just a woman he'd spend a week or two entertaining before moving on to the next poor soul. Most of the women any of the lads were shagging were part of our set, and those who weren't never stuck around after they learned just who their new partner kept company with. Not that I could blame them. If I was in their shoes, I wouldn't want to be around scumbags either, and that was exactly what the Disciples were.

Scumbags.

Kara, however, wouldn't be able to get out, soon enough. She'd hung around some of the other Disciples before she came to my set, and that told me that eventually she'd become one of us and this life would become hers.

"D'ye want a line?" Anto asked Kara, brushing her blonde hair out of her face. "I got a fresh batch this mornin'. I can have a runner bring me some if ye' want?"

She shook her head. "I don't wanna do the white stuff anymore. It makes me sick as a dog the day after. I think I'll just stick to smokin' weed."

Anto patted her arse.

"Good," he praised. "I told ye' anythin' other than weed wasn't worth it. When ye' start sellin', ye'll fuck yourself over if ye' use your own product."

We may be scumbags who sold drugs, but we were scumbags who didn't use drugs . . . except for weed. Nearly all of us smoked weed, but so did Mrs Dowling, the seventy-year-old woman two doors down who had a bad back, so it wasn't that big of a deal. If you used hard drugs within our little family, bad shite happened as a repercussion. I once had to enforce the rule of no drugs after I broke a member's leg when it turned out he'd been doing coke from the stash he was supposed to be selling. I didn't want to hurt him, but I had to; the boss would have someone else do a lot worse otherwise.

My boss, Mr Nobody, was a ruthless bastard, but abiding by his rules was what we signed up for when we got involved with him. Not that we knew better – when myself and Anto had joined his unit we were only thirteen. We were young and dumb, which is exactly why most of us got roped in. We would get fifty quid a pop for every job we did for Nobody's Disciples. Easy jobs like delivering a parcel to someone, of course, changed and got harder as time went on, and by the time we realised we didn't want to do it anymore, it was too late.

We didn't have rituals where you'd get jumped into a gang or go through an initiation like you'd see in films. No, what we had to do was much worse. We had to give our fingerprints, dental impressions and DNA. If we decided that one day we wanted to have a life away from the one we'd previously chosen, then Mr Nobody would kindly remind us that he had our lives in his hands. He wasn't big on killing his Disciples, as he, and everyone else, called us. If we didn't do the job we were given, those fingerprints, teeth impressions and DNA samples might just end up on a rape victim, a murder victim or – my personal favourite – on a tortured and left-for-dead politician or Garda.

Spending the rest of your life in prison for a crime you didn't commit was worse than dying. It was a prolonged death, where every minute felt like an hour and every hour felt like a day. A person had an abundant amount of time to sit and think of Mr Nobody – and that he was the one who had power over you. To be honest, that was true of the day-to-day too. The life I chose was hell, but I had to live it; my choice was taken from me when I jumped at the chance to make a lousy fifty quid.

With my mood sour once more, I left my mates to their own devices and headed upstairs to my bedroom to get changed out of my work clothes. I worked full-time for a construction company that had me out of the house every weekday. Even if I hated the job, which I didn't, I needed it in order to keep the guards off my back. Not having a job, while having a mortgage, health insurance, a hell of a nice home and raising a kid, wouldn't bode well for the tax man in the Irish Revenue office, or the social services for that matter.

My lifestyle had to match up to what I was earning at my job. Of course, I bought what I want when I wanted it, but previous encounters with the law had led me to be less materialistic. After my house was raided for the tenth time in two years, I'd stopped buying expensive decor items, because the guards would purposely ruin them during the raids just to piss me off.

You live and you learn.

Once I'd changed into grey tracksuit bottoms and a white long-sleeved T-shirt, I went into my little brother's room to make sure he had done his chores and left his space tidy before he went to school that morning. Checking up on him was a habit I'd formed – after all, I'd been doing it since I was twelve. I'd taken over being the man of the house when my piece-of-shite father left us and never looked back.

I had hated the man for as long as I could remember. The only memories I had of him were of him being drunk and beating on my ma and me, every chance he got. The day he left our lives was the happiest day of my life, but it did add weight onto my small shoulders.

Our father left us when Sean was four, so I knew I had to grow up fast to help my ma. I'd get up earlier so I could get us both ready for school and she could get breakfast and lunches prepared for our day. I'd walk him to school ten minutes away, then run to my school to make it on time before first period started, just so Ma was never late to work.

When school was over I'd collect him and care for him until our ma got home from her job. I'd have the dinner ready so she'd have one less thing to do in her hectic day. I wasn't perfect, though, and it took multiple ruined dinners until I caved and asked her to teach me how to cook properly. It wasn't long after that that I learned the rocket science that was the washing and drying machines.

I did all the duties of a father while still being a kid myself, but I never regretted my lost childhood. Even though I got involved with Mr Nobody early on in my life, and made my ma sick with worry, I was a good son. I did everything I could to ease her struggle, but I couldn't help what happened to her. I was eighteen when she got sick. We found out that she was in the mid-to-late stages of kidney failure, and after her diagnosis things happened at a rapid pace. For three years she fought long and hard, but the day after my twenty-first birthday she died in her sleep at the hospital. Her body couldn't fight anymore, and she slipped away.

That was the first time in my life that I could remember crying like a baby.

"Stop thinkin' about it," I said out loud, to rid myself of my thoughts.

I loved my ma dearly, but I couldn't think about her without feeling down. I hoped one day that would change, but right now thoughts of her made me struggle. I always tried to focus on the now. Thinking about what had been, and what could be, was too much for my brain to handle. I took it day by day, and that had been working well for me . . . until some prick added new worry to my life by breaking into my house.

"Good man," I mumbled as I glanced around my brother's room and saw it was clean and tidy.

I reached for the door handle and was about to leave when a piece of folded white paper on Sean's pillow caught my attention. I furrowed my brow as I stepped back into the room. I picked it up, unfolded it and read the sentence written in red ink.

U took who I love, so I'm takin who u love. Expect me.

"What the fuck?" I mumbled as I read the words, then reread them.

I felt fear. Not for myself, but for my little brother. This message, though on my brother's pillow, was meant for me. Sean was the only living person on the face of this miserable Earth who I loved with every fibre of my being, and I would die before I let anyone harm him. Not my brother.

"Anto!"

Loud laughter and talking came from downstairs, but no response to my call. Instead, I heard footsteps coming up the stairs.

"Where are ye'?"

"Sean's room," I answered.

My friend appeared in the doorway, and once he looked at me, he lost his usual happy-go-lucky grin and his face became expressionless.

"What's wrong?"

I held out the piece of paper. "It was on Sean's pillow."

He stepped into the room and took the paper from my hand. I watched as he read the words, paused, then reread them. When he looked up at me, I saw worry in his blue eyes.

"Someone's threatenin' Sean to get to ye'."

I nodded. "I have no clue who it's from, and I don't understand what they mean. I've never taken anyone from anybody."

Anto read the note once more before shaking his head.

"Did ye' fuck someone's missus?"

I scrubbed my face with my hands. "Maybe? I have no fuckin' clue. I don't ask about a mot's relationship status when she's up for sex."

I sat down on Sean's bed, and Anto sat beside me.

"We'll figure this out," he said, and placed a hand on my shoulder. "We know which neighbours have security cameras, I can go and check them out—"

"What're ye' both doin' in me room?"

Anto and I jumped to our feet, swung our attention to the bedroom's doorway, and it made my little brother burst into laughter.

"What the fuck!" Anto shouted. "Don't ye' know how to make noise?"

"I did make noise," my brother said, still chuckling as he wiped at his eyes. "Ye' both weren't payin' attention."

I took the piece of paper from Anto's hand, folded it and shoved it into my pocket. The action caught the watchful grey eyes, identical to mine, of my brother.

"What was that?"

I grinned. "Your Christmas list."

My brother regarded me, not knowing if I was telling the truth or not. Christmas was only a few weeks away, so for all he knew, I was.

"Can I see it?" he chanced.

Anto clicked his tongue. "Nice try."

My friend looked at me and said, "I'll be back later. I'm goin' to get that thing we talked about sorted."

Knowing he was talking about the neighbours' security cameras, I nodded. Anto made a fake jab at my brother's balls as he left the room, and it caused Sean to yelp and jump away, making Anto laugh as he made his way down the stairs. When my brother looked at me, and found me grinning, he stuck his middle finger up at me.

"D'ye want me to break it?"

"Like ye' would," Sean mused as he kicked off his shoes.

I ruffled his hair as I passed him by.

"Stop doin' that!" he snapped as I left the room. "How many times do I have to tell ye' to leave me hair *alone*?"

My only response was to laugh as I headed back downstairs. A glance into the sitting room showed everything was still in order, but all my friends, and Kara, were gone. The kitchen was empty too. I wasn't surprised that they'd all left. They knew I hardly ever had big groups in my house, for two reasons. One, I hated being around loads of people, and two, I didn't want Sean to be around the people I had no choice but to be around.

I grabbed some food items from the freezer, and preheated the oven so I could get a start on dinner. My brother came down the stairs, sounding like a baby elephant in the process. I looked out of the kitchen doorway and saw him walk into the sitting room. I waited for him to say something but he didn't. The kid didn't even notice a single difference in the room, which made me smile. He was oblivious to everything now that a girl was a factor in his life.

"Homework," I reminded him just as he went to put his school bag in the storage press under the stairs.

Sean looked like he wanted to thump me.

"Why do I even have to do homework, or bother with school at all?" he asked, frustration lacing his tone. "I don't need an education to deal."

I walked over to him and whacked him across the head, not caring if I hurt him.

"Ye' keep talkin' rubbish, and I'm gonna smack the sense that ye' seem to be lackin' into ye'," I bellowed. "D'ye hear?"

Sean rubbed his head and said, "Yeah, man. Jaysus."

"I've told ye' that ye' aren't gonna be doin' what I do," I said as I turned and went back to the oven. "Ma made me promise ye'd finish school and go to college before she died. She never wanted me in with Nobody's crew, so she *definitely* wouldn't want *you* in it – and I intend to keep it that way."

A glance his way showed that Sean was as mad as a bull.

"Look," I sighed, placing my hands on the counter, "being a Disciple isn't cool, man. D'ye think people look at me with respect, or fear?"

My brother thought about this for a moment.

"Fear, I guess."

"Exactly. Everyone round 'ere is scared I'll hurt them. D'ye think I'll get me a nice bird with a bright future, or a slag from the flats who uses or needs the protection of a Disciple?"

My brother swallowed. "I get it, okay?"

"I don't think ye' do," I informed him, and leaned forward. "The Disciples are only as loyal to me – like 'family' to me – because I do what Nobody wants. If I turn me back on them, on *him*, then I'm goin' to prison for somethin' I didn't do. Don't forget that. It's not cool, it's not fun and it's *not* safe. The people I ride with would ruin me life if they thought for a split second that me loyalty wasn't to Nobody. D'ye hear?"

Sean nodded.

"Good." I folded my arms over my chest. "Now, do your bleedin' homework."

"I already finished it."

I could tell he was lying; he couldn't look me in the eye when he was being dishonest.

I set my jaw. "Try again."

"Ash."

"Sean."

"Jaysus," he huffed. "It's two subjects, I can do it later. Be reasonable."

"Now."

"For once," he argued, "can ye' just let me do it later? Come on, man. I have a date."

"Your date can start fifteen minutes later because you're doin' your homework. The longer ye' argue with me, the later ye'll be."

With a glare of fury shot my way, Sean grabbed his bag and angrily sat at the kitchen table, dumping out the bag's contents. Most of the items remained on the table top, while others bounced off it and fell to the floor.

"You're goin' to be pickin' up every single thing that just fell before ye' leave this house, so if I were you, I'd rein it in before ye' piss me off entirely and I ground ye'. Ye' won't be goin' on no date if that happens."

He didn't reply, he only grabbed the items that had fallen onto the floor and roughly shoved them back inside his bag.

"You're not Da," was all he spat as he began doing his work.

Whenever he was angry with me, he tossed those words my way, and they stung like a bitch.

"Ye' think I don't know that?" I snapped. "I'm not Da, you're right, but I've been fillin' in for the piece of shite since I was twelve, and fillin' in for Ma since she died, so give me a fuckin' break, Sean. I didn't get an instruction manual on how to raise a kid while *being* a kid. I'm doin' the best I can, so just do your homework – and for God's sake, stop answerin' me back. First and only warnin'."

The oven needed to preheat for another ten minutes, so I left the room so Sean could do his work in silence. I went into the sitting room, and the first thing my eyes went to were the new picture frames, with copies of the photos the intruder had ruined sitting nicely beneath the glass. Just seeing the smiling face of my mother relaxed me a little. I sat down on the settee, grabbed the remote and turned on the television, making sure to avoid the news channels. I didn't watch the news, or read the papers. I did enough bad shite in my life and had my own problems without hearing about everyone else's. Ten minutes later, I heard Sean approach the sitting room, even though he was doing his best not to make noise and draw attention to himself.

"Ashley," he mumbled from the doorway.

Once he said my full name, I knew an apology was coming. I made him sweat for a moment by not looking his way and acknowledging him.

He cleared his throat, and he repeated, louder, "Ashley?"

I didn't look at him, but I did answer him.

"Yeah?" I said as I flicked through the stations on the TV.

Out of the corner of my eye, movement caught my attention. The settee dipped as Sean sat down next to me. He was tense. I didn't have to look at him to know that either, I could sense it on him.

"Can I talk to ye' for a sec?"

I muted the TV, set the remote down and turned his way, giving him my full attention.

"Go for it."

My brother's shoulders slumped, and his eyes were on his jeans as he picked at the fabric. Just then, he looked like the kid he was, and it only fuelled my desire to protect him further.

"I'm sorry about what I said, about ye' not bein' me da. I didn't mean it."

"I appreciate ye' apologisin', but I want ye' to stop throwin' that I'm not Da in me face. A lot of things don't faze me, but that gets to me. I'm tryin' to do right by ye', and bein' firm is the only way I know to keep ye' in line."

I *had* to keep him in line; I couldn't let him turn out like me. I just couldn't.

"I know. That's why I say it, to get ye' mad for makin' me mad. I won't say it again though, because I know that you're both me brother *and* me da, it's just . . . ye' really piss me off sometimes and I get mad. I know that's no excuse, so yeah, I'm sorry."

I knocked my knee against his so he would look up at me, and when he did I said, "I'm hard on ye' 'cause I don't want ye' to turn out like me. Your future is *my* future, and I want ye' to give it everythin' in school so ye' can have opportunities that I didn't."

"I know." Sean nodded. "And I'm doin' good in school because of ye'. I know that."

I bumped his arm with my fist. "You're a good kid."

A ghost of a smile touched his lips.

"I did me homework. It's on the table for ye' to check it."

"I'll do it after I make dinner."

My brother nodded, and remained sitting next to me.

"I thought ye' had a date?"

"Oh, shite. Kerry!" Sean's eyes almost popped out of his head. "She's goin' to bloody *kill* me."

I laughed. "Be back no later than half nine, and text me back when I text you."

"I won't be late, and I'll text back whenever ye' text me. Promise."

"And don't eat out," I warned. "I'll leave your dinner in the mic for when ye' get back."

"Okay."

That was all he said before he jumped up and fled the house without a backward glance. I shook my head, amused.

I love that kid.

But my joyful mood almost instantly turned sour as the message from the person who broke into my house ran through my mind.

U took who I love, so I'm takin who u love. Expect me.

What the *fuck* did that mean? Who did I take from someone, and why was it bad enough that they'd want to hurt my little brother? I had no fucking clue what this person was talking about, or planning to do, and the not-knowing terrified me.

CHAPTER FOUR
RYAN

I had been awake hours before I heard movement from Eddi's room. It was five to six in the morning, and I'd had barely four hours of sleep for the second night in a row. Between cars driving by, people walking by, dogs barking and cats screeching, it was too loud. But I'd somehow managed to contain the screams that had wanted to break free all night long.

I didn't dare leave my room and go downstairs because I kept thinking of the Disciples that Eddi had warned me about. In my mind, if I went downstairs, they would be there waiting for me. It was a stupid thought, but it scared me enough to stay in my room. I wanted to wait for either Eddi or Andrea to head down ahead me before I showed my face, and when that didn't happen, all I could do was stay in bed and think. When thinking started to give me anxiety, I grabbed my phone, opened my Kindle app, and read a book to take my mind away from my worries, even if only for a little while. But one of the characters stuck out and reminded me of someone I knew in real life.

Ciara Kelly.

I rarely thought of the woman, because I made it a priority not to. She was supposed to be my stepmother – her and my da had been due to get married, but he was arrested nine weeks before the big day and squashed those plans. However, if I was being honest, if there was any good that came out of my da's arrest, it was Ciara no longer being in my life. I had silently objected to her from the start, and it seemed my prayers had been answered in a sick and twisted way.

I personally believed that the title of mother was earned, not awarded, and that was something Ciara didn't understand, which was why I didn't understand her. From the moment she entered my life four years ago, she just assumed that she would take over the role of mother without asking me if I wanted her to do so. My da did a wonderful job in raising me for eleven years by himself as he rose through the ranks of his profession. I was at an age where I didn't need a mother; I could have used a friend, but all of five minutes after meeting Ciara, I knew neither mother nor friend would be what I considered her.

All my objections, worries and dislike of her aside, my da saw something in her that was worth loving. I loved him enough to accept that Ciara would be a new, permanent part of my life, and for a while, I tried with her. I tried to understand her, to befriend her, to make an effort with her, but she made things very . . . difficult. Everything about her was too much for me to handle, her personality being the main issue.

She seemed to expect me to act a certain way, and when I didn't, we butted heads.

I personally found their relationship rather clichéd. My da was rich, handsome and in a very respected occupation. He had everything going for him, including his age. He was only forty years old when they met, and even I could see what a catch he was. My da didn't, though. He thought Ciara, an attractive woman who'd just turned forty and who was a solicitor he'd hired a year before they started dating, was out of his league. Ciara was beautiful, there was no denying that. She had jet-black, shoulder-length hair, blue eyes, freckles, and a curvy body that caused people to do a double take.

Ciara had been chasing my da from day one, and I knew from the get-go that her end goal was to get hitched. I met her two weeks after they started dating, and she was already talking of marriage. There was no such thing as a prenup within Irish marriage law, which I found to be too convenient for her. I believed that she wanted my da's money, and she was either going to get it through spending it in a lifelong marriage or by getting a hefty sum through a divorce settlement.

Maybe my dislike for her had made me think the worst of her and her intentions, but I realised that I'd never know what her motive was because the marriage never came to be.

They'd spent two full days a week together because of their busy schedules. I didn't know anything about relationships, having never been in one, but I couldn't work out how they could have a genuine, loving partnership when they had such little time for one another. They did appear to make it work, because whenever my da spoke of Ciara, he did so with an enormity of love and respect, so I held my tongue as best as I could for his sake. It was their personal relationship, it didn't involve me, and even though it ground my gears, I had to respect it.

Even though Ciara wasn't someone who I wanted in my life, she was part of it for a long time, and then all of a sudden, she wasn't. Before, I'd disliked Ciara simply because I didn't like her character, but now I loathed her because she abandoned my da when he needed her the most, and to me that was unforgiveable.

Thinking about Ciara made me think about my life before it went to shite. I'd had a great upbringing, with more ups than downs, so I really couldn't complain all that much. I had my da and Johanna, and I had my books. I was a massive bookworm, so much in fact that my da turned one of the spare rooms at our house into a library for me. I was a boring person with a boring life, but I loved it . . . and that's why it hurt so much when it was turned upside down.

"Ry-on," Ciara hollered.

"Jesus, give me the patience to deal with this bitch."

I thought of that word, and mentally sneered it, at least fifty times a day, but only when she was present. Ciara Kelly, unbeknownst to my da, was royalty amongst bitches, and she wore her Queen Bitch title with pride. Whenever I saw her, or simply thought of her, it made me regret not having an active social life to get me out of the house. Spending more time than need be in the same vicinity as her was hell on Earth. She was the Devil incarnate, and everyone apart from my wonderful – but clearly personality-blind – father could see it.

I rolled my eyes to the heavens as she forcefully pounded on my bedroom door instead of knocking like a normal person. Everything about the woman irritated me, but the way she said my name took the cake. She added an "o" to the pronunciation, so instead of Ryan, it became Ry-on. It pissed me off, and she knew it did, so that was the only reason why I never corrected her on it. I didn't want to give her the satisfaction of knowing she got to me, so I dealt with being called Ryon.

"Ryon who-never-answers-me Mahony," Ciara shouted louder, "can you hear me?"

My sigh was long and dramatic.

"The whole of Ireland can hear ye', Ciara."

She fiddled with the handle. "I knew you were in there."

"What d'ye want?" I asked, barely containing a groan of despair. "I'm busy."

If painting my toenails counted as busy.

"Don't talk to me in that tone, Ryon. I'm going to be your mother, you have to respect me."

"Step," I corrected. "Stepmother, and FYI, you don't get that title until you and me da tie the knot, which is nine weeks away . . . plenty of time for 'im to come to his senses and dump your arse."

A thump sounded, and I knew that Ciara had kicked my door in frustration, and it made me grin.

"You listen to me, you smart-mouthed little terror," she sneered. "Your father asked me to come and figure out your dress-fitting schedule for the wedding, so open the poxy door so we can get this over and done with."

I gritted my teeth in annoyance.

"Why don't ye' just pick the dates and I'll go to the fittins?" I angrily suggested. "There, it's over and done with. Have a nice day, ye' life-suckin' monster."

Another thump.

"Once your father and I are married, things will be changing around here, and I'll make sure that your attitude is at the top of the list of things that need to be re-evaluated."

With that, the sound of heels clapping against the floor was heard, and I relaxed – knowing Ciara had stormed off and I didn't have to deal with her any longer.

"Not until dinner, at least," I grumbled to myself.

I finished off the last coat of varnish on my nails, then proceeded to stick my toes, very carefully, into my large UV lamp to help the varnish set quicker. I impatiently tapped my fingers against my mattress as I waited for the lamp to switch off so I could move without fear of ruining my nails. I tried to focus on my toes in the hopes it would put Ciara out of my mind, but it didn't work. I was antsy – I always was after a conversation with Queen Bitch, but today I was more wound up than usual, and I knew it was because time was running out for my father to remove her from our normally perfect lives.

Perfect lives that Ciara Kelly was sure to tarnish.

When my nails were done, I grabbed my iPod, placed the earbuds in my ears, lay back on my bed, hit "Shuffle" and closed my eyes. I loved music. I loved how it could close the door on reality and take you to another place, giving you a sense of peace, even if only for a few minutes. When I was in a tense situation, like after a conversation with Ciara, music was my go-to stress reliever. If it weren't for music, and the clarity and peace it brought me, there wasn't a doubt in my mind that things between me and Ciara would get bad, fast.

After calming down, I got up, dressing warmly for the autumn weather outside and making sure to wrap up. I left my bedroom and walked down two flights of stairs before I reached the ground floor of the house. I saw Johanna walking towards me.

"Are ye' off, Ryan?" she asked, sounding out of breath.

Johanna was in her mid-fifties, and had been our live-in housekeeper for as long as I could remember. She had asthma, and every so often it seemed to act up.

I nodded. "I'm goin' to stretch me legs . . . d'ye need me to get your inhaler?"

She waved me off. "I'll get it in a minute."

I gave her a stern look, which only made her smile.

"Dinner will be ready at six on the dot. Don't be late," she said firmly. "Your father expects ye'."

I winked. "I wouldn't miss your cookin' for all the money in the world."

"Ah!" She chuckled, squeezing my arm affectionately as she passed.

I left the house and began the thirty-second walk to get off our property. We lived in Kildangan in County Kildare, a beautiful area and a village in itself, but instead of owning a home on one of the private estates, my parents had bought a couple of acres of land just outside the Stud and built a six-bedroom house. The front garden had a huge driveway with lush gardens on either side, that I got to help decorate when I was old enough.

When I left the grounds, I made sure to stick as close to the hedges as possible as I walked. We lived in the countryside, surrounded by farmland, which meant back roads, speeding cars, and no pavements until you reached a village or town. Wearing high-visibility clothing was a must when walking at night, otherwise one of the oncoming vehicles would be your end.

I walked for close to thirty minutes before I spotted the street lights of the village. It was tiny – Kildangan itself only had a population of five hundred or so people. It consisted of a crèche, a primary school, a church, a chipper, a petrol station, a few stunning housing estates and, of course, a pub – the Crosskeys. My da liked to have a pint there occasionally, mainly after he won a case that he had spent months, possibly years, working on.

I loved the village. I loved how small it was, how tidy and well kept; I loved the people; but most of all, I loved the views. At night, it was nothing to look at, with poor street lighting so you could barely see your hand in front of your face, but during the day, our sweet countryside was something to behold. We had every shade of green imaginable, trees of all heights and widths, fields of wheat that were so perfectly sowed, it seemed a shame to see them harvested.

I may have been born in Dublin, but I was a Kildare girl. It was where my heart belonged.

When a chill set into my bones, I headed for home. Thirty minutes later, I made it back without a scratch. I had just shut the door when the grandfather clock in the entryway chimed, alerting to me to the time.

Six o'clock.

After I removed my layers and hung up my coat, I went straight into the downstairs bathroom and washed my hands. My da was already seated at the head of the ten-person table, but Ciara was nowhere in sight. Da looked up from his phone when he heard me enter the room, and the smile he flashed my way brought a big one to my own face.

"Baby." He beamed. "How was your day?"

I crossed the room to hug him, then sat at my usual seat, on his right-hand side.

"Long," I answered. "And borin'."

He chuckled. "It won't be long until ye' start college, and then your days will be busy and full."

"I know . . . but I was thinkin' of gettin' a job in the meantime, to keep me occupied."

My da gave me his full attention as he silenced his ever-vibrating phone. I knew this would interest him, as he already thought it was foolish of me to take a gap year when I had no plans to do anything during it. But

I had been home-schooled and tutored for over a decade; I wanted a year off before I jumped back into that.

"A job?" he asked. "Where?"

"I was goin' to ask Mary down in the village if she needs any staff to work at the garage." I shrugged. "I haven't given it much thought, I just want to be out of the house. I'm always on me own, and while I like that, I wouldn't mind gettin' some work experience. What d'ye think?"

Heat flooded my cheeks at the beaming smile of pride my da shot my way.

"I support this venture one hundred per cent."

I laughed. "Thanks. I'm glad to have ye' in me corner."

He winked. "Always."

I glanced across the table, and noticed the placemat where Ciara usually sits wasn't set.

"Where's Ciara?"

"She had to take a rain check," Da explained. "She's buildin' her files for her next case, and since she's briefin' the team tomorrow, she wants to make sure it's sound."

Ciara wasn't going to be around for dinner?

"What a shame," I said as sincerely as possible, as I unfolded a white napkin over my thighs.

"Ryan," Da said, his tone displeased.

I looked up and smiled wide. "Yes?"

"Ye' could at least pretend *to miss Ciara's presence."*

That irked me.

"I'm devastated." I lost my smile. "I'm missin' out on business discussions, and me absolute favourite, weddin' discussions. How will I cope?"

Da set his jaw. "You're being ornery this evenin'."

"And you aren't?"

"Ryan!" he said in a voice so low it made the hairs on the back of my neck stand up.

I lowered my gaze to the empty plate before me. "Sorry."

There was a moment of silence.

"What's goin' on with ye' lately?"

I shrugged. "Nothin'."

"I thought we agreed that we'd never lie to one another?"

I rolled my eyes. "We made that agreement when I was seven."

"So?" Da questioned. "As far as I'm concerned, there wasn't an expiration date on that promise."

I looked up and found him grinning at me. All annoyance fled as I grinned at him.

"You're such a . . . da."

"I try my best."

"I know ye' do."

"Thanks for noticin'," he said. "But back to you – are ye' okay? Be honest with me if ye' need to talk about anythin'. Nothin' is off limits with us, absolutely nothin'. Not even girl talk."

My lips twitched.

"Da, I'm grand, I promise. I'm just bored, but I've a plan in place to sort that out, so don't worry about me."

"I always worry about ye'," he said with a one-shoulder shrug. "It's somethin' I excel at."

I grinned as Johanna brought in our dinner. I made a move to get up to help her, and as always, she told me to park it and let her serve me. I knew it was her job to "serve" us, but now that I was older – and could see Johanna was getting older – I wanted to help her, but getting her to allow it was most difficult.

"Why won't she let me help 'er?" I asked my da when she'd left the room.

"She's a proud woman," he answered.

"She can let me help 'er and still be proud."

"Keep at 'er, you'll wear 'er down eventually," Da chortled. "Ye' always do."

◆ ◆ ◆

I opened my eyes, smiling at the memory of my last meal with my da. That memory was precious to me. It was the last time we'd laughed and joked together before everything changed. It felt like a hell of a lot longer than fourteen months since that day took place.

I shook my head, and turned my thoughts to something positive, like my interview. I couldn't wait until it was over and done with, because if everything went well, I'd have a job and be working with my cousin. I just hoped that today, for my sanity's sake, things went smoother with Eddi than they had so far.

CHAPTER FIVE
ASHLEY

"How come ye' aren't at work?"

I glanced over my shoulder at Anto, who had entered my kitchen. He had a key to my house, so a random drop-in from him was a common occurrence. I turned back to reading the sports section that Mr Joe had given me that morning from the newspaper as he went about searching the presses for food. It didn't matter what time of the day or night it was – Anto was always hungry.

"I could say the same to you."

"Fridays are me day off, but it's not yours, so I'll ask again, how come ye' aren't at work?"

"I phoned in and told them about the break-in yesterday, and the boss told me to take the day off and that he'd see me on Monday."

I was glad for the day off, if I was being honest. I needed to figure out who'd been in my house, and I had to figure it out fast. The longer this person's identity went unknown, the longer my brother was at risk. I'd even had to do something I'd never done before: I called up a few of the seniors in Sean's school that were Disciples and I had them watching out for him, just to make sure this son of a bitch didn't try anything when I wasn't around to protect him. I didn't give the kids any details, I just told them to keep an eye on him and those around him, and if anything happened, for them to intervene to keep him safe and then phone me.

"Well, that's good," Anto said. "At least ye' have the weekend to relax a little."

"I am relaxed."

"You're takin' the piss sayin' that," my friend grunted. "You're wound tighter than a nun's fanny."

I couldn't help it, I burst into laughter.

"You're goin' to hell for that!"

Anto clapped me on the shoulder as he fell into the chair next to me, his lips turned upwards into a smile.

"And we know who's goin' to be sittin' right next me, talkin' shit with the Devil."

I shook my head. "Yeah – me."

Anto, who was eating a packet of Tayto crisps, said, "I checked in with all the neighbours yesterday, and some of them this mornin' before they headed to work. None of the cameras on their houses caught any-thin', so I think whoever it was came in through the back since those are the camera blind spots."

I balled my hands into fists. "The more I think about not gettin' cameras of me own in sooner, the more pissed off at meself I get."

"Don't start," Anto warned. "Ye' hardly knew this bollocks was goin' to kick off."

"But still."

"Nah, mate, no 'but still' anythin'. Ye' can't predict the future."

"No," I agreed. "But I can be prepared for it."

Anto froze. "What'd ye' do?"

"Phoned up Angle and ordered their newest alarm system to rig every window and door, along with cameras on every corner of the house and motion sensors for the inside. I'm gettin' cameras inside too, pointin' at all the entrances, just to double up. I can check all the cameras, inside and out, from me phone as well, so when no one is home I can make sure everythin' is okay."

Anto stared at me. "Ye've gone mad."

I leaned back in my chair. "Everyone around 'ere has these kind of security systems in their house. It's the norm."

"Yeah," Anto agreed tentatively. "But we're Disciples. We don't need that kind of protection. Who we are *is* our protection."

"Bein' a Disciple didn't do me any favours yesterday, did it?" I quizzed. "Whoever broke in 'ere isn't afraid of us, and *that* is bothersome because *everyone* fears us."

Anto considered my words, and when he looked at me, I knew just what he was thinking because I was thinking the exact same thing. I needed answers, and we both knew of one man who had them all.

"I was thinkin' of goin' to Mr Nobody." I rubbed my fingers along my jawline, feeling the bristles of hair already growing back.

"That's a good idea. If whoever broke into this house told someone about it, Nobody's ears would have heard about it." Anto pushed his packet of crisps aside, and scrubbed his face with his hands. "We haven't met with 'im face to face in four years though."

"Because there hasn't been a need to," I reminded him. "We've been sellin' and meetin' our quotas. There's no reason for 'im to want to see us as long as we do that."

"But how do we contact 'im about this?" Anto asked, baffled. "No one knows who he is, and he wore a ski mask the last time we met with 'im."

"I have an idea, so just hear me out."

"Jesus Christ," my friend groaned. "I'm not goin' to like this, I know I'm not."

"It'll be grand."

"That's what you always say, and then I somehow get punched in the face."

I thought back to the last time Anto got punched in the face because of me, and I cringed. "I didn't know the girl's fella was built like The Rock."

"Well, fuckin' trust me, I felt his dig, and he may as well have *been* The Rock."

I snorted.

"Go on." Anto waved a hand. "Tell me how we're goin' to get in touch with Mr Nobody. I can't wait to hear it."

"I'm keepin' the money from November's sales."

Anto stared at me. "Repeat that. Slowly."

"I'm not lettin' me runners deposit any money earned from this month on the deadline," I said. "When someone checks the log and sees my quota unmet, Mr Nobody will come to me. Problem solved."

Anto continued to stare at me, unblinking.

"Are ye' okay?" I asked, concerned.

He shook his head. "I think I just crapped meself on your behalf."

Truth be told, I was on the verge of doing the exact same thing, but I had to remain calm.

"It's the only thing I can think of." I shrugged. "We don't have someone who oversees us, so it's not like I can give them a buzz and ask to arrange a meetin'."

"I know," Anto groaned, scrubbing his face with his hands once more. "But what if he's pissed about ye' not sellin'?"

"I'll have the money. I'll just be holdin' off givin' it until he meets with me," I said, cracking my knuckles. "I'm not worried about it."

That was a massive lie, but I was trying to save face.

"I am," Anto commented. "I'm fuckin' worried."

"It'll be—"

"Don't say grand. Don't ye' dare say that word."

I held my tongue. Anto grumbled under his breath, as if he was arguing with himself.

"Ye' don't have to come to the sit-down with me," I told him. "This is on me."

"Shut the fuck up," he said with furrowed brows. "Where you go, I go. End of."

I leaned forward and clapped my hand against his arm. "Thanks, man."

"Thank me *after* we survive the meetin' with Nobody," he said, just as the doorbell rang. "Just pray I don't get punched, 'cause if I do, I'm gonna kill ye'."

I grinned as I left the kitchen and headed down the hallway to open the door. It was Deco and his boyfriend, Beanie. I gestured for them to enter and followed them into the sitting room.

"What's the crack, man?" Deco asked me, as he sat down next to Beanie on the settee under the window.

I sat on the one opposite them. "Fuck all."

I looked at Deco's face, and my lips thinned to a line. He was sporting *another* shiner, and Beanie looked anywhere but at me when he saw I noticed the bruises. Deco's muscular frame was really just about fitness to him, because he never used his body as a weapon, even when it was to defend himself. I'd caught Beanie once before knocking Deco around, and I put a stop to it then, but it looked like he hadn't understood my message. It took all my restraint not to stand up and kick the shite out of him for it.

Beanie was in my set – he was a Disciple, someone who I'd have to protect if push came to shove – but he wasn't my friend. He was only in my company because Deco cared for him, and since Deco was my friend, I tolerated Beanie.

"What did I tell ye' about hittin' 'im?" I growled, my body tight with tension. "Touch 'im again and I'll break both of your legs."

Deco widened his eyes, and looked from me to his boyfriend and back at me. Beanie was nervous, I could tell by the way he looked at me. The fear in his eyes was plain as day, which both amused and disgusted me. I hated when weak members became Disciples, but there was jack shit I could do about it because I wasn't the boss.

"I won't," Beanie said to me. "I was just tellin' 'im that before we came 'ere."

I looked at Deco, who said, "It's cool, Ash. Thanks."

I nodded. Beanie had a lot of grovelling to do from the looks of things, though I thought Deco forgiving him was bullshit. He'd hit him before and he'd do it again. The lad was an abusive piece of filth, but Deco was going to have to see that on his own, because other people interfering didn't seem to work.

"Why're ye' pickin' on the fag?" Anto asked as he entered the room, dropping down on the settee next to me.

Both Deco and Beanie glared at Anto and told him to fuck himself, which he found amusing. He was going to slag them off for being gay one too many times, and one day they'd beat the shite out of him for it – and then *I'd* give him stick for it for the rest of his life.

I spared Anto a glance. "Why d'ye fuck your second cousin when she visits?"

"Because she's got a mouth like a Hoover."

"You're a sick bastard," I said, but I chuckled as I spoke the words.

"Ye' were right about Eddi Stone's cousin, Anto," Deco suddenly said. "She's gorgeous."

Anto bopped his knee with mine. "Even *he* thinks she's a cracker, and he's a cock gobbler."

Beanie chuckled, earning an elbow from Deco.

I focused on Deco. "When did ye' see 'er?"

"Two minutes ago?" he guessed. "She was runnin' over to the shop. I reckon she's still there – she's new, so Mr Joe will wanna know all about 'er. Ye' know how he is, the nosey bastard. He'll keep 'er there until he gets his fill of gossip."

I stood up, and without a word walked out of the sitting room and towards the front door, grabbing my jacket on the way.

"Where's he goin'?" Beanie asked.

"To satiate his curiosity," Anto answered, then cheered. "Go get 'er, fuckboy."

CHAPTER SIX
RYAN

When I went downstairs, my auntie asked if I'd slept well and I lied to her face. I didn't need her to be any more worried about my settling in, so I wanted to appear as relaxed as possible . . . though that was hard, knowing I had an upcoming job interview. Eddi called me at ten a.m. from her job and said my interview with her boss was at two p.m., and that she'd swing back to the house and collect me at ten minutes to. Both she and my auntie left for work at nine a.m., so I'd been milling around the house trying to keep myself busy.

I read a book, and began another before I started to get ready.

This was my first job interview, so I wanted to look presentable, but I also didn't want to overdo it. I had originally picked out a long-sleeved black top and jeans, but that felt too casual. I settled on a loose-fitted, royal-blue knee-length dress, with black tights, black ankle boots and a thick grey cardigan. I divided my hair into two sections and plaited them tightly, allowing each braid to hang over my shoulders. I went light on my make-up, and only added a touch of liner and mascara to my lids and lashes to define them.

I walked out onto the landing and looked at myself in the full-length mirror that was fixed on the wall next to the bathroom door. I studied myself from my dark brown hair to the tips of my booted feet, and decided that I looked nice. I hoped "nice" was what Eddi's boss was looking for.

I was ready and waiting for Eddi, so when she pulled up outside the house, I was out the door, locking it behind me before she had a chance to beep.

I slid into the passenger seat of her car.

"Ye' look like you're about to be sick; your face is as white as a ghost."

I blanched. "It's not, is it?"

"Calm down," she chuckled. "Ye'll be grand."

"I can't help me nerves." I swallowed as I buckled my seat belt. "They won't go away."

Eddi pulled away from the kerb, completed a three-point turn, then drove out of the estate and onto the main road. I'd been in the car only a few minutes when we suddenly pulled into a crowded car park. There was a single large building, just one-storey tall, but it was divided up into multiple shops. A chipper, a Ladbrokes, a hair salon, a nail salon, a toy shop, a Chinese takeaway, and lastly, a supermarket. I followed Eddi towards the supermarket when we exited the car.

She silently led me into the shop, then through a heavy plated door you could only access by punching in a key code. I followed her, observing everything around me, and came to a stop when she knocked on the large oak door that had a sign saying "MANAGER" fixed to it. We both entered when a voice hollered, "Come in."

"Afternoon, sir," Eddi said, gesturing to me with her hand. "This is me cousin, Ryan Mahony."

Eddi's boss was in his mid-to-late fifties. He had grey hair on the sides of his head, while the top was completely bald. His grey beard was very thick and didn't show signs of hair loss, unlike his head. He had a warm smile and a round frame. He reminded me of Santa Claus.

"Ah." The man stood up. "Lovely to meet ye', Ryan. I'm Mr Conroy, the manager of this fine establishment."

I held my hand out to him, and he shook it eagerly.

"And you, sir." I smiled. "Thank you for givin' me this opportunity."

Eddi moved towards the exit. "I'll be on the floor if ye' need me, boss."

She left, closing the door behind her.

"Sit, sit," the manager ushered me, pulling out a chair for me.

I thanked him and took a seat as he rounded the desk and sat down too.

"Is it rainin' out?" he asked as he sorted through some papers in front of him.

"Surprisingly no, but it is a bit nippy."

"Winter is comin'," he mused.

I chuckled.

"So," he said, intertwining his fingers and leaning his chin on them. "Ye've got the job."

I blinked a few times, unsure I'd heard him correctly.

"I got the job?" I repeated, my surprise obvious.

Mr Conroy bobbed his head. "Yep. Eddi had some great things to say about ye', and I trust 'er."

I didn't know what shocked me more, that I'd got the job without interviewing or that Eddi had said nice things about me.

"Is this a joke?" I asked, unsure of what was happening.

Mr Conroy sat back in his chair. "No, I'm as serious as a heart attack."

I was speechless, for all of two seconds.

"Thank you." I beamed at my new boss. "Thank you so much. I can't believe this. When do I start?"

"Tomorrow at two," he answered enthusiastically. "Ye'll be on the same shift as Eddi for the next few weeks. She'll be trainin' ye', first on the floor and then on the tills."

I resisted the urge to clap my hands together. I wasn't exactly looking forward to Eddi barking orders at me, but I *was* excited that I would be a working woman. A job was a job, and I had one now.

"Thank you," I repeated.

"No worries." He smiled. "Bring your bank details tomorrow, as well as your ID and proof of address. Eddi already told me your home address is different from hers, but that won't be a problem. We can get everythin' together then when ye' come on shift."

I nodded, absorbing his instructions.

"Also," Mr Conroy added, "stop by the storage room on your way out and take a uniform, it's down the hall and to your left on your way out. There are a bunch of different sizes. Grab yours and ye' can get on out of 'ere until tomorrow."

I stood. "Yes sir, and thank you again."

I shook hands with Mr Conroy once more and left his office, grabbing a uniform from the storage room as instructed on my way out to the shop floor. Things were quiet, and Eddi was leaning against the side of the counter, laughing at something her friend behind the till had said. When her friend saw me walking towards them, Eddi turned, folded her arms across her chest and eyed my uniform.

"Ye' didn't mess it up then?"

"Not yet," I answered, making the girl behind the counter chuckle. "He said I start tomorrow at two, can ye' believe that?"

Eddi only grinned, while the other girl said, "Congrats."

I turned my attention to her, and held my hand out in her direction.

"Thanks. I'm Ryan, nice to meet ye'."

"Amber," she replied with a smile as she took my hand and shook it. "Welcome to the team."

I thanked her again, and turned my focus back to my cousin.

"I'll head back to your house and get dinner started, so it'll be ready before you and your ma get back."

Eddi eyed me. "What're ye' makin'?"

She sounded wary.

"Haven't decided yet." I paused. "But whatever it is, it won't poison ye'."

Amber laughed, and Eddi's lips twitched ever so slightly.

After that, I walked the ten minutes from the shop to the house, taking the laneway Eddi had told me to. It was impossible to get lost, as once I cleared the lane and looked across the public park, I could see where the housing estate was and headed towards it. When I entered the house, I headed up to my room, hung up my uniform on the back of my bedroom door, removed my cardigan then went down to the kitchen. I did a mental inventory of the food in the presses, fridge and freezer, so I could think up a nice meal.

I settled on stuffed pork, veggies, mash and gravy. Once I got everything prepared, I placed it in the oven and set the timer. I had the gravy granules to the side to make at the end, and I placed the mixed vegetables aside for boiling later, too. Then I went in search of potatoes, and came up short. There was a bag in the press, but there wasn't enough inside it to feed three people.

"Shite."

I stood up and placed my hands on my hips, before walking out of the kitchen and down the hall to come to a stop at the front door. I leant down and peered through the frosted pane of glass as best I could before I stood upright. I knew there was a corner shop across the road, and surely it sold potatoes.

Everywhere sold potatoes.

I grabbed some money from my bag in my bedroom, then picked up the set of keys my auntie had given me and left the house. Once the door closed behind me, I instantly regretted not taking my cardigan with me. My dress, on its own, was definitely not part of an autumn wardrobe.

"Crap, crap, crap," I sang, and hopped from foot to foot as I locked the front door.

I hesitated for moment, pondering on whether or not I should go back inside and get my cardigan, but it seemed like too much of a hassle now that I was already outside. I turned and scurried out of the garden before jogging over to the shop once I saw that the road was free of cars. The shopkeeper looked up and stared at me with unblinking eyes as I bolted inside.

He clicked his tongue as he assessed me. "Ye'll catch your death."

I agreed with him.

"I know." I shivered, firmly closing the door. "I regretted not takin' me cardigan the second I left the house. I thought I could run over 'ere and back before it became too much of a bother."

The man chuckled. "I'm Mr Joe. And *you* are?"

I stopped in my tracks. Eddi's warning that this man could possibly be a sleeper for the Disciples was front and centre in my mind, and I had to be smart about the information I freely gave to him.

"I'm Ryan. Nice to meet ye', Mr Joe."

He folded his arms across his chest. "D'ye have a surname?"

"I do," I answered, and looked at the shelves behind him, trying to turn his attention back to selling me his goods.

"I've never seen ye' around 'ere before, and I knew *everyone* in Jobstown."

I bet he did.

"I'm just visitin' family. D'ye sell—"

"What family?"

Jesus, he was nosey.

"The Stones," I eventually answered.

"I didn't know Andie and Eddi had other family."

He didn't seem to like the fact that he hadn't known that piece of information. I just smiled in response as I approached the counter. A phone rang from the back of the shop, so he excused himself to answer it. It was about five minutes before he returned.

"Sorry about that."

"Don't worry about it."

"Did ye' just arrive?" he then asked. "I've never seen ye' before today, and I see everybody."

He *definitely* had to be a sleeper for the Disciples, or if he somehow wasn't, he was a gossiping old ninny.

"I actually just got 'ere the other night," I answered. "I'll be stayin' a while . . . ye' know . . . spendin' time with me auntie and cousin."

"Ah." Mr Joe nodded. "Christmas with the family."

I smiled, my lips tight together.

"A wonderful thing, is Christmas," he continued. "Why, I think it's the best time of the year."

Staring at him, I said, "Me too."

"Where are ye' from?"

I hesitated. "Kildare."

"Ah, the countryside."

When he was about to waffle on again, I quickly cut in and said, "D'ye have any potatoes, Mr Joe? I've left the oven on, so I hafta be quick before I burn the house down."

Hint hint, mister.

"We only have the fifteen-kilo bags," he answered. "Is that okay?"

I nodded, and paid once he told me the price. I heard the squeaking of hinges as the door to the shop opened and closed. A rush of cold air slammed into me and caused a shiver to run up the length of my spine.

"It's colder than a witch's tit out there."

The voice that spoke was deep and had a husky hue to it, as if the man had just woken up from a deep sleep and hadn't spoken until now.

Mr Joe grinned at the newcomer. "At least *you* wore a jacket, son."

I playfully rolled my eyes at the jibe intended for me, which made Mr Joe snort. He pointed over my right shoulder. "Potatoes are there, love."

I turned, walked over to the bags, bent down and tried lifting one by the handle, but the heavy weight told me I needed to get my hands under the base of it to get a good hold. I positioned myself, and was bending my knees to do just that when a voice stopped me.

"Don't hurt yourself, babe," the deep, alluring voice teased from behind. "I've got it."

I stood upright. "Thanks, but I've got it under—"

I froze mid-sentence when I turned and looked at the man who'd spoken. The first thing I noticed was his height. He was tall, easily a couple of inches over six foot, which towered over my five-foot-nothing frame. One part of my mind told me instantly that I had never seen a more attractive man in my life, while the other part reasoned it was because I'd seen so few whilst living in Kildare.

His eyes got my attention almost straight away. I had never seen grey eyes on a person before. Light blue, hazel brown or emerald green, sure, but never a lustrous grey. They were gorgeous. His hair was the next thing to snag my attention. It was fiery red, and though short, his head was covered in thick, individual curls.

"Like what ye' see?"

His words registered instantly, and I felt mortified at having been caught staring. No, not staring. Gazing. His amused eyes roamed over my cheeks. I felt them burn with heat, and knew he could see my blush.

"Where d'ye live?"

My tongue flattened to the roof of my mouth.

"Babe," he said, tilting his head to the side. "I haven't got all day. Which road do ye' live on so I can drop the potatoes off at the door?"

I opened my mouth to speak, but no words came out, so I closed it. The actions caused the stranger's lips to twitch. I most likely looked like an eejit to him, because I most definitely felt like one.

"Corner house across the road," I managed to say in a mumble.

He leaned his head towards me slightly and squeezed his eyes, as if doing that would help him hear me clearer.

"One more time," he requested. "I didn't catch a word of that."

I cleared my throat.

"The corner house across the road . . . the Stones' house," I said, louder, firmer. "Please."

A ghost of a smile graced his plump but slightly marred lips. They were full, but a thick scar cut through his lower lip on the left-hand side of his face in a diagonal pattern, and ended just before it met his Cupid's bow. I wondered how it had happened, then found myself deciding that I liked the scar, even though it added a mist of danger to the man. I liked the stranger's mouth overall . . . and that thought alone embarrassed me.

"Sweetheart," his soothing voice asked softly. "Is everythin' okay up top?"

I blinked. "Huh?"

The corners of his eyes creased as he smiled.

"I said," he emphasised, "are ye' okay . . . up 'ere?"

When he lifted his hand and tapped on his temple with his index finger, it took me a moment to understand what he was asking me. He was asking if I was crazy because I'd frozen when talking to him. Embarrassment quickly fled, and a smouldering fire of anger began to build within me.

"There's nothin' wrong up top with me," I said, standing up straight. "Thanks for your offer, but I can manage meself."

I didn't understand why he looked so amused.

"I didn't mean to offend ye'."

"Ye' didn't?" I questioned, not believing him for a second. "Ye' thought askin' if I was in me right mind was anythin' other than offensive? God forbid I get nervous talkin' to a *stranger* who gets in me space."

"Christ in Heaven, young one," the shopkeeper almost screeched. "Stop talkin' to 'im like that."

I looked at Mr Joe. "D'ye not hear *him*?"

"She's new around 'ere, kid," Mr Joe said to the stranger. "Doesn't mean any harm."

I didn't get why Mr Joe called him "kid". Sure, he was young, but there was nothing childlike about him. He was a grown man.

The stranger laughed. "I figured that."

I had the urge to flee. I knew I was out of my depth with this man, so I turned and focused on the stupid potatoes. However, before I could act, a hand reached over my shoulder, grabbed the handle of the bag and plucked it from the floor like it weighed nothing.

"Excuse me." I spun around and scurried after him as he walked out of the shop, Mr Joe staring after us with his jaw agape. "Excuse me, mister!"

"You're excused," he replied.

I slowed down a bit, shocked at his harsh reply. Then I snapped out of it and hurried up, crossing the road to catch up with him. My heart was pounding, I had never been in a verbal altercation in my entire life, and I hated every second of it.

"I can't believe you're doin' the opposite of what I want," I shouted over the wind. "I don't need your help, mister."

"I know," the man replied. "But you're gettin' it anyway."

He had a neck like a jockey's bollocks and knew it, but he didn't give a fuck. I followed him into my auntie's garden, not quite believing his audacity. I stopped a metre away when he dropped the bag at the front door. He straightened, then turned to face me.

"If you're expectin' thanks," I said wryly, "ye'll be a long time waitin'."

The man's mouth curved in a grin that would rival any Cheshire cat. He lazily slid his tongue along his lower lip, his eyes not leaving mine for a second. When I swallowed, he winked at me. Then, without a word, he walked out of the garden, back over the road and into the corner shop. I watched him until he disappeared, not quite being able to believe how dismissive he was.

"Arrogant arsehole," I groused before hurriedly unlocking the front door. Then, with all my might, I dragged the potatoes into the house, sliding them along the floor because they were too heavy for me to lift off the ground.

I put the encounter with the stubborn man at the back of my mind, and focused on making dinner. Just after five, everything had just finished cooking. My auntie and cousin got home five minutes apart and were ready for eating, and I beamed with delight when I heard them groan about how good the house smelled thanks to my cooking. There wasn't much idle chat from Eddi. She gulped down as much food as she could before she went upstairs to her room.

Both me and my auntie weren't finished, so we chatted while we ate.

"Eddi rang earlier today and said ye' got the job." Andrea beamed as she took a sip of her tea. "I knew ye' would."

"I'm delighted," I expressed. "I start tomorrow at two, so after dinner I'm goin' to shower and have an early night to get meself ready."

"Ye'll do great," Andrea encouraged. "Ye've got a good head on your shoulders."

"Thanks," I chuckled. "I just hope I catch on quick. I think Eddi will crack 'er whip otherwise."

We laughed, and the rest of dinner continued like that. Us laughing over nonsense until we couldn't talk. With smiles, we cleared the table and washed our plates in the sink before drying them with tea towels. Andrea left the room before me, and the happiness I'd felt moments before slipped away and a frown took up residence on my face.

I thought of my da, how I was here laughing and having a cracking time with my auntie, while he was in prison suffering God knows what. I knew there was nothing I could about it, but I still felt guilty.

I went upstairs and had my shower. Afterwards, I sat on the edge of my bed with my towel still wrapped around my body, and suddenly I was fighting off tears. I hated crying, but it was all I seemed to do as of late, and it made me even more miserable. I could feel the sense of melancholy that I radiated, and I couldn't make it go away.

I was heartbroken.

"Suck it up, Ry," I told myself, lifting my chin. "Da isn't dead, he's in prison, and he *will* be home one day."

I just hoped to God that day was sooner rather than later.

CHAPTER SEVEN
ASHLEY

"I need to talk to ye', Ash."

I looked up from my phone when Sean spoke. He was standing at my bedroom door, hands on his hips and a stern expression on his face. He looked like he meant business, so I put my phone to one side and gestured him into the room with a jerk of my head.

"What's on your mind?" I asked, then waited patiently.

Sean furrowed his brow. "The Disciples at school, why're they followin' me around?"

Fuck!

I held off sighing out loud. Instead, I lied and asked, "What're ye' talkin' about?"

"Don't do that," Sean grumbled as he began to pace left to right in front of me. "Don't lie, when I *know* ye' know what I'm talkin' about."

I watched him for a moment.

"When ye' say followin'—"

"I *mean* followin'. Everywhere I turned today, one of them was there. When I asked what they were doin', they didn't even answer me, they just walked away as if I didn't speak."

I shook my head, silently vowing to smack the little fuckers around for failing to complete a simple task.

"They're just lookin' out for ye'." I shrugged. "They've always been doin' that, but for some reason they're just now bein' obvious about it. I'll have a chat with them about it, don't worry."

Sean stared at me, and I knew he was deciding whether he was going to believe me. When his body relaxed, I knew what decision he'd come to.

"Right." He nodded. "Thanks."

He left my room without another word, so I grabbed my phone and sent a text to one of the seniors at the school, scolding them for fucking up. I received an apology a minute after I sent the text, and a promise that it wouldn't happen again. Satisfied with the answer, I left my room and headed downstairs.

"If ye' want food," I called out to Sean, "get it now. It's past ten, and I want ye' out cold by eleven."

Sean's response was muffled, but I could guess what his reply was and it made me grin.

I had barely pressed my foot on the last step of the stairs when a knock sounded at the front door. Not expecting anyone to stop by, I approached it cautiously.

"Who is it?" I called out gruffly.

A laugh sounded.

"Mrs Brown's boys," Anto hollered. "Who the fuck do ye' think?"

I relaxed, rolled my eyes and unlocked the door, pulling it open wide. Standing tall, with a six-pack of Bulmers in his raised hand, was Anto. He shrugged. "I figured ye' could use a cold one."

I stepped back, and waited for him to enter the house.

"Ye' never were one to turn away a free drink," Anto chuckled.

I shook my head, amused, but before I could close the door fully, laughter got my attention. I opened the door wider, and when I saw Deco and Beanie walking into my garden, talking and laughing, I leaned against the door frame and scratched my neck.

"Don't ye' have houses of your own?"

Deco looked my way. "Yeah, but yours is much nicer."

I guffawed. "Well, at least you're honest."

After welcoming the two more unexpected guests, I joined them in the sitting room and closed the door behind me.

"Keep it down," I said. "I want Sean to go to sleep at a reasonable hour."

"Fuck that, daddyo." Anto clapped. "Bring the lad down and let 'im have a few—"

"D'ye want to go home?" I interjected.

Anto frowned. "No."

"Then shut up."

He pulled a face. "Way to piss on me party, little bitch."

I forced myself not to laugh at his stupid antics, but it was hard not to. Anto had no filter, and no matter what the situation, or how bleak something seemed, he had a way of bringing a smile to people's faces. Whether it was by being stupid, or making dumb comments, he didn't care. It was one of his best qualities, and I was glad to say he'd been this way since we were kids.

I sat down next to him, taking the can of Bulmers he extended my way.

"So," he said, a grin in place, "I've heard rumbles that the new country bird down the road ruffled your feathers today."

I opened the can and took a swig of cider. "When are me feathers ever ruffled?"

"Never, which is why this bit of information interested me."

"Information?" I repeated. "*What* information? And how d'ye know she's from the country?"

"Well, Mr Joe said—"

"Mr Joe," Deco, Beanie and I said in unison, followed by chuckles.

"That man may as well have a fanny on his forehead for all the gossipin' he does." I shook my head, taking another swig of my drink. "He's unreal."

"Just listen," Anto requested as Deco and Beanie started their own conversation, ignoring him. "He said that she was from Kildare, and that she went off on ye' in the shop, and that she gave ye' grief over a bag of potatoes. He *also* said ye' barely said a word back to 'er."

I resisted the urge to pinch the bridge of my nose.

"Like ye' said, she's *new*, so she doesn't know any better," I said as I leaned my head back on the settee cushion. "I'm sure she won't look at me again, though. 'Er cousin will no doubt tell 'er to stay away from me – to stay away from all of us."

Anto blinked at my amused grin. "And *why* is that funny to ye'?"

"Because . . . since when do girls give me lip, whether they're new or not?"

Anto thought about it. "Never, I guess."

"Exactly." I nodded. "It's refreshin'."

"What's refreshin'?" Deco asked as he and Beanie paid attention to our conversation again instead of their own. Beanie was focused on rolling two joints, but he glanced up at us every so often, showing he was listening.

"The weirdo likes that the new mot down the road gave 'im lip," Anto explained, getting them up to speed. "I'm tellin' ye', lads. Gingers aren't like us, they're fucked in the head."

They both laughed at Anto insulting me.

"She's Eddi Stone's cousin, right?" Deco quizzed.

I nodded.

"Like I said earlier, she's gorgeous, but even if she was oblivious that you're a Disciple, she wouldn't touch ye' with a ten-foot pole."

I stared at him. "What the fuck are ye' talkin' about?"

"She's a country bird," Deco smirked. "She looks down on lads like us. She was probably told scary stories about this county when she was little. I've met a few culchie mots over the years; they aren't like Dublin birds. North *or* Southside."

"Dublin birds are in a class of their own," Anto mused. "I've never met one that gave bad head to date."

The lads laughed, and my own lips twitched in amusement.

"Let's get one thing straight," I said, sitting upright. "If I wanted to fuck 'er, then I'd fuck 'er. Country bird or not."

"You're talkin' outta your arse, Ash."

This came from Beanie, just as he lit one of the spliffs and tossed the other one to me, followed by his lighter.

"Ye' wanna bet?" I challenged as I lit up.

"No," Anto cut across, glaring when he caught my eye. "He doesn't."

I felt peeved at Anto's sudden interruption, so I took a couple of drags of the joint then passed it to him, my eyes burning into his to show my displeasure.

"We've other shite to focus on," he pressed, noticing my expression. "*Remember?*"

The direct reminder of the stranger who'd broken into my house and threatened my brother burned a hole in my mind. I roughly bit my lower lip and nodded curtly. I wasn't pissed at Anto; I was pissed at myself. Losing focus wasn't something I could afford to do right now. I had to be alert at all times, not putting my energy into a stupid bet that I knew I could win without trying.

"Get some girls round 'ere," Anto suddenly demanded as he blew a cloud of smoke into the air. "There are *way* too many dicks for me likin'."

"You have half a dick, so it doesn't count."

The lads laughed at my joke, and I was relieved – glad neither Deco nor Beanie asked what Anto and I had been talking about. They continued to talk about women, sports and, of course, our drug shipments. My mind wasn't on the conversation, though; it was torn between two things. My brother, and the country girl down the road. My brother should have been my only focus, but there was something about the timid yet feisty brunette that had me thinking about her.

She'd left an impression on me, and that was something no other girl had done before.

CHAPTER EIGHT
RYAN

"That's not how ye' do that, princess."

I held my tongue.

"Nope," Eddi chirped. "Still not how ye' do it, princess."

I felt all the muscles in my body tighten, but somehow I managed to stay mute.

"Princess, that's not—"

"If ye' call me princess one more time, or correct me on stackin' shelves one more time, I'm goin' to stab ye' in the face with this can of soup."

Eddi looked at the soup in question. "How can ye' stab someone with a round can?"

"Keep talkin'," I warned, "and ye'll find out."

My cousin laughed at me, not caring about my threat in the slightest, and it drove me up the wall. She was making my first day at my job harder than it needed to be, and it frustrated me.

"Why're ye' over 'ere with me?" I asked, tired of being in her presence. "I can finish this on me own."

"I'm trainin' ye'," was all she said.

I silently counted to ten. "I know ye' think I'm a princess, but I don't need *help* to put cans of soup on a shelf, Eddi."

"Judgin' from the angles of those cans, I'd say ye' do. The labels are supposed to face forward for the customer to *see*."

I was two ticks away from throwing a can at her head; she was grating on my last nerve and she didn't even care. In fact, I was confident she knew how much she was annoying me. It most likely amused her.

"If I straighten them," I began, "will ye' leave me alone for five minutes?"

"Yes," she answered.

I straightened the cans, stepped back and looked at my cousin.

"I'll be back," she warned.

I waved her on. "Okay, Arnold."

When she was out of sight, I sent a silent prayer of thank you up to God, then placed my hands on my hips and turned to the remaining crates that I still had to empty. I had got the soup crate empty, so I lifted one full of tinned tomatoes and got to work on stacking those cans onto their correct shelf, but when I grabbed some more tins and accidentally let one fall, I stumbled back and tried to catch it with my foot before it rolled under the shelves. I managed to catch it, but I bumped into someone in the process.

"I'm sorry," I squeaked as the stranger's hands gripped my waist, helping me keep my balance. "I'm *so* sorry."

When I was steady on my feet, I turned to apologise again to the person I'd trampled, and my breath got caught in my throat.

"*You!*"

The stranger from the corner shop yesterday grinned and said, "Me."

I was so surprised to see him that for a few moments, I simply stared at him.

"I'm sorry about that." I swallowed. "I didn't see ye'."

"Obviously," came his teasing response.

His voice was so deep it sent chills up my spine.

"I'll just get out of your wa—"

"What's your name?" he asked, his eyes scanning my face.

I cleared my throat. "I'm sorry?"

"Your name," he repeated, leaning on the trolley beside him. "What is it?"

"Ryan."

"Ryan?" he repeated.

I nodded. "Yeah, Ryan."

He snorted. "Where are ye' from?"

I glanced around the empty aisle before refocusing on the man in front of me.

"Kildare," I replied. "I just moved in with me auntie and cousin. I got 'ere the other day."

I had no idea why I was giving him details, but my nerves wouldn't allow for anything less. I wanted him to turn around and walk away, but he didn't look like he planned to do that.

"D'ye have a boyfriend?"

I frowned. "No, but I don't see what that has to do—"

"I'm Ash. Your cousin is Eddi, right?"

I nodded, slowly.

"She lives a few houses down from me."

I widened my eyes when his words triggered Eddi's warning from my first night in Dublin.

Don't look or speak in Ash's direction. Ever.

"Ash," I said, stunned. "*You're* Ash Dunne."

The corner of Ash's lips curved upwards, the scar that marred them stretching with the action. His grey eyes seemed to light up with amusement at my obvious horror.

"I'm sorry," I blurted out. "I've got to go."

I turned, and without another word I scurried down the aisle, with Ash's laughter following me. "Whatever ye've heard about me," he called out, cheerfulness in his tone. "I'm sure I'm far worse."

Oh my God.

I slowed my pace all the way down to a brisk walk, but didn't stop moving until I punched in the key code to get to the break room. The room was small, but it was empty, and it gave me a moment to gather my jumbled thoughts. When I had a second to calm down, the first thing I was sure of was that Eddi was going to absolutely kill me. She had told me, point blank, *not* to talk to Ash Dunne, and not only had I spoken to him, I'd had a mild argument with him over potatoes the day before to boot. Granted, I hadn't known who he was when I argued with him, but still, Eddi had also told me to be wary of everyone around me, and I wasn't.

She was *definitely* going to kill me . . . or maybe Ash would. He was the one who Eddi said did horrible things. Maybe he was stalking me, trying to get me on my own so he could get rid of me. My mind was conjuring up all kinds of horrible scenarios and it sent my blood pressure skyrocketing.

"Don't be so stupid!" I scowled, cursing my overactive imagination. "It's fine, everythin' is *fine*. Why would he want to kill ye'? He doesn't even *know* ye'."

I inhaled a deep breath and forced myself to relax. It was okay. Everything was . . . okay.

I screamed when the break-room door suddenly opened, and jumped about a foot into the air. I covered my head with my arms, and in my mind I spoke to Jesus and asked him to protect me.

"What in God's name are ye' doin', princess?"

I slowly lowered my hands, and straightened myself to my full height.

"Eddi?" I said, my heart deflating. "It's you."

"Who else? Ye' bloody lunat— what the *hell* are ye' doin'?"

Before I realised what I was doing, I had thrown my arms around her in a bone-crushing hug. Not because I wanted to hug her, but because she wasn't Ash Dunne. I stumbled backwards when she shoved me away.

"Ryan," she said as she brushed her uniform off. "What the heck is goin' on with ye'?"

"Sorry," I said. "I'm just . . . thankful ye' got me this job."

My cousin glared at me. "Get back out on the floor before ye' lose it and get me sacked right along with ye'."

She turned, and was gone from sight before I could respond. I licked my lips, took a few more calming breaths, then I left the break room and carefully made my way back to the aisle I'd been working on. I must've looked like an owl as I walked, because my head was twisting and turning in every direction, hoping to God I didn't catch sight of Ash. As I reached my aisle, a quick glance out from behind a shelf showed me it was empty.

"Thank you, God."

I hurriedly got back to work, and finished stacking the shelves I had been assigned to in record time. I stacked the empty crates into one another, lifted them and scurried into the back, placing the crates in their designated spot. When I was about to turn away, I saw another crate full of beans and my head thumped. I heaved it up, put it on a trolley, found what aisle I had to go to and got back to work.

As I turned to see which section I had to place the items in, I jumped when I found a person's chest mere inches from my face. My body took on a role of its own as I lurched backwards. Once again, I tripped over my own two feet during my stumble, and I began to fall backwards onto my behind. Hands as quick as lightning shot out and grabbed hold of my forearms, halting my tumble.

"Oh my God!" I screeched as my hands flattened against the hard chest.

"Careful, nightmare," a voice I knew to be wary of said. "You're beginnin' to form a habit of fallin' when you're around me. Is that a sign that ye've fallen *for* me?"

A teasing tone was wrapped around the words, but I couldn't begin to form a polite smile; I was frozen.

"Hey," Ash prompted, giving my forearms a squeeze. "Anyone home?"

Why is he still holding on to my arms?

I seemed to snap out of my trance, and shook my near-fall – and Ash's hands – off.

"Sorry," I said, taking a hefty step backwards without looking up at him. "I was in a world of me own. Pay me no mind."

I turned around, got down on my knees and began to stack the beans onto the bottom shelf, hoping to God above that Ash would take the hint that I didn't want to talk to him and that he should go away. He either didn't get my hint, or he didn't care because he didn't move a muscle.

"I'm workin'," I said after a few seconds.

I still felt him behind me. In fact, I could still almost feel the gentle strength of his grip on my arms, and that sent a small shiver up my spine.

"Ash," I said hesitantly.

"Yeah?"

I closed my eyes. "Leave me alone."

"No."

I opened my eyes, stood up and faced him.

"Why not?" I demanded.

I sounded like I was annoyed, but in reality I was so scared that my knees wobbled.

He shrugged. "I have no fuckin' clue, nightmare."

I squinted my eyes. "Nightmare?"

His lips twitched. "Seems fittin'."

I looked around. "This is stalkin'."

"Hardly." He grunted. "I came in 'ere to get bread, milk and some other bits of shoppin', like I do every other day, and this time *you* just happen to be 'ere."

I exhaled a deep breath. "I don't want to talk to ye', okay?"

He tilted his head to the side. "Why not?"

"Because."

Ash smiled at me, and a very stupid part of my brain decided it liked his smile. And his lips. I couldn't forget about those. I was horrified to find that I wanted to run my tongue over his scar to see what it felt like.

"Because," he prompted.

Still staring at his mouth, I missed what he said.

"Huh?"

His smiled changed to a grin as he stepped forward, crowding me.

"Ye've got nice lips," he said, dropping his gaze to my mouth. "I wonder what they taste like."

He smelled of Lynx and a splash of rich cologne, and those scents invaded my senses and turned me to mush. My brain no longer had a say in what I would do next – I was acting on instinct alone – which is why, instead of answering Ash, I leaned up and kissed him.

If he was surprised by my forwardness, he didn't act like it. I heard his basket drop to the ground with a thud as his hands went to my waist, where his fingers bit into my flesh. He kissed me back. My lips parted, and his tongue touched mine before I pulled back with a gasp.

What did I just do?

"Chocolate," Ash rumbled. "Ye' taste like chocolate."

The tips of my ears were burning.

"I ate a Dairy Milk on me break," I replied, dumbfounded.

I swallowed when the hand on my right hip dipped and slid down to the curve of my behind. I widened my eyes to the point of pain when he suddenly closed his hand around my bum and fisted a handful of it.

"Christ," Ash growled. "Ye've a great arse."

I opened my mouth to speak, though I had no clue what to say. Words eluded me, but fate did not. Eddi chose that exact moment to be my knight in shining armour.

"*Ryan?*"

I jumped away from Ash like he was a pile of scalding hot coal, and swung to face my slack-jawed cousin.

"Hi," I said, breathless. "D'ye need some help?"

Instead of waiting for her reply, I rushed forward and grabbed the tray of tinned peas in her hands. I turned to my right, placed the tray on the floor, then got on my knees and began placing them on the empty section of the bottom shelf.

A minute or so of silence passed.

"Is he gone?" I whispered.

"No," Eddi and Ash answered in unison.

I closed my eyes and let my shoulders slump as I grudgingly got to my feet. I opened my eyes and turned to my cousin, who looked like she'd seen a ghost.

"I don't even know how it happened," I said in a rushed breath. "I asked 'im to go away, he said no, and then we were kissin'. I'm sorry. I swear, I am."

Eddi stared at me long and hard.

"D'ye want 'im to leave ye' alone?"

I bobbed my head.

Eddi looked over my shoulder at Ash. "Ye' heard 'er. She wants ye' to leave 'er alone."

"She said that before she kissed me too," he answered, mirth in his tone. "If anyone is confused, it's me."

Eddi widened her eyes as her gaze darted back to me.

"*You* kissed *him*?"

"I don't understand it either," I blurted out, wringing my hands together. "He was standin' really close to me, and he smells good and I acted before I realised what I was doin' and . . . and . . . I'm so sorry."

Ash's laughter made me tense. "Why're ye' apologisin'?"

I didn't turn to look at him.

"Because I promised 'er I wouldn't get involved with ye', or any of your friends."

Eddi's eyes bulged at my admission, and her worried gaze flicked to Ash. A knot of sickness formed in my stomach. Ash was an incredibly handsome man – he was beyond the term "hot" – but that didn't excuse him being a gang member, which was something I had to remind myself of. I had only just got here and I'd already thrown my cousin in the deep end with him, and I was so worried about what he would do because of that.

"I see," Ash replied. "She told ye' horror stories?"

"I told 'er the truth," Eddi said with a confidence I knew she didn't feel.

We all fell silent when an old lady passed by, grabbing a few items from the shelves as she went. "Eddi!" Amber's voice hollered from the end of the aisle. "Come give us a hand on the tills."

"Shite," Eddi said, gnawing at her lower lip. "Just get back to work. He'll get bored and leave."

I nodded, dropped back to my knees and quickly did as she instructed. I counted to sixty in my head, peeked over my shoulder and saw Ash's legs, then turned back around as quick as lightning.

He laughed. "I'm not gonna bite ye', so ye' can relax."

I felt like a yoyo as I reluctantly got back to my feet and turned to face him.

"I don't understand why you're still here."

"If I'm honest," Ash answered, "neither do I."

I shook my head and made a move to walk by him, but I tripped over my own two feet *again*. I sucked in a sharp breath, and before I could even prepare myself for a hard landing, hands shot out, gripped my shoulders and steadied me.

"Jesus Christ!" I squealed. "What is *wrong* with me? I swear to God I'm not doin' this on purpose."

Ash kept his hands on my shoulders. "Okay?"

Words failed me, so I swallowed as I bobbed my head. There was no one on planet Earth that was as big a disaster as me. I understood why I thrived on my own; being around people was hard.

"Ryan?"

I glanced up and Ash looked deep into my eyes, and from his expression, I knew he saw the fear I felt.

"Ye' don't have to be scared of me."

He sounded so sincere that I almost believed him.

"That's not what Eddi says, and me auntie says, and what Mr Joe seemed to think."

He was so close to me, and he smelled *so* good. I felt my brain preparing to have another stupid moment, so I shut it down before anything could happen. I stepped back from him, and his hands fell to his sides.

"Anyone who's told ye' somethin' 'bout me doesn't personally know me."

I considered this.

"That's a lot of people sayin' the same thing though."

Ash's lips twitched. "I'm no angel, but I'm no demon either."

I sighed. "What does that even mean?"

"That ye' shouldn't listen to bullshit."

I blinked. "Does that include the bullshit *you* spew?"

Ash snickered, bent down and picked up his basket, and then began to back away. I wanted to slap myself. I was saying what I was thinking without realising it, and I knew it could easily get me in trouble, but Ash . . . he didn't seem to mind it in the slightest. In fact, when I answered him back, he appeared to get a kick out of it.

"I'll see ye' around, nightmare."

He turned and walked away.

"I'd prefer it if ye' didn't," I called out.

The only thing to answer me was Ash's laughter, and I found that long after he'd gone, I was still thinking of the last thing he'd said to me. He said he'd see me around, and for the life of me, I didn't know if it was a threat or a promise.

CHAPTER NINE
ASHLEY

"Why d'ye keep smilin'?" Anto asked as we leaned against the tall wall of my garden. "You're freakin' me out, Ash."

I spared my friend a glance before looking back up to the sky. It was a clear night, cold as fuck but not raining, so – like most nights when the weather permitted us – Anto and I were hanging about and talking outside.

"What?" I asked without looking at him.

"Don't 'what' me," Anto joked as he passed me the joint he was smoking. "Why d'ye keep smilin'?"

"No reason."

"Bullllllshit."

Laughter bubbled up in my throat. "You're a pest."

"Which is why ye' might as well answer me." Anto shrugged as he brought his bottle of Bud to his lips. "Otherwise I'll just keep botherin' ye' about it."

I knew that to be the absolute truth.

"It's nothin' . . . I just ran into Ryan at the supermarket earlier today."

I held back a grin at the thought of her. She was somewhat of an enigma to me. She knew who I was, and was obviously scared of me, but she was interested in me too, even if she didn't want to be. She wouldn't have kissed me otherwise.

I shifted my stance, thinking about her soft but hungry kiss. She took that kiss from me, and I'd be damned if it wasn't one of the sexiest things I'd ever experienced . . . and it was only a chaste little kiss.

Anto lowered his bottle and pulled me from my thoughts with a single question. "Who?"

"Ryan."

"Who the fuck is Ryan?" he quizzed. "You're sayin' that name like I know it."

"The new bird down the road," I corrected. "'Er name is Ryan."

Anto's jaw dropped. "Shut the front door."

"Nope."

"Your name is Ashley, and hers is Ryan?" he questioned, and at my nod he said, "Bagsy bein' best man at your weddin'."

I rolled my eyes as I took a hit. "This is girl talk."

"This is a casual conversation, ye' 1950s brute."

My lips twitched as I exhaled the smoke from my lungs. "She kissed me."

"She *kissed* ye'?" Anto asked, his face blanched with shock. "On the lips?"

"Yeah, on the lips, ye' dirty bastard."

My laughter flowed free, and it was at moments like this that I really appreciated Anto.

"How did ye' manage that?" he asked, clearly intrigued. "Mr Joe said she wanted nothin' to do with ye'. He said she was as skittish as a rabbit and could barely get 'er words straight when ye' were talkin' to 'er."

I drank from my bottle, took a deep drag of the doobie, then passed it back to Anto. "I have no clue. I got in 'er space to ruffle *her* feathers just to see what she'd do, and she seemed to lose all sort of rational thinkin', and the next thing I know she was kissin' me."

"Yeah, but *why* were ye' in 'er space at all?" he asked. "Ye' aren't doin' that stupid bet with Beanie, are ye'? 'Cause that doesn't sound like ye' at all, mate. Ye' love women, I can't imagine ye'd try and use one by fuckin' 'er just to prove Beanie wrong."

I shook my head.

"No, I'm not doin' the bet, ye' were right about that. I have other things to focus on . . . I don't know why I walked towards 'er when I saw 'er today. I just did."

"It's probably because you're not used to a bird givin' ye' lip."

"Yeah." I scratched my chin. "I'm sure it is, it just gives me a laugh . . . I guess."

As I spoke the words, I wasn't sure if they were the honest-to-God truth. Ryan's attitude towards me *did* amuse me, but I also liked it, and I didn't know what to think about that. Liking something about a girl's personality wasn't what I was used to. As shallow as it sounded, I never got past liking the body a woman came in.

I shook the ridiculous thoughts away.

"No more talkin' about birds."

"Then what else are we supposed to talk about?" Anto asked with a frown. "I have no suggestions."

I vibrated with silent laughter. "Shipments."

Anto groaned. "It's always work and no play with you."

I shrugged. "Work never stops."

He looked down to the ground. "You're right about that."

I noticed the change in his demeanour.

"What's up?"

He glanced at me, then back down to the ground as he smoked. "D'ye ever wonder what we'd be doin' if we weren't Disciples?"

I looked back up at the night sky and took a swig of my beer.

"Nope," I answered. "There's no point in wonderin' about what we can't have."

I hoped I'd said it with enough conviction that he believed me. The truth was that I *did* wonder about a normal life, one where I wasn't the bad thing that lived up the road, but I tried not to. It was wishful thinking, and if I could help it, I tried not to tease myself with other possible life scenarios. I was a Disciple, and I always would be. Plain and simple. Dreaming of a different life, one I'd never have, was self-torture, and I wasn't into that.

"Yeah," Anto said, clearing his throat as he passed the joint back to me. "No point . . . so, shipments?"

I felt sorry for him.

I, at least, had my brother. Anto had no family, except an uncle who he hardly saw. Both of his parents were junkies and overdosed on the same day when he was just sixteen, and he'd been on his own since then. He hated dealing, I knew it killed him to sell the shite that killed his parents, but he had no other choice. This was the life he chose when we first got involved with Mr Nobody.

Like me, Anto had a regular job. He worked in a Ladbrokes so he had a front for supporting himself. He rented a one-bedroom flat about ten minutes away from my house, which he barely decorated because of raids on his home. Everyone, especially the guards, knew who we were, so keeping our "dirty work" out of our homes was vital. They couldn't pin anything on us when they came around because we were clean. The Gardaí kept tabs on all of the well-known Disciples, so we had to play our cards carefully so as to not fuck up and reveal our hand.

"Mine is gettin' collected tonight," I said as I smoked. "Is yours?"

Anto nodded. "At three in the mornin'. The docks won't be quiet until then."

All of our shipments came in the dead of night, no matter which part of the country they were coming from.

"Are ye' still payin' a score per bag or quarter-block sold?"

Anto grumbled, and I knew what he was thinking about. Money. Since neither of us physically sold our own product anymore, and ran it through the younger members, we had to pay them a part of our cut. Every monthly shipment that was mine was worth a hundred thousand euros. Each year, that number, and the weight of my shipments, grew. I got ten per cent of each shipment's cut, per month, and my runners got ten per cent of what I got – and they divided that equally amongst themselves.

It was easy money for them to earn – when I was a runner, I didn't earn nearly as much.

I'd had to do the job for a long time before I led my own set, so I knew the hardship of it, which was why I gave a good cut. We had a certain price each drug sold for, but if a runner found a gullible person, and got more money for a deal than necessary, then they kept that money along with their original ten per cent.

People didn't like to think so, but dealing was a business, and you had to treat it as such if you wanted to get paid *and* make a profit.

"Still ten per cent." Anto nodded. "You?"

"Yeah. I'm not increasin' that unless things become harder for the runners," I said. "They sell the shite so easy, and they don't even go for the street junkies anymore to make a few quid. These fuckers are goin' for the business folk and high-earners. We had to start at the bottom of the barrel to sell when we were runners. These little shites are skippin' that stage and goin' straight for the rich feckers."

Anto chuckled. "As long as they sell it, I don't care who they sell it to."

As heartless as that statement was, I agreed with it. People always blamed drug dealers for the problems that junkies faced, and in all honesty, we *were* the suppliers that fed a bad habit, but we never approached people to take what we offered. I used to when I was a runner, but when I headed my own set, I made some changes. The only people my runners sold to were the people who came to them.

I had one rule: no kids. If I found out a runner of mine was selling to kids, they wouldn't be in my set anymore, and he, or she, would have a bone or two broken for good measure. Simple as that.

"Did ye' have your runners bring their money to the point?" Anto quizzed as he took the joint from me and inhaled deeply. "The deadline was last night, since today's the first of December."

The "point" was a money-collection point. When the runners picked up their batch from the shipment after it arrived, they were each given a point of delivery at the end of the month to bring the money they garnered from selling. Since I made the decision that I needed to talk to Mr Nobody, I'd put out word to my runners not to go to their collection points last night. Instead, they were to hold on to the money until I said otherwise.

"Nope," I answered. "Me plan is in effect. I missed the deadline, so Nobody will see that on the log and he'll come to me. He won't let a hundred and twenty-two grand slip through the cracks without an explanation from me. He knows my set makes a good profit on what I'm given, he'll notice."

"What if he doesn't?" Anto asked, a flash of worry appearing in his eyes. "What if he sends someone else?"

I shrugged. "I'll have to deal with them and hope they can help me."

"I'm nervous over this." Anto took a gulp of his beer. "Are *you* not nervous?"

I chuckled. "I'm shittin' it, mate."

We clanked our bottles together, laughed and drank. I felt relaxed for the first time in a few days, and I knew it was because of the weed I was smoking and the beer I was drinking. That peace, however, was shattered moments later. We both jumped upright when the tyres of a car skidding could be heard. Anto and I dropped our bottles, hopped over the wall and into my garden as a car spun around the corner and into our estate at rapid speed. I burned my finger on the joint in my hand before I threw it on the ground. I had no idea who was driving, or what was going on, but I couldn't take any chances. Rivals had driven by in the past and shot at us for no reason.

"Ash!"

I looked over the wall upon hearing the familiar voice, and when I spotted Doyler as he got out of the white car, I stood upright.

"What the fuck, Doyler?" I snapped. "Ye' scared the shite out of—"

"Help me," he pleaded as he rounded the car and pulled open the back door.

It was then that I noticed the bloody handprint he left while grabbing the handle. I stared at it, and didn't move until I heard a feminine cry. As if on instinct, I moved forward to help.

"*Kara?*" Anto sucked in a sharp breath when Doyler lifted a battered, and hardly recognisable, Kara from the back of the car. "Jesus Christ, what happened?"

"I found 'er on me porch like this," Doyler grunted as he adjusted his hold on her. "She's hurt bad."

Anto shut his car door, wiped the visible blood away with the sleeve of his jumper, then together we ran into my house. Doyler lay Kara down on the leather settee, and Anto instantly got onto his phone and called up our personal doctor. I focused on Kara as he did this. She was breathing, I could see her chest rising and falling, but she was in bad shape. Her face . . . Christ, it was swollen all over, and she had so many gashes that her skin was coated with blood.

"Get a blanket for 'er," I told Doyler. "I'll get the kit."

We both acted quickly, Doyler grabbing a throw-over from the back of the chair, and me running out to the hallway press where I kept the first-aid kit. It was a big one, packed with everything a paramedic would use. I came back into the sitting room, opened it and grabbed the items I'd need to clean Kara up as best I could before the doctor got here.

"Ten minutes," Anto said. "He'll be 'ere in ten."

"D'ye hear that, babe?" I said to Kara, my voice louder than needed. "The doc is on his way, you're goin' to be grand. Don't worry a hair on that pretty head of yours."

She groaned in response.

"Christ," Anto whispered. "Who'd do this to 'er?"

"Crazy boyfriend?" Doyler suggested as he mimicked me and put purified water onto gauze and carefully cleaned away any visible blood.

"No," Anto answered Doyler. "She wasn't with anyone. We were messin' around, and it was the first thing I asked before we started."

"Maybe she was mugged?" Doyler then suggested.

"And they conveniently left 'er on your front porch?" I questioned with a knowing look.

He exhaled a deep breath. "I don't know then, all I know is I just about died when I heard 'er cryin' and found 'er. This is sick, even by our standards."

I looked over Kara's battered body. "I'm just glad ye' heard 'er, and found 'er when ye' did."

"Me too," Doyler agreed.

We spoke softly to her over the next few minutes, then I suddenly heard footsteps on the stairs. I jumped to my feet and rushed to the sitting-room door, pulling it closed behind me as I stepped into the hallway. Sean was in the middle of coming downstairs, in just his briefs, staring at me.

"What's goin' on?" he asked tiredly. "I turned off me telly to go to sleep and heard a bunch of talkin'."

"Nothin', man," I answered. "Doyler's just gone and hurt 'imself. The doctor's comin' round shortly to patch 'im up."

Sean froze. "Is he okay?"

I hated that he knew the doctor only came when it was a bad injury.

"Yup." I smiled to appease him. "He needs a few stitches is all, nothin' to worry about."

Sean eyed me for a moment, then nodded. "I'll go back to bed and put me earphones in then."

"Good man," I said. "I'll see ye' tomorrow. I'll let ye' have a lie-in since it's Sunday."

Sean was hesitant for a moment, but when he turned around and walked back up the stairs, I released a breath I hadn't realised I'd been holding. He wasn't a stupid kid, he knew something was going on, but I was glad he respected me enough to mind his own business when I needed him to. When I heard his bedroom door click shut, I re-entered the sitting room, shutting the door firmly behind me.

"She's talkin'," Anto said the second his eyes landed on me. "Can barely make out what she's sayin' though."

"Stand at this door," I told him. "Just in case Sean comes back down. I don't want 'im to see this."

Anto did as asked, while I moved over to the settee Kara was on and kneeled on the floor beside her.

"Kara?" I said softly. "It's Ash, babe."

I wasn't sure if she could open her eyes even if she tried; they were almost swollen shut.

"Ash," she murmured.

I reached for her hand and gave it a gentle squeeze so as not to hurt her further.

"I'm 'ere. You're goin' to be okay."

"He said," she rasped, "it was for you."

I shared a look with my friends before looking back down to Kara.

"I don't know what you're sayin', babe."

She swallowed, and the action caused her to cry out in pain. Her throat was discoloured with bruises on the outside, so I could only imagine how damaged it was on the inside. I stroked my thumb over the hand I still held and hushed her, hoping it would ease her into a sleep she desperately needed.

"Ash."

"I'm 'ere."

"He said . . . he said he hurt me . . . for *you*."

My heart stopped and a chill fell over me. I looked over at Anto, and found his eyes locked on Kara. He was focusing on what she'd just said, so I looked back down at her.

"Who did?" I pressed. "Who hurt ye'?"

"Don't know," she mumbled, her words sounding gargled, most likely from blood in her mouth. "Didn't see his face."

"It's okay," I told her. "Ye' didn't have to, it's okay."

"He gave . . . me a message for ye'."

I leaned in closer. "What, honey?"

"I have," she groaned, "a message for ye' . . . from 'im."

My palms became sticky with sweat, and my stomach swirled with sickness.

"What's the message?"

"He said . . ." she replied, her breathing shallow. "Nobody can't help ye'."

CHAPTER TEN
RYAN

"Ryan!"

I jumped, and barely managed to tighten my hold around the jars of carrots in my arms. When I stilled, and neither of them fell to the floor and smashed to pieces, I exhaled a relieved breath. I gently set them onto the correct shelf, then turned to face the wicked witch of the Southside.

"What, Eddi?"

She stormed towards me, armed with her trusty clipboard.

"You're *still* stockin' the shelves?"

I placed my hands on my hips. "Nothin' gets past you, Sherlock."

She overlooked my comment and asked, "*Why* are ye' still stockin' the shelves?"

I looked at the remaining crates filled with jars of carrots, then turned back to my cousin.

"Because I'm not finished yet?"

Eddi blew out a breath of what I think was frustration. "Ye' were supposed to finish doin' that fifteen minutes ago, then come find me in the back to take inventory. Ye' need to learn all of this."

I huffed with annoyance.

"It's me *second* day," I stressed. "I don't want to rush around and do a half-arsed job."

"While ye' take your sweet time, I'm stuck 'ere after me shift has *already* ended."

I blinked. "What?"

"It's twenty past nine," my cousin snapped. "The shop closes for customers at nine, and we're supposed to be finished and out the door by half."

My heart stopped.

"Bollocks."

"Bollocks is right," Eddi quipped. "I've done the inventory already. Ye' can double up tomorrow. I'm goin' home, ye' can just leave the jars there until tomorrow."

I didn't move. "I can't just leave them sittin' out on the floor."

"If ye' want a lift home, ye' will."

I curled my lip up into a snarl. "I'll walk then."

"Suit yourself."

I turned away from her as she stormed down the aisle towards the exit, grabbing her jacket and bag that was sitting on the countertop waiting for her. I thought about picking up a jar of carrots and lobbing it after her, but I kept my temper in check. Getting sacked on my second day for assaulting my cousin with carrots wasn't how I saw my day panning out.

I pushed Eddi from my mind, and as quick as I could, I finished my task and put the now-empty crate in the back and stacked it with the others. I jogged out of the back, squealing when the lights began to switch off one by one.

"I just about locked ye' in, Ryan," Timmy, the security guard, teased.

I grabbed my jacket and bag from the staffroom, ducked under the half-drawn shutter, and waited for Timmy as he set the alarm and locked up the shop.

"Sorry I kept ye'," I said as he bent down and clicked the padlock on the shutter, securing it. "I just had to put the empty crates out in the back."

Timmy straightened to his full height, which towered over me, and smiled. "It was no bother . . . though your cousin did tell me to lock ye' in before I left."

I gritted my teeth, but laughed for Timmy's sake.

"She's always messin' around," I assured him. "See ye' tomorrow, Tim."

He waved as he walked in the opposite direction to me. I looked around to see if I could spot Eddi's car, and when I didn't, I stood still for a moment and absorbed the fact that she'd left me on my own. Granted, I was only a ten-minute walk away from the house, but it was night-time, and I was still new to the area and she'd just . . . left me.

I refused to believe that the pain I felt in my stomach was anything other than hunger. I zipped up my jacket as I passed by the chipper, which was filled with lads and girls of all ages. I just wanted to get home without an incident, so I kept my head down and walked. When I was clear of the car park, I crossed the main road and headed towards the laneway that I would have to walk through to get home.

As I approached the unlit lane, the hairs on the nape of my neck stood up. I paused before I walked any further, and looked left to right. There wasn't anyone around, and I couldn't see another road that I could take to get out of this end of the estate. I didn't want to walk a different way in case I got lost altogether.

I looked ahead, and I could see the street light at the other end, so I decided to run for it. I held on to my bag and jogged down the lane, tensing and holding my breath at every sound. As I approached the end of the laneway, I exhaled a relieved breath, but fear struck as a dark figure suddenly jumped from the shadows on my right and grabbed hold of my arm.

I screamed, and the person – who I assumed to be a man from his strength – moved behind me, reached around and clamped his hand over my mouth, silencing me. I felt his hot breath on my face, and heard his wheezing breaths as he pressed his mouth against my ear. Dread surged through me, and fear almost paralysed me.

"Aren't *you* a pretty little thing?" the gruff voice spoke into my ear, causing me to squirm with discomfort.

The movement dislodged his hand from my mouth.

"Please," I panted, my breathing laboured as my heart pounded against my chest. "I don't have money but I have a phone. Take that."

The man's laugh caused him to cough and choke, the sound turning my already upset stomach. He reeked of stale smoke and cheap alcohol. My hands, which were somehow on the arm he had hooked around my neck, instinctively flexed. My fingernails dug into his arm, causing him to hiss.

"That hurt," he bellowed.

His anger was evident, and I took the opportunity to scream once more. The man struggled to quieten me, but when we both heard a voice we went as still as statues, until I remembered that I needed that person to hear me.

"Help!" I shouted. "Please, help me!"

The man thumped me in the back and it hurt. Pain shot up my spine, and a pulsing throb settled on the spot his hand had hit. I continued to fight against his hold, and when I saw a tall figure jog towards the lane, I cried out with relief.

"What the fuck is goin' on 'ere?"

That voice. I *knew* that voice.

"Ash!" I screeched. "It's me, Ryan. Help!"

He didn't answer me, but his movements sped up. One moment I was in a creep's hold, and the next I was behind Ash, hidden and protected. My hands went to his jacket and I gripped on to it for dear life as he placed his body between mine and the man harassing me. I pressed my face against his back as my body trembled.

"I hope to God," Ash growled, "that ye' weren't doin' what I think ye' were doin'?"

"I'm sorry," the man stammered.

No bullshit excuses, no silence or long, drawn-out pauses, just instant apologies. Ash moved away from me, grabbed hold of the man, and because of the darkness I couldn't see what he was doing but I heard a sickening crack followed by the man crying out in pain.

"I don't think it's me ye' should be apologisin' to, *d'you*?"

Ash shoved the man and stepped aside, and the new view showed me that the man who'd attacked me had now backed up considerably. In fact, he looked like he might bolt at any given second. He was leaning forward and cradling his hand to his chest.

"I'm so sorry, miss," he choked out. "I didn't mean to scare ye', I swear."

Ash continued to stare at the man as he said, "Is that a good enough apology for ye', nightmare?"

I frantically bobbed my head just so the stranger would leave. I didn't want to be in his presence a second longer.

Ash growled. "She's new to the area, so ye' best thank 'er for bein' so kind when any other girl from round 'ere would want your balls cut off and stuffed in your mouth."

My stomach churned some more at the vivid description.

"Thanks, miss," the man practically cried. "Thanks so much."

I remained mute.

Ash and I both watched the man run and disappear into the night, and for a long moment we were silent. Then Ash took out his phone and spoke to someone briefly. He was giving them a description of the man who'd attacked me, and told them which direction he was running in.

"Make sure he thinks twice about attackin' a woman again."

He hung up, put the phone back in his pocket and then turned to face me, placing his hands on my shoulders. "Are ye' okay?"

I was shaking. "I think so."

"Did he hurt ye'?"

I ignored the pulsing pain in my back where I'd been hit.

I shook my head. "No. Just scared me."

Ash nodded but left his hands on my shoulders. I was trembling, and I knew he could feel it. I saw that he shook his head, and I heard him sigh.

"Ye' may be a good-lookin' girl," he commented, "but you're very stupid."

I stared at him, aghast.

"What d'ye me-mean?" I stammered. "I was just walkin' back to me auntie's when he came out of nowhere and tried to mug me . . . I think."

I hoped to God that he'd just wanted to mug me.

Ash shook me. "I can take a wild guess what he wanted to do to ye', and it wasn't mug ye', ye' feckin' eejit."

I blanched. "*I'm* an eejit?"

"Yeah, ye' are." Ash said with a shake of his head. "It's pitch-black out, and ye' decide to take a stroll home through the laneway. Ryan, I shouldn't have to explain why that is a fuckin' *terrible* idea."

I couldn't argue with him, because he was absolutely right.

"I didn't know another way to get to me auntie's house," I admitted. "I was afraid I'd get lost."

Ash considered this, then asked, "Where's your cousin?"

"She drove home without me," I sniffled, hiking the strap of my bag up my shoulder. "We had a fight."

Ash cursed. "And she just up and *left* ye'?"

I nodded, and when he didn't say anything, I said, "Yes."

"Fuckin' bitch," he growled. "I'll be havin' a word with 'er."

Fear shot up my spine.

"No!" I almost screeched. "No, please don't."

Ash paused. “I’m not goin’ to hurt ’er, Ryan. I’m goin’ to explain to ’er what almost happened to ye’. She’s from round ’ere, she’s grown up knowin’ how dangerous things can be, so she knows fuckin’ better than to let ye’ walk home alone at night. I bet your auntie is havin’ murder with ’er about this right now.”

I imagined exactly that so I didn’t disagree, and instead I sniffled once more. I wasn’t crying, but I was on the verge of it. I rubbed my eyes and took a few deep breaths to calm down.

“Hey,” Ash said, moving a hand from my shoulder to flick underneath my chin. “You’re okay. I’ve got ye’.”

Without thinking, I stepped forward and placed my arms around his waist, and hugged him tightly. It hit me in that moment what had almost happened to me, and terror wrapped itself around me like a blanket.

“Thank you,” I whimpered. “I’m so sorry for thinkin’ the worst of ye’. Ye’ saved me tonight, and I won’t ever forget it.”

Ash’s arms came around me after a moment’s hesitation. He placed one hand on the middle of my back, and with the other he stroked up and down my side. The motion, or Ash’s presence overall, helped me relax a bit.

“Don’t mention it, nightmare.”

An unexpected laugh burst free of my lips, and then, tears. Ash hugged my body to his and swayed me from side to side. Luckily, it was only a minor breakdown and my tears didn’t last long.

“God,” I said, stepping out of his warm embrace as I quickly wiped my tear-streaked cheeks. “What must ye’ think of me?”

“I think,” he said, jamming his hands into the pockets of his jeans, “that both of us got off on the wrong foot. I’ll level with ye’, okay? I know ye’ know that I’m a Disciple, but I’m not a horrible person, I don’t go around hurtin’ people for shits and giggles. I just have a really crap job that I’m not allowed to quit.”

That seemed to be an extremely honest thing for him to say. A job he wasn't allowed to quit . . . that sentence made me feel for him. Did that mean he became a Disciple because he was forced to? Or did he join because he had no other choice?

"I'm sorry for how I've acted around ye'," I said, folding my arms across my chest and shifting my stance. "I promise I'm not a bitch . . . not all of the time, anyway. I'm just not really used to bein' around people."

Ash snorted. "I'll take your word for it."

I swallowed. "Can . . . Can I ask ye' a favour?"

"Go for it."

I glanced around. "Can ye' walk me home?"

"Ye' thought I wasn't goin' to?"

I was glad of the darkness when heat stained my cheeks.

"I didn't want to assume. I'm sure ye' have other plans."

"I don't," he answered. "I was headin' home from a friend's house. She hurt 'erself last night and I was just stoppin' by to check on 'er."

"Oh," I said. "Is she okay? Your friend?"

"Yeah," he nodded. "She had a nasty fall yesterday, but she's on the mend and will be okay."

"Thank God for that."

"Yeah," Ash agreed. "Come on, let's get you home."

He gestured towards the path, and we both fell into silence as we walked, but a comfortable one. After we crossed the road close to the laneway, I could now see Ash better thanks to the street lights so I looked up at him. As if he sensed my eyes on him, he glanced down at me and I quickly averted my gaze.

"I have questions," he suddenly announced.

I looked back up at him. "Huh?"

"Well, we don't know much about each other, so I have questions."

I nervously swallowed. I wasn't prepared for questions. I couldn't let on about my background, especially not about my da, so I tried to play it cool.

"Like, what's me favourite colour?"

Ash chuckled. "I bet it's pink."

"Wrong. It's silver."

"I've read ye' completely wrong," he teased. "This changes everythin'."

I hid a smile. "What's *your* favourite colour?"

"Black."

"Black isn't a colour," I playfully argued.

"Of course it is," Ash debated. "It's as much of a colour as white is."

"White isn't a colour either."

He snorted. "Next you'll be tellin' me that water isn't wet."

"It's not wet. Wet is what we experience when we touch water, but it's not *actually* wet."

Ash's laughter was deep and rumbling, and I liked how it sounded. It reminded me of the disastrous moment of weakness I'd had in the supermarket with him, and my ears burned with heat. I couldn't believe I'd forgotten about the most daring thing I had done in my entire life.

"I'm very sorry about kissin' ye'," I told him, looking down at the road as we walked. "I'm mortified about it."

"Don't be sorry," he said. "I enjoyed it."

My stomach did a silly little flip.

"Ash!" I breathed, embarrassment running through my veins. "Ye' aren't supposed to say that."

"Why not?"

"I don't know, ye' just aren't."

He continued to laugh. "It was a kiss, don't overthink it."

If he knew just how much I overthought everything, he wouldn't have made that joke.

"Why Ryan?" he asked, changing the subject.

"Why Ryan what?"

"Why is your name Ryan?"

"Oh." I chuckled. "Me ma and da didn't want Eddi to go through life on 'er own with a lad's name, so they saddled me horse to hers and gave me a bloke's name too."

Ash laughed. "I like your ma."

"I think I would have liked 'er too."

Ash slowed down his pace. "What d'ye mean?"

"She died when I was four." I answered. "Kidney failure."

Ash stopped walking completely. "Are ye' serious?"

His reaction was what I would call flabbergasted. I'd had the same reaction when Eddi told me what his ma died from. It was something we had in common, though I knew we both wished that we didn't.

"Yeah, why?"

"Because *my* ma died of kidney failure two years ago."

"I'm sorry, Ash."

"Small world," he said, and began walking again. "For both our mothers to have died from the same thing."

"A cruel world, ye' mean."

"Yeah," he nodded. "It's definitely a cruel fuckin' world."

We continued to walk in silence for a moment or two, then I said, "Why Ashley? Eddi told me what Ash stood for."

"I don't have a funny story like you do. Me parents just liked it."

"Well, that's not very fair. I was hopin' for somethin' laughable."

Ash's lips twitched. "Sorry to disappoint ye'."

"Ashley isn't all that bad, since ye' can shorten it. When ye' shorten mine to Ry, it's still a lad's nickname."

"Yeah," Ash snickered. "You're shit out of luck there, nightmare."

"Nothin' gets by you."

He stared down at me for a moment, then grinned. "I know what you're tryin' to do when ye' get all sarcastic with me, ye' know?"

"Enlighten me," I said. "What *am* I tryin' to do?"

"Be ornery so no one wants anythin' to do with ye'."

I didn't think that's what I was doing at all. I was just really inexperienced talking to men, or people in general. I'd mentioned that I wasn't used to being around people, but Ash really had no clue just how little experience I had.

I blinked. "Or maybe I'm just ornery."

"Maybe," Ash agreed, "but only time will tell."

"It could be a waste of time. I could be completely evil for all ye' know."

Ash shook his head. "I deal with girls a might meaner than you on the daily, big head. Ye' don't scare me."

He didn't scare me either, and I couldn't believe it when I realised that. According to Eddi, he was a big shot in the Disciples, someone who people feared, a name that people only whispered, and yet I didn't get that vibe from him. Not even in the slightest.

"I'm about to," I quipped. "Did ye' just say I have a big head?"

Ash stared at me, unblinking. "No. I called ye' big head . . . I didn't *say* ye' have a big head."

"That doesn't make sense."

"It does round 'ere."

"To who?"

"Everyone." Ash laughed. "Ye' really are foreign."

I bristled. "I'm Irish, just like you."

"Ye' were born a planet away from growin' up in estates though."

"Just because I didn't grow up in a welfare family doesn't mean I'm not Irish."

I regretted the words the second I spoke them, because I knew not every family in an estate lived on welfare. My auntie and cousin being one. I blurted the stereotype before I could catch it, and I cringed.

"Ye' just downgraded from big head to arsehole." Ash clicked his tongue. "Half of the people on these streets are on the welfare, and the other half own their homes and have nine-to-five jobs, but do ye' know what they all have in common?"

I shook my head.

"They're some of the nicest people I've ever met, and they all come from different backgrounds and had different starts in life. No one on these streets has a stick up their arse, not until *you* moved 'ere, at least."

Ash continued to walk beside me, but we fell into a silence that *was* awkward.

"I'm not stuck-up," I said after a minute or so. "Or at least, I don't mean to be."

"If you're goin' to live round 'ere, you're goin' to have to see things through our eyes . . . ye' aren't in the countryside anymore, nightmare."

He didn't need to tell me that; every little thing reminded me that I wasn't at home. I was out of my element here, tonight's events had proved just how much.

I sighed. "I know."

"To be honest, I don't really believe that you're a culchie."

I raised an eyebrow. "Why?"

"Ye' don't sound like one."

I blinked. "I was home-schooled me entire life, and grew up around people who're from Dublin. That's why I don't have a Kildare accent. I am very much a culchie though, and I'm proud of it."

"Well, ye' sure told me."

I didn't reply.

"Why were ye' home-schooled?"

My palms got sweaty, because I was worried that I was speaking too much about my home life when Eddi had told me *not* to do that. I had to watch what I said, but it was hard, because conversation seemed to flow easily with Ash. Conversation flowing easily with anyone was never something I'd thought I could achieve.

"Where I lived was far away from local schools. It was easier to be home-schooled."

Telling that lie was easier than saying my father kept me close to him because he grieved the loss of my mother. I knew that Ash knew how my ma died, but it felt a little too personal to reveal another person's grieving process to a stranger, and that was what Ash was. I was also worried that mentioning it would invite unwanted questions about my father. When I didn't expand on it further, he didn't press me about it. He nodded in understanding.

"I'm a Kildare girl, though. Don't get that twisted, just 'cause I sound like you and everyone else around 'ere when I talk."

Ash held up his hands. "I didn't mean to offend ye'."

"Ye' didn't," I countered. "Ye' asked a question, and I answered it."

"So you aren't mad?" he quizzed.

"No," I answered instantly. "Not at all."

He laughed. "*Right.*"

"I'm not mad," I emphasised. "But you suggestin' I am is makin' ye' a little irritatin', if I'm honest."

Ash looked at me like he couldn't believe I'd called him irritating, and then he cracked up laughing. He didn't seem angry. If anything, he seemed thoroughly amused by me.

"You're somethin' else, nightmare."

"Somethin' bad?"

"No." He sounded thoughtful. "Not somethin' bad."

We approached my auntie's estate, and it was quieter than usual, but I couldn't put my finger on what was different.

"Eddi's not at home," Ash said as we approached her house.

He was right; her car wasn't in the garden. A sick feeling churned in my stomach as I quickly hurried up the driveway and fumbled with my keys to open the door. Before I could get my key into the lock, the door opened and my auntie was there. Her eyes were red and swollen, and she looked absolutely beside herself with worry.

"Ryan!"

She practically dove on me, hugging my body tightly to hers.

"What's wrong?" I asked, hugging her back.

"Are ye' okay? I was worried sick because it took ye' so long to walk home." She pulled back and said, "I can't *believe* she left ye'."

It didn't take a genius to figure out who she was talking about.

"It's fine—"

"It bloody well *isn't*." Ash's voice cut me off.

My auntie leaned forward and looked over at Ash, who was halfway inside the garden, leaning against the wall. She widened her eyes a little, but she didn't look like she was scared of him, she just looked surprised to see him.

"Ashley?"

He nodded. "She was attacked by some creep, Andie. If I hadn't of been there, I don't want to know what would've happened."

My auntie's hold on me turned vice-like.

"I'm okay," I assured her, before looking over at Ash and glaring at him.

He shrugged, uncaring.

"Are ye' *sure* you're okay?" Andrea asked. "Ye' can tell me if ye' aren't."

"Not a single hair is outta place. I'm grand."

It was at that moment that Eddi pulled her car into the driveway and got all our attention. She killed the engine and jumped out, her eyes blazing as she trained them on me. She was furious, but I didn't miss her shoulders sag with relief when she realised that I was okay.

"Where the *hell* were ye'?"

"I think," Ash cut in, "the main question 'ere is, why the fuck did *you* leave 'er on 'er own? Ye' fuckin' dope."

Eddi visibly paled when she realised Ash was in the garden. Unlike her ma, she *did* look scared of Ash, and there was a part of me that wanted to assure her that there was no reason to fear him, but I kept my mouth shut because I didn't know that for certain.

"Why are *you* 'ere?"

"Because if I wasn't," he answered with a growl, "Ryan probably wouldn't be either."

Eddi's eyes widened as she looked at me. "What does he mean? Did somethin' happen?"

I shot Ash a warning glare to be quiet, then returned my gaze to my cousin.

"A man attacked me but I'm *fine*," I said, emphasising the word. "Ash saved the day."

Eddi blinked her eyes in disbelief, then to him she said, "Thank you."

If he was surprised by her thanks, he didn't show it; he simply inclined his head in acknowledgement. Eddi locked up her car, and passed Ash on her way into the house.

"Give me a minute," I said to her and my auntie.

They were hesitant, but then nodded and went inside. Ash approached me, but stopped a metre or two away from the doorway. I pulled the door closed and leaned my shoulder against it.

"I can't thank ye' enough for what ye' did."

"Like I said, don't mention it," he said with a wave of his hand. "I'd have done it for anyone."

I believed him. Behind me, I heard my auntie and cousin arguing, and I sighed. Knowing that I was the subject of their fight left me feeling sick.

"I better go in and act as a buffer," I said, looking at Ash. "I don't want them fightin' over me."

"Before ye' do," Ash said, stepping forward. "I want to ask ye' somethin'."

I wasn't sure why, but my heart beat faster with his words.

"Ye' do?"

He nodded, his eyes never straying from mine.

"Okay." I licked my lips. "Shoot."

"Will ye' go out with me?"

There was no hesitation, and from what I could see on Ash's face, no trace of uncertainty as he asked the question. He looked the picture of confidence as he stood before me, and it made my knees a little weak. I really liked that confidence, even though I knew I shouldn't.

My teeth grazed my lower lip. "Go out where with ye'?"

"Out out." Ash shrugged, putting his hands into the front pockets of his jeans. "On a date."

Words eluded me, so I simply stared at him.

"Ryan," he prompted, his tone amused. "Anyone home?"

I blinked. "I can't."

He quirked an eyebrow in question. "Can't, or won't?"

"Can't. Won't," I blurted out. "I don't know, both."

He didn't look surprised, or upset, he just looked amused. He always looked amused.

"Okay." He nodded. "I'll ask ye' again tomorrow."

For some reason, I wanted to smile at him. He was charming, I couldn't deny that. It wasn't so much that he was a man of many words, just that he had a way with them. He always sounded so sure of himself, like he knew exactly what he wanted and wasn't afraid to ask for it.

"The answer will still be no, Ash."

He turned and began to walk out of the garden. "I'll try again the day after that."

"It'll still be no," I called out.

"Then I'll ask the next day, then the next day," he hollered. "I'll wear ye' down eventually, nightmare."

I did smile then, at his back as he walked home, and when he was out of sight, the thought crossed my mind.

Maybe Ash Dunne isn't as bad as everyone thinks he is.

CHAPTER ELEVEN
ASHLEY

Two weeks later . . .

"I'm beginnin' to wonder if Nobody has even noticed that ye' haven't paid your money for November."

I glanced at Anto as he hung a bauble on my Christmas tree. He was very focused, messing with it until it hung straight, and the sight amused me greatly. His eyes were squinting, and his tongue stuck out of the corner of his mouth in concentration. He took decorating a Christmas tree *very* seriously, it appeared.

"What makes ye' say that?"

"No one's showed up ready to cut your bollocks off because ye' missed the deadline, that's what makes me say it."

I'd been thinking the same thing. I'd thought that, since I didn't have my runners pay my monthly quota, then Mr Nobody would seek me out to find out why, but that hadn't happened. Not yet, anyway.

"Maybe he's busy?"

"Yeah." Anto mused. "He's probably puttin' up his Christmas tree today, too."

The corners of my lips curved upwards into a grin.

"Ye' know I put it up for Sean," I said. "Me ma loved this holiday – she made a huge deal about Christmas when we were growin' up – and since she's gone, I want to keep that alive for 'im durin' this time of year. I need as much normalcy as possible where he's concerned."

Anto didn't make a joke, and instead he said, "I know, man. You're very good to 'im."

"Of course," I said. "He's me little brother."

Footsteps sounded on the stairs as said little brother descended them.

"Speak of the Devil," Anto murmured with a sly grin on his face, "and he'll appear."

We both looked at Sean as he entered the room wearing the ugliest Christmas jumper I had ever seen in my entire life. Anto placed his hands on either side of his head and stared at it, his eyes burning with judgement. Sean, completely unfazed, was grinning from ear to ear, and the festive jumper made him look younger than he was.

A memory of the moment he'd received it from our mother, four years ago, rolled through my mind like a scene from a film.

◆ ◆ ◆

"Ma," Sean practically squealed. "I'm not wearin' that."

Our ma frowned. "Why not? Don't ye' like it?"

Sean caught the pointed look I shot his way, and before he was about to answer her honestly, he cleared his throat and said, "It's way too big."

"I did make a bit of a mistake with the measurements, but ye'll grow into it. We can just roll up the sleeves for now."

Sean looked like he would rather drink vinegar, and it drew a chuckle from me. His eyes cut to mine after he tugged the jumper on, and he cast a frustrated glare my way. But my amusement was short-lived when soft fabric suddenly whacked against my face.

"Ha!" Sean laughed. "You've got an ugly jumper too!"

"Ugly?" Ma admonished. "Ye' little shite, it's taken me weeks to make them for the pair of ye'!"

"Sorry, Ma." Sean cringed. "It's the best ugliest Christmas jumper I've ever got though."

I held my own jumper out, and stared at the overweight Mrs Claus and said, "I have to agree with 'im, Ma. They're hands down the best ugly Christmas jumpers to have ever existed."

I pulled mine over my head, and was pleased to find the sizing was perfect.

"Well," Ma huffed as she got to her feet, "if that's how ye' both feel . . . I'm eatin' the rest of the trifle on me own."

She burst into laughter when Sean and I darted out of the sitting room after her. I hooked my arms around her waist just as she reached the fridge in the kitchen and hoisted her up into the air, giving my brother a chance to steal the dessert from right under her nose.

"Put me down, ye' little shite."

"Little?" I repeated. "I'm a foot taller than ye'."

"Tall or not, I'll cut ye' down to size real quick, boyo." She laughed as I set her down on the floor. "Now, say ye' love your jumpers or you're gettin' no trifle."

I could tell that Sean was contemplating running out of the room with the dessert, but he thought better of it and said, "I love me jumper, Ma, even if it's ugly."

"You're so talented at creatin' ugly Christmas jumpers, Ma," I added with a grin. "We'd be lost without ye' and your obvious knittin' skills."

"Get three spoons, ye' charmin' little feckers," she chuckled. "Before I eat it all to meself and leave ye' with nothin' but *your jumpers."*

◆ ◆ ◆

I looked at Sean, and I knew our ma would have loved to see him finally fill that godawful jumper out. There was a dull pain in my chest with the thought of her, and like always, I pushed her from my mind. I could handle a lot of shitty things, but talking or thinking of my ma wasn't one of them. Not yet, anyway.

"I found it," he announced. "It was in the back of me wardrobe, but I found it."

I nodded. "That ye' did, buddy."

"It's brilliant, isn't it?"

"Yeah." I nodded. "Was it always *that* red though?"

Sean nodded. "Ma wanted it to be extra Christmassy when she made it."

"It looks like a knittin' machine blew up," Anto commented. "Your ma was a lousy seamstress, mate."

"Don't speak ill of the dead," I warned, but I couldn't help chuckling because he spoke the truth. "But you're spot on, she was terrible at it."

"She was right, though. She always said I'd finally grow into this jumper." Sean laughed. "I use to dread when I'd outgrow a jumper, because I knew it meant she'd make a new one for me, an uglier one. This, hands down, has to be the worst one she ever made, though. I love it."

My smile was as wide as his when I said, "Me too, bud."

Sean happily got involved with decorating the tree, like he did every year. He'd always enjoyed this part the most with our ma, so I tried to make it as enjoyable as I could without being over the top. He missed her every day, just like I did, but unlike me, he could happily talk about her without feeling like his chest was caving in.

I stepped back from the tree to inspect our work so far. Mine, and Sean's, side was coming along great, but Anto's . . . Jaysus.

"Why don't ye' just unravel the lights?" I suggested to him. "That'd be a massive help, mate."

"Why?" he queried, his tongue still sticking out the side of his mouth as he focused on his bauble-hanging task. "I'm havin' fun doin' this."

"You're rubbish at it though," Sean remarked under his breath, but both Anto and I still heard him. He may as well have slapped Anto across the face for the look of disbelief my friend shot my little brother's way.

"I'll kindly ask ye' to take that back, ye' lyin' little bastard."

I rubbed my hand over my mouth in an attempt to stop myself from laughing.

"Ash said I'm not allowed to lie." Sean smirked. "So I'm afraid I can't do as ye' ask."

"Ash," Anto growled as he scowled at my brother. "Did ye' hear what he just said to me?"

"Yeah?"

Anto's wild eyes flashed to mine. "*And?*"

"Annnnddd . . . I agree with 'im."

My friend's mouth dropped open. "How fuckin' *dare* you?"

My lips curved up into a big smile that I knew would hurt my cheeks if it remained on my face for long.

"Don't start," I said. "I haven't got time for one of your outbursts tonight."

"No," Anto stated, setting down his baubles and placing his hands on his hips. "Let's fuckin' talk about this."

"'Ere we go," Sean chuckled. "He's gonna have a bitch fit."

"Mind your business, Bilbo."

I laughed, the sound bubbling up out of me as joy filled me. This was Christmas. Decorating, having fun and spending time with people you cared about. That was what my Christmas was all about.

"Can't we just finish the tree?" I suggested, gesturing to it. "We've been at it ages already, and we *still* haven't got the lights on."

"I don't think so," Anto announced. "All our years of friendship have just been ruined, and ye' want me to sweep it under the carpet?"

"Ye' sound like me bird goin' off on me when I don't notice she got 'er hair done."

When Sean finished speaking, I bumped into him as my laughter flowed freely and filled the room. I slapped my open palm against my brother's, and tears of joy stung my eyes. I had to sit down and rub them to relax.

Anto's reaction, as always, was priceless. I hadn't laughed like that in a while, and it was only then that I realised I'd needed it.

"That's made me happy," I said, merrily. "Very fuckin' happy."

Anto didn't agree, but I did see his lips twitch one or twice when he flicked his eyes to a still-cackling Sean, which told me he was playing up being offended just to make my brother smile.

"Okay, lights time," I announced, slapping my palms against my thighs. "Sean, you grab—"

I was cut off when the doorbell rang. We all turned, and when Sean automatically moved to leave the room and open the door, for some reason I stopped him.

"What?" he asked, confused.

"I'll get it."

It was only six p.m., but it was dark outside, and I didn't want Sean in harm's way. Not that he *would* be in harm's way, but I couldn't take any chances. Since Kara was attacked two weeks ago and delivered a message from the man who had it out for me, things had been quiet. She had, thankfully, healed wonderfully. Faded bruises were all the evidence that remained of her attack.

Physically, she was nearly back on her feet, but I wasn't sure what emotional damage was done. During my last visit with her, I offered to pay for her to speak to someone should she need to, but she refused. She kindly asked me if I could place her in a new set within the Disciples now that she had become a member. I didn't blame her for not wanting to be around me; if I was her, I wouldn't want to be near me either.

I'd keep an eye on her, and check in on her with the head of her new set every now and then, because I felt somewhat responsible for her after what she went through because of me, but I respected her decision to move on. Considering the threat that was dangling over my family, it was the best decision she could have made.

"I'll only be a second," I said as I left the room, closing the door behind me.

I hovered by the front door.

"Who is it?" I called.

"Nobody," a voice answered.

My breath caught in my throat, and a cold wave of misery washed over me. On the other side of my front door was the very man who'd bound me and my friends to a life we loathed.

I shook my head, stood up straight, got myself in gear and quickly opened the door. I knew I shouldn't look directly at him, but it wouldn't have mattered either way. Mr Nobody was wearing a balaclava, and only his eyes were visible. But he didn't look out of place with his disguise on, as everyone outside was wrapped up in layers to protect themselves from the bitter winter cold.

"We need to talk, Ash."

I nodded, stepped aside and let my boss into my house. I glanced out at my empty garden, then closed the door, locking it from the inside. My heart pounded erratically against my chest; it was so loud that I could hear each beat in my ears.

"Kitchen," I said quietly. "Me brother is in the sittin' room."

Mr Nobody nodded once. "Bring Anto in too. I know he's 'ere."

Shite.

"Okay."

He walked towards the kitchen, and didn't look like he was going to make an attempt to remove any of his clothing, so I hustled into the sitting room.

"Sean," I said as calmly as I could. "Get the lights on the tree as best ye' can. Me and Anto have to talk business in the kitchen with a mate of ours."

Anto instantly walked out of the room and headed for the kitchen. I gave my brother a firm look, and waited for his nod to acknowledge what I'd said. I left the room, closing the door fully, and headed into the kitchen, shutting that door too. It wasn't until I looked down at my hand as I removed it from the handle that I realised it was shaking.

"D'ye want a drink or somethin', sir?" I asked, fisting my hands to get control of myself.

"No," Mr Nobody answered from the kitchen table, where he was sat across from Anto. "I won't be 'ere long."

His voice was just as I remembered, deep, gruff and scary as hell. I took a seat next to Anto and waited.

"Ye' know why I'm 'ere?"

"Yes, sir."

"So," he began, tapping his fingers on the table. "Where's me money?"

"With the runners," I answered. "I told them not to deliver it to their checkpoints on the deadline date because I needed to meet with ye'."

I could only see the man's green eyes, so I couldn't gauge his reaction to my news.

"How'd ye' know I'd come and meet with ye'?"

"I didn't," I answered honestly. "I just hoped ye' would."

"And *why* did ye' want this meetin' to take place?"

"I needed to see if ye' could help me." I leaned back in my chair, trying to appear relaxed and confident when I was anything but. "Someone is threatenin' me. Whoever it is broke into this house and ransacked the sittin' room, and left a note on me brother's bed." After I explained what the note said, Mr Nobody remained mute, so I continued. "Two weeks ago, Kara, one of our new Disciples, was attacked by this man. He battered 'er up good, and left 'er a message for me."

"What was the message?"

"It was 'Nobody can't help ye'.'"

That made him sit forward.

"Meanin' me?"

"Yes, sir." I nodded. "It had to be about you."

Things were silent for a few minutes as the boss thought.

"What did ye' think I could do for ye'?" he asked of me. "Ye' know I don't involve meself in personal matters of Disciples."

"I know that, sir. I just wanted to know if any of your associates heard about someone who had it out for me," I explained. "I have no idea who this person could be, or why they'd want to hurt me and me family. I don't have bad blood with anyone, so I'm at a loss."

Mr Nobody nodded. "Nothin' has been said to me, but I'll put the word out and see what gets back to me."

I exhaled a relieved breath. "Thanks, sir."

"In the meantime," he stood up, "November's collection is to be delivered with this month's collection on New Year's Eve, with an extra ten per cent added for missin' the deadline, understood?"

"Yes, sir," I said, standing up too. "Thank you, sir."

I thought he was about to leave the room, but then he turned his gaze on Anto.

"*You* need to tighten your runners up," he said, his voice gruff. "Two of them came up short at November's collection. Only by a grand each, but leavin' me short of a penny is *never* acceptable."

Anto paled. "D'ye have the names of which two?"

"I'll have them sent to your phone," Mr Nobody answered. "Those two are out. I don't want body bags since they're kids, but I don't want them to go unpunished either. Stealin' from me is a big no-no, lads."

Anto robotically nodded.

Mr Nobody began to walk out of the room, and as he walked, he said, "And Anto, *you're* the one who let rookie runners handle me money and make a mess. So, *you'll* be the one to clean it up. Pick a limb and snap it. Make an example of them, or one will be made of *you*."

My friend looked like he was about to be sick, but he said, "I'll get it done, sir."

We didn't have to walk the man out; he left as quietly as he came, the front door clicking shut behind him. He moved like the wind but you knew he was always there, you could always feel his eyes on you. Anto turned to me, his face filled with panic.

"Fuck," he swallowed, his face paling. "*Fuck!*"

"It's okay," I told him. "Once we know who the runners are that's caused the problem, we'll filter them out and get two new ones. Better ones."

Anto sat down. "I have to hurt the other two though . . . how am I goin' to do that? I've never broken someone's bones before, Ash."

"Maybe we can just pretend—"

"He has eyes everywhere, Ashley," my friend said solemnly. "I can't risk it, he'll have me thrown in prison for rape or murder if I disobey 'im . . . ye' know he will."

He was right. No one disobeyed Mr Nobody and got away cleanly.

I ran my hands through my hair. "I'll help ye'."

Anto looked up. "What?"

"I'll help you deal with the runners," I stated. "We'll batter them good, and break their legs . . . we'll do what we're told and nothin' will happen to us."

Anto placed his head in his hands. He looked as sick about the situation as I felt.

"We aren't those people, Ash. We don't hurt people, we just sell fuckin' drugs."

"Not anymore."

Anto was silent, which was very unlike him, so I knew he was having a rough time processing what we had to do.

"This was a bollocks of a meetin'," he angrily growled. "We didn't even get any information on the cunt whose gunnin' for ye'!"

"But we *did* alert Nobody's attention to it," I reminded him. "He said he'd have his ears to the ground."

Anto shook his head. "This has turned into a poxy day."

I nodded in agreement. "Let's just go and help Sean finish the tree . . . there isn't much more we can do until ye' find out the runners' names and I get the information I need."

If I get the information I need, that is.

Anto nodded, but I could tell he was only trying to appease me, and that made me feel like shite. Our good day had gone from fun to hell in the matter of ten minutes.

So much for a happy fucking Christmas.

CHAPTER TWELVE
RYAN

"Ryan Mahony!"

I just about jumped out of my skin when my name was hollered. I had heard it shouted like that twice a month since my da was sent to prison, and it still scared me half to death. It was alerting me that it was my time slot for my visiting hour with him.

I quickly gathered up my things and proceeded towards the security gate. I had already passed through two of these stop-and-search checkpoints since entering the prison, but I had nothing on me to hide so I wasn't worried about them.

I stood still and followed the instructions given to me by the guards as they patted me down, searched my bag and had me stand in an X-ray scanner of sorts so they could triple-check that I wasn't smuggling anything illegal into the prison on my person or inside my body. Not that I would ever consider it. I'd be too terrified of getting caught to even attempt it.

"Thank you," I said to the guard who handed me back my bag after I passed through the checkpoint.

I made sure my visitor's badge was visible as I headed towards the small shop, where I purchased coffees, snacks and some sandwiches. I bought a lot of extra goodies for my da to bring back to his cell after our visit. He worked in the kitchen and got paid for it, but the amount he earned wasn't enough to splurge on sweets, so I did that for him.

Once everything was placed into a plastic bag, I checked my badge for the room number I was assigned and headed towards visitor room six. I showed my badge to the guard who was stood outside the room. He checked his clipboard to make sure my information matched up with his.

"Go on in, Ryan," he told me. "Your aul' lad will be in shortly."

I smiled my thanks and entered the tiny room. It was nothing special; it had a small table with two chairs, a window overlooking the mountains, a chair off to the side for the guard, and a rubbish bin. Two cameras were on the ceiling, but I never looked up at them if I could help it. I had always got a small room whenever I came visiting. The more people you had in your visiting party, the bigger the room you were assigned.

I had passed by one of the family rooms before, and saw it to be colourful, with toys of all sorts on the floor. Obviously, that was a room for inmates whose young children came to visit.

Once I was settled in my chair, I placed mine and my da's piping-hot coffees down, then emptied out some of the sweets and sandwiches onto the table. Everything else that I'd bought for my da to bring back to his cell I left in the bag on the floor, knowing the guard would have to document each item, then take away the plastic bag and replace it with a paper one. That part always bothered me – I didn't understand why they used plastic bags in the prison shop if the inmates couldn't have them.

I exhaled, and bobbed my leg up and down as I waited for the door to open. When it did, I jumped to my feet.

"Da!"

My da's entire face lit up when he saw me, and like the emotional wreck I was, upon seeing him tears stung at my eyes and splashed down onto my cheeks. I quickly wiped them away so as to not upset him more than he already was.

I waited for our assigned guard to undo the cuffs on my da's wrists, waist and legs. Da always turned his back to me while this was carried out, and I think he did it to shield me from seeing him wearing them. The guard took his time with the task, and I was on tenterhooks waiting for him to give me the all-clear so I could hug my da. When the guard finally stepped back with the cuffs and handed them to a person outside the room, my da and I lurched forward and wrapped the other in a tight embrace.

"I've missed ye' terrible, love."

"I've missed ye' too." I squeezed him so tight I probably hurt him. "So much, Da."

We hugged for a long while, as usual, and when we separated, my da jokingly clicked his tongue as he thumbed away the tears on my cheeks.

"Sorry," I said, helping him rub them away.

"Don't be sorry," he said as he straightened my chair for me.

After I sat down, so did he. The guard was already sitting in his own chair, with a newspaper in hand. Every time I came here, each guard assigned to our visiting hour did the exact same thing. They rarely talked, they just sat in the corner and read the paper. I always did my best to pretend they weren't there.

"How are ye'?" I asked. "Are ye' gettin' on okay? Are men still bein' nice to ye'? How's your job in the kitchen treatin' ye'?"

Da's joyous laughter burst free.

"Slow down," he said, beaming. "We have time to talk."

I wanted to tell him that we had hardly any time together. A quick glance at the clock on the wall told me it was already ten past two, and our visit ended at three p.m. sharp – so we barely had any time in the other's company, and I hated that.

"Sorry." I smiled, taking his hand in mine from across the table. "I feel like I haven't seen ye' in forever."

"I know." He nodded. "It's tough, but this won't last forever, Ry."

"I keep tellin' meself that, I do," I assured him, "but it's very hard."

He squeezed my hand. "I know, love."

I shook my head clear. "I don't want to be a Debbie Downer, so tell me everythin'."

Da laughed. "There isn't much to tell."

"How are ye' gettin' on?" I asked, repeating my earlier question. "And be honest with me. I'm a nervous wreck when I think of you in 'ere."

"Ry . . ." He smiled. "I'm in a high-security wing because of me profession outside of these walls. I'm not in with the general population because I've most likely put a lot of the inmates in 'ere."

The guard suddenly snorted, without taking his eyes off his paper. "Ye' have, Joe."

I ignored his comment.

"I know that," I said to my da, "but is it okay?"

He nodded. "It's no picnic, but I keep meself busy. I've been readin' a lot more since I joined the library."

My lips parted with shock. "They have a library in 'ere?"

"Yup." Da grinned. "I even have me own card with me picture on it, so I can check out books. It's pretty cool."

I laughed. "You're a spanner."

"It passes the time quickly, so that's really helped."

"And your job?"

"Kitchen work is fine." He shrugged. "I'm not involved in any of the meals, just clean up after they have ended and the inmates are back in their cells or out in the yard."

"What about the inmates ye' *are* around?" I questioned. "Are they okay?"

"I don't talk to any of them durin' work in the kitchen," he answered. "And I'm in me cell the rest of the time, readin' and writin'."

He was stuck in his cell for twenty-three hours a day. He hadn't committed a crime to warrant maximum security; he was in the high-security wing simply because it was safer for him to be away from other inmates. I knew the men he'd got locked up would kill him if they could, and it seemed that the governor of the prison knew it, too.

"Writin'?" I blinked. "*You're* writin'?"

"Yes. Why the amazed expression?" he teased.

"Like, a book?" I asked, ignoring his question.

"Yes, like a book."

"What kind of book exactly?"

"A fictional one." He shrugged. "It's just a hobby I've picked up. It's really helped me mental state. When I'm writin', me mind brings me to a new place and I sort of forget where I am, at least for a little while, ye' know?"

I squeezed his hand. "I'm so glad, and when you've finished it, I'll read for ye' . . . I'll tell ye' if it's shite or not. Ye' can count on me for honesty. Always."

At that, he laughed.

"How's life in Dublin?" he asked after we began eating the items I'd bought at the shop.

"It's good," I said, making sure I stayed away from the topics of the Disciples, Ashley Dunne and my close call with my attacker almost three weeks ago. It would only worry him, and I didn't want him to worry about me while he was in prison.

I couldn't believe I had already been living in Dublin three weeks. It felt like so much had happened since then, but at the same time, nothing at all. I worked a shift at work every single day, six days a week. I didn't mind all the long hours, because it was money of my own that I was earning. My job kept me busy, and I loved it. It wasn't what I wanted to do for the rest of my life, but for now it would do.

"It's very loud, if I'm bein' honest."

Da grinned. "Can ye' sleep with the noise?"

"I couldn't at first," I admitted, "but I must be gettin' used to it because I'm out like a log every night."

My da laughed, and asked me more questions about my new living arrangements. We talked about my job, about Eddi, and about Andrea too. I lied when I spoke about Eddi – I pretended like we got on like a house on fire, but in reality that wasn't the case. Since I was attacked, things with my cousin had been really tense. She'd apologised profusely the night it occurred, but we hadn't spoke about it since. We only spoke about work, or about what to cook each night for dinner and other mundane things.

She hadn't even brought up Ash, though I knew she'd seen him talking to me whenever he came into the supermarket.

I knew that he was a Disciple, and I knew that my auntie, and cousin, had warned me off having anything to do with them, but Ash didn't seem to be the horrible person Disciples were portrayed to be. He was funny, cocky, charming, kind, and he'd saved me from something that most likely would have scarred me for life. I liked him, or what I knew of him. I was also fiercely attracted to him, that much was obvious, and I think he was attracted to me too. He asked me out on a date every time he saw me, and I had already planned on saying yes the next time I spoke to him, just to see what he'd do.

In the back of my mind, however, I constantly reminded myself that he *was* a criminal. I'd grown up around the law, around my father putting people like Ash in prison, and I couldn't allow myself to turn a blind eye to that. It was very hard, though. I didn't have the easiest time socialising with people, but with Ash, it was like riding a bike.

"Will they be comin' to visit next time?" Da asked.

I blinked. "Huh?"

"Andie and Eddi." He smiled, not commenting on me zoning out. "Are they comin' to visit next time?"

I nodded.

"Eddi's in the car park, waitin' for me. She didn't want to impose today since ye' thought it was just goin' to be me, but she and 'er ma told me to let ye' know that they'd both come for the next visit in the new year."

Da blew out a breath. "Can ye' believe it's Christmas in six days?"

"No," I said with a shake of my head. "It's insane."

"Hopefully next Christmas or the one after that, I'll be home."

I looked down. "Ye' don't know that."

"Hey," he said, not speaking again until I looked up at him. "I'm goin' to get time suspended. I'm doin' everythin' I'm supposed to be doin'. I was a year into my sentence on the tenth of last month; I'll be home before ye' know it."

I knew just how long he'd been away from me. I felt every minute as if each one was a whole year.

"What are ye' doin' for your birthday?" he then asked, turning the conversation towards something he thought was lighter to talk about. "New Year's Eve will be 'ere before ye' know it."

I shrugged. "I don't have anythin' planned."

I never did anything on my birthday, other than read a book by an author I hadn't read before.

"Don't have anythin' planned?" he repeated incredulously. "But it's your nineteenth birthday, honey. *And* it's New Year's Eve."

I wasn't sure why he was so surprised, I never did anything for my birthday. I never did anything in general – a night out for me was when we went to the cinema together.

I smiled sadly. "It's just another day to me."

Da frowned, but he didn't press me any further about it.

"Have ye' seen or heard from Ciara?" he asked me offhand.

I shook my head. "No, but I'm goin' into your office to see what the hell 'er problem is. I've already decided on it."

I'd been thinking about her a lot in the past few weeks, and not knowing why she had abandoned my da was killing me. I wanted to confront her and find out what her problem was, once and for all.

"Don't," Da pleaded. "If she doesn't want to see me, that's 'er own decision."

He was hurt by that decision to stay away, I knew he was, and I wanted to wring the bitch's neck over it.

We continued with our visit, talking about everything that we could think of, and before we knew it the guard stood up and announced it was time up and that I had to leave.

"Already?" I frowned.

"Sorry, kid," the guard said, pity in his eyes. "Have you brought anythin' for your da that you'd like brought back to his cell?"

"Yeah." I picked up the plastic bag of sweets and sandwiches and gave it to him.

I watched as he counted out the items, then wrote them down on his clipboard. He opened the door to the room and called, "Paper bag, please."

A few seconds passed, then a hand passed a paper bag to the guard, and he closed the door and bagged all the items. I hugged my da tightly, not wanting to let go, but when we separated, I was proud of myself for not crying like I normally did when we said goodbye. I was being strong for him.

After he was cuffed once more, we shared one last look before the guard handed him his paper bag of goodies and led him from the room.

"I'll see you soon," I called. "Merry Christmas, and Happy New Year."

"Same to you, love," he shouted. "And happy birthday!"

"I love ye'!"

"I love ye' too, baby."

The door to the room closed, and I felt like the walls were suddenly closing in on me. I grabbed my stuff, and placed all the rubbish accumulated during the visit into the small bin. I quickly left the room and headed towards the barriers that led towards the exit. I had to sign myself out and return my visitor's badge along the way.

Walking out of the prison, each footstep I took felt heavier than the last. I was weighed down with the knowledge that every time I left this building, I was leaving my da behind.

It's not like you can take him with you, I told myself.

With slumped shoulders, I headed towards the car park, and scanned the rows until I spotted Eddi's car. She was sitting inside it, doing something on her phone. When I was next to the car, I tapped on the passenger window, and Eddi nearly jumped out of her skin. She dropped her phone in her lap and put her hand against her chest. Then she quickly unlocked the car by pressing a button on her door.

"Sorry," I said, settling into my seat. "I thought ye' might have seen me comin'."

"It's okay," she answered. "I was just playin' a game on me phone to pass the time."

I buckled my seat belt, and Eddi did the same.

"How's your da?" she asked as she reversed out of the parking spot.

I sighed. "He seems in good spirits. He said he's readin' and writin' and it's helpin' 'im pass the time."

"That's good," Eddi commented. "That should keep his mind occupied."

I nodded, but said nothing further.

"Are *you* okay?" she asked as she pulled out onto the main road and headed towards the motorway.

I played with my fingers.

"Not really," I replied, honestly. "I love when I get to visit 'im, but it gets harder leavin' 'im in there. Me stomach gets so sick over it."

"I can't imagine what it feels like," Eddi said. "I'm sorry you're goin' through this, Ry."

That was the first genuine thing I'd ever heard her say to me. She'd been nice to me after my attempted assault, but I knew that was mostly because she felt guilty for leaving me behind that night. This time, she'd said this not because she had to, but because she wanted to. It made me look at her and really study her. And before I knew it, I said, "Why aren't we friends, Eddi?"

She swallowed. "I don't know, Ryan."

"We're cousins," I said, stating the obvious. "We're each other's *only* cousin, and we're like strangers."

"I know."

"It never bothered me before I lived with ye', but if I'm bein' honest, it bothers me now."

Eddi was silent for a moment as she got us onto the motorway.

"It bothers me too," she said, minutes later.

I cleared my throat. "I want to be friends with ye'. D'ye think we can manage that?"

"Yeah." Eddi nodded. "Once we understand the other, I think."

"Why don't we admit why we never bothered bein' in the other's life and go from there?" I suggested. "I'll go first, if ye' want."

"Okay," she said slowly. "I'm a little worried, but okay."

I cleared my throat once more.

"Right, so, I never liked bein' around ye' because ye' look like a double of me ma."

Eddi glanced at me, and I saw surprise in her eyes before she returned her gaze to the road.

"I do?"

I nodded. "I've dozens of pictures of 'er, and ye' could be 'er twin when she was your age."

"Me ma's said the same thing to me before, but I never gave it much thought." She licked her lips. "Am I a reminder that she's dead?"

"Ye' were before I lived with ye', then I got used to seein' ye' every day," I explained. "I think your appearance was more of a reminder that I never had a relationship with 'er, and the time I had with 'er is just a montage of foggy memories. That's what I hate the most – the bond I've missed out on now that she's gone."

"That's deep."

I huffed a laugh. "I know."

"I never wanted to be around *you* because ye' had everythin' that I didn't," Eddi said, and her cheeks were aflame as she spoke. "I don't just mean materialistic things, I mean havin' your da there."

That surprised me.

"I only know a little about your da," I admitted. "I can't remember what he looks like. Me da said he and your ma separated when you were ten."

Eddi nodded, exhaling a deep breath. "Jaysus, I've never talked about this to anyone."

"Then this conversation is probably long overdue for ye'."

"Yeah," she said softly.

"So, your da?"

"He . . . he was an alcoholic."

I blinked, my eyes wide with shock.

"I'm sorry, Ed."

"He was into the hard stuff a long time," she continued. "I drank from one of his whiskey bottles when I was eight by accident, and that was when he told me it was his medicine, and I shouldn't touch it ever again. I never understood how he could drink so much of it because it burned like hell. I thought it was crap medicine."

She spoke with so much venom in her tone, it was obvious the feelings she harboured for her da were of anger and, clearly, pain.

"Me ma kicked 'im out when I was ten after he almost hit 'er in a drunken rage, and he's been in and out of me life since then."

I shook my head. "That's crap."

"Yeah," she huffed. "Tell me about it."

"D'ye talk to 'im at all?"

"I stopped when I was fifteen," she said, her fingers flexing on the steering wheel. "I was sick of all the promises he'd break, and all the times he let me down, so I cut 'im out."

"I don't blame ye'," I said, hoping that would somehow help. "I'd have probably done the same thing had I been in your position."

"He always said he was goin' to stop drinkin' and get sober, but it was always just talk. But when I was seventeen, somethin' changed in 'im and he gave up the bottle and everythin' attached to it."

My lips parted. "That's brilliant."

"Me ma thought so too," she muttered.

"But not you?"

"Not me," she said firmly. "I didn't believe he could change, so I didn't let 'im back in."

"Did he though?" I pressed. "Did he change?"

She nodded, and from what I could see of her face, her expression was one of surprise.

"Yeah, and no one's more shocked about it than me. He's been sober for two years now."

"Wow!"

"Yeah."

"But ye' still don't want a relationship with 'im?"

"Honestly," she sighed, "I'm terrified that if I let 'im back in, everythin' will go back to the way it was." She reached up and scratched her neck before returning her hand to the steering wheel. "I know that's the only reason me ma isn't open to the idea of them gettin' back together for real."

"What?" I gasped. "Your ma and da?"

"Yeah," she snorted. "They started datin' a few months ago, which is how I knew his sobriety was real, because she wouldn't have 'im back in 'er life otherwise. They text all the time, but only meet up once a month. I think she's fallin' in love with 'im again."

"I don't know whether to say congrats or not."

Eddi laughed. "Neither do I."

"So that was your reason for not havin' a relationship with me?" I questioned. "It hurt ye' that I had me da?"

"I was jealous," she said, not ashamed to admit it. "Plain and simple. It hurt me that your da was so great to ye'. Me ma always sung his praises. It made me angrier at me da as well that you had no choice in the death of your ma, but me da's selfish decisions kept 'im from bein' a constant factor in *my* life. That was all targeted on you then. I needed someone to focus me anger on, and since me da wasn't around, I picked you."

I whistled. "Ye' have daddy issues, and I have mammy issues . . . aren't we a pair?"

Eddi chuckled. "A right pair."

We rode in comfortable silence for a few minutes.

"D'ye think ye'll warm up to your da?"

"Normally, I'd say no," she answered. "But when I first brought ye' 'ere the week after ye' moved in, I realised that ye' drop everythin' in your life just so ye' can spend an hour with your da. Ye' said ye've never missed a visitin' day in nearly a whole year – that's two visits a month. Ye' don't get a choice in the matter, ye' just do what ye' have to do to see your da and that's that."

I didn't speak; I let her say what she needed to.

"Me da is a stranger to me, but he *is* me da . . . and I'm beginnin' to realise that I do want 'im in me life. I've always wanted 'im in me life. I just have to figure out a way to get over me fear of 'im goin' back to his old ways."

"What about baby steps?" I suggested. "Maybe set up a meetin', just an hour or so, with 'im and your ma and go from there."

"Yeah," Eddi mumbled. "Maybe."

I looked out the passenger window then back to my cousin, and said, "I feel lighter havin' talked to ye' about all this."

"Me too, princess," Eddi said, saying my once-hated nickname teasingly. "Me too."

CHAPTER THIRTEEN
ASHLEY

"What has your knickers in a twist?"

I bet I looked stupid, angrily scrubbing a pot, but I didn't care.

"I got a phone call today from Sean's year head at school," I grunted. "He wanted to let me know, before school closes for the holidays, about Sean's Christmas exam results, because the little fucker never showed them to me. He was supposed to get the report card signed by me and return it to his year head, but he never did."

Anto whistled. "Is he gettin' coal off Santa for bein' a naughty boy?"

"Piss off," I said, shaking my head. "This is serious. The little shit has failed four of his exams. *Four of them*. Maths, English, Irish and History."

"Mate, I failed *all* of mine and I turned out fine."

I looked over my shoulder at Anto, and said in a sarcastic tone: "You're a Disciple who has no education past secondary school."

Anto waggled his eyebrows. "But I get *allllll* the bitches."

I grunted, and turned back to scrubbing the pot.

"I'm gonna deck 'im," I said firmly. "That's exactly what I'm gonna do to the little shite."

"Maybe he has a good reason?" Anto suggested. "Hear 'im out first before ye' jump down his throat."

"What reason?" I demanded. "His feckin' girlfriend?"

"Most likely."

I huffed with annoyance.

"Ye' can't be this wound up just over Sean."

"Why can't I?" I pressed. "*Well?*"

"Because ye'd be annoyed, sure, but not this put-out over some failed Christmas exams," Anto speculated. "It's somethin' else."

"Okay, Oprah, go on," I said, dropping the pot and turning to face my friend, then leaning back against the counter. "Tell me what's botherin' me, since you're filled with knowledge."

Anto held up his hand and extended his fingers.

"Mr Nobody hasn't gotten back to ye' with any information about the sicko who has it out for ye', and it's been a week since we spoke to 'im." With that said, a finger went down. "Sean's schoolin' *is* botherin' ye', so that counts too." Another finger went down. "We're still waitin' on the names of me runners that we have to deal with." Another finger dropped. "And lastly, the country bird hasn't just ruffled your feathers, she's plucked them all out. Ye' love 'er."

"Fuck off." I scowled as he wiggled all his fingers at me.

"Okay," Anto grinned, "ye' don't love 'er, but you like 'er. Why the fuck would ye' keep askin' 'er out whenever ye' see 'er? *Especially* after she turns ye' down each time? No man would put 'imself through that much rejection just for the fun of it."

I set my jaw. "I don't wanna talk about Ryan."

"I do." Anto smiled. "She's fun to talk about."

"Anto," I glared. "Leave it alone."

"Okay, okay," he acquiesced, holding his hands up in defence. "Sean is out with his friends and won't be home till later. I want some chips, so let's go to the chipper to calm ye' down before ye' go all WWE on your baby brother."

"That's probably the smartest thing I've ever heard ye' say."

Anto stood up. "I have me moments."

After I switched everything off in the house and locked it up, making sure I set the alarm system that was recently installed, I sent a text to Sean to tell him where I was going, and then started the ten-minute walk with Anto to the chipper. We talked about mundane things along the way, and it wasn't until we got inside the chipper than I realised how hungry I was. The smell caused my stomach to rumble.

"I'd murder a kebab."

Anto hummed. "I'm feelin' a burger tonight, and some garlic cheesy chips."

We were both scanning over the menu when I heard soft laughter flow in through the open chipper door. I looked over my shoulder and watched as Ryan and her cousin Eddi walked towards the chipper, laughing at something one of them had said. They were both still in their work uniforms, and came from the direction of the supermarket, so it was obvious they'd just finished their shifts.

I whistled as they entered the shop. "Well, well, well. I'm beginnin' to think that you're stalkin' me, nightmare."

Ryan clapped her eyes on me, and was brought to a stop when Eddi hooked her arm through her cousin's and muttered, "Let's just go home."

Anto turned to the pair. "Don't run off yet, ladies, we don't bite . . . unless ye' ask us to."

Eddi scoffed in his direction. "You're such a pig."

"I'm a pig?" Anto dramatically gasped as he clutched a hand to his chest and looked my way. "Why'd ye' never tell me that?"

"Don't mind 'er, buddy." I patted him on the shoulder. "You're nothin' of the sort."

Anto turned back to Eddi and smugly said, "D'ye hear that? I'm not a pig. Ha."

"You're a child, though," Eddi said with a shake of her head. Then to Ryan she said, "Let's go, Ry."

Ryan, however, was trying, and failing, not to smile at the Anto-and-Eddi show happening before us. I saw that as my chance to ask her out again, seeing that she was in a good mood.

"Ryan," I said, causing her green eyes to flick towards me. "Can I get ye' a bag of chips, babe?"

Her lips twitched ever so slightly. "No."

"Come on," I urged. "I'll throw in a battered sausage, what d'ye say?"

Another twitch of her lips. "No."

"Fuck it," Anto announced. "Ye' can get me a bag of chips and a battered sausage if she doesn't want it. I'll go on a date with ye' for a hell of a lot less than that, buddy."

Ryan laughed, and the look of horror on her cousin's face made *me* laugh.

"We aren't goin' to maul ye', Eddi," I said to her. "Relax."

"Speak for yourself, my guy," Anto cut in, his eyes raking over Eddi. "I may do a bit of maulin' with 'er *fine* self."

"Not with me ye' won't," Eddi countered, the quiver in her voice not going unnoticed. "Don't start fake chattin' me up again, Anto. Ye've been doin' it for years and I've never said a word to ye', but you're gettin' on me last nerve now."

Eddi had lived on my road for as long as I could remember, and she'd never, not once, got lippy with Anto when he jokingly hassled her. It seemed that with Ryan by her side, she'd developed a backbone. It also appeared that my best friend really liked that new backbone of hers.

"Where is Eddi Stone and what have ye' done with 'er?" Anto demanded, placing his hands on his hips. "Who are *you*, imposter?"

"What?" Eddi asked, bemused. "What're ye' talkin' about?"

"Anytime ye' see me, ye' run in the opposite direction, but today you're full of beans. What gives?"

"She has *me* around now to back 'er up," Ryan interjected, standing tall beside her cousin, though she didn't look that confident in herself. "She knows where I'll put me foot if ye' bother 'er."

I snickered. "Ye' may have met your match in these two, bud."

"Do any of ye' actually plan on *orderin'* somethin'?"

All our attention turned to the man behind the counter, who looked fed up with us being in his shop.

"Yes, we do," Ryan said, tugging Eddi over to the counter.

Anto was inches away from Eddi, and kept grinning and looking her up and down, and Eddi caught him in the act.

"Stop lookin' at me, creep."

"Creep?" Anto repeated, rapidly blinking his eyes. "First I'm a pig. Now I'm a creep. You're mean when you're hungry."

Eddi glared at him before turning her attention to the menu, but not before Anto and I saw her lips twitch. She was fighting off a smile, and I bet it was killing her inside. Her and Ryan then placed an order, quickly followed by Anto and me. The four of us lingered in the shop as we waited, and for some reason I wanted to laugh, because Eddi looked like she'd rather be anywhere else but in our presence.

"Anto," Eddi suddenly snapped. "*Stop* lookin' at me."

"I can't help it," he said with a shrug of his shoulders. "You're beautiful."

Eddi looked like she'd stopped breathing, and I wondered if Anto's declaration was one of interest to her, because it was to me. I'd heard him call women a lot of things, but beautiful wasn't one of them.

I looked towards Ryan, who was smiling as she glanced between her cousin and Anto. When she caught my gaze, she nodded towards the pair and shrugged, clearly amused.

"Ye' shouldn't say things like that," Eddi said to Anto after clearing her throat. Twice.

"Why not?" Anto queried. "It's true."

"Shut up," she countered, her face turning bright red. "Just shush. Please."

"Ye' might as well marry me now," he stated, noticing her blush. "We're clearly meant for one another."

Eddi turned her back to Anto, and got into a battle of whispered words with Ryan. She was snickering, and earned a thump from Eddi because of it. I looked at Anto and muttered, "Leave 'er alone."

"Not a hope," he mumbled back. "This is the most conversation I've ever gotten out of 'er in, like, *ever*. Did ye' see 'er eyes when she stuck it to me? Mate, I'd throw 'er over me shoulder and run away with 'er if I didn't think Ryan would enlist you to hunt me down."

I shook my head. "It's your funeral, man."

We lingered in silence a few more minutes, then Ryan caught me staring at her and she smiled shyly. I wanted to shake her. She was into me, it was obvious, but she kept saying no whenever I asked her out, and I didn't understand why. Maybe me being a Disciple really *was* a deal breaker for her, which sucked because there was fuck all I could do about it.

"C'mere," I said, not sure if she'd listen. "Just for a second."

She said something to Eddi that her cousin didn't like, then she walked towards me, her eyes never leaving mine. She was being brave, but I saw the hesitation in her eyes as she neared me.

"Yes?" she asked, stopping not far away. "What d'ye want?"

"When are ye' goin' to put me out of me misery and go out with me?"

Ryan's smile caused my stomach to do a little flip, and I momentarily wondered what that was about, before I dismissed it and focused on her.

"I don't know," she hummed with a tilt of her head. "Maybe ye' should ask me again and see what happens."

I wasn't sure where this flirtatious side of her came from, but I fucking liked it.

I grazed my lower lip with my teeth. "Why do I feel like you're challengin' me, nightmare?"

"Maybe because I am."

My heart thumped against my chest.

"Okay," I grinned. "Ryan, will ye' please go out on a date with me?"

She beamed at me, and purposely delayed her response to keep me on edge.

"Don't do it, Ry," Eddi warned. "Don't ye' *dare* do it."

"Stay out of this, Debbie Downer," Anto interjected. "Let me lad get this date. He deserves it after practically beggin' like a gowl for weeks."

"Ash," Ryan said, tilting her head to the side. "I'd *love* to go on a date with ye'."

As if it were planned, Eddi, Anto and I said, "Really?" in unison, and it made Ryan chuckle.

"Yeah." She bobbed her head. "Really."

I blinked, not sure what to say now I'd received the answer I wanted.

"Right," I said slowly. "When are ye' free next?"

"Tomorrow," she answered. "It'll be me first weekend off since I started workin' at the supermarket."

I rubbed my hands together.

"Perfect." I smiled joyfully. "I'll pick ye' up at seven."

"Where are we goin'?" Ryan challenged. "What will we be doin'?"

I had no bloody idea yet. I was making this up as I went along.

"That's for me to know," I mused, my voice laced with forced confidence, "and *you* to find out."

CHAPTER FOURTEEN
RYAN

"Ryan, *why* are ye' doin' this?"

I exhaled a deep breath. I was tired of hearing that question. Ever since I'd accepted Ash's proposal of a date last night in the chipper, Eddi had been breathing down my neck to back out of it. It had been a few days since our lengthy discussion, and since then we'd gone out of our way to get to know one another. It was amazing how close we'd become in such a short space of time. We weren't the best of friends yet, but we were friends, and we'd continue to build on that relationship.

"He saved me a few weeks ago," I answered my cousin. "I know ye' think he's a horrible person, but he's been so nice to me, Ed. I know he's a Disciple, and trust me when I say that red flags go off everywhere in me mind because of that . . . but a big part of me wants to go on this date."

"*That's* why you're goin' out with 'im?" she questioned, her tone fill with shock. "Ye' feel like you owe 'im somethin' for savin' ye'?"

"Of course not," I answered, surprised she'd even think that. "I'm goin' out with 'im 'cause I like 'im."

That earned me a scoff, which was probably deserved.

"You've only been around 'im a handful of times though. How can ye' know if ye' like 'im?"

"Based off those handful of times, he's made me laugh, smile, and even annoyed me once or twice, but I still like 'im. I'm not sayin' he's the best thing since sliced bread, but I'm interested in 'im. This has never happened to me before, Eddi. I've never been on a date, I've never even been asked to go on one. I don't know. I guess I feel special."

Every word I spoke seemed to go in one ear and out the other.

"Ryan, listen to me," my cousin stressed. "You're forgettin' that he's a *Disciple*."

Like I could forget something like *that*.

"I'm definitely not," I assured her. "I'm just goin' on a little date with 'im. It's not *that* big of a deal."

"But it *is*," Eddi argued. "What if it goes badly?"

"Then there won't be a second date." I shrugged, glancing at her in the mirror on the landing as I applied a coat of mascara. "I'm not sure what ye' think he's goin' to do if the date doesn't work out."

"I've a few ideas," she grumbled.

I couldn't help but smile at her.

"Look," I said as I turned to face her. "He said to me that bein' a Disciple is a job he isn't allowed to quit, and when he said it, I could tell he hated bein' associated with the Disciples. Good people get stuck in bad situations all the time, and I think that's the case with Ash. I just . . . I just think there's more to 'im, even though *you*, and the people around 'ere, don't think there is."

"You're makin' a mistake, Ry," Eddi said, unconvinced. "I'm tellin' ye'."

"Then let me make it and learn from it," I almost pleaded. "This is a first for me. I'm as excited as I am nervous, and I don't want to think about Ash's 'job' right now. I just want to think about 'im and me, goin' on a date. That's it."

"Ryan—"

"Eddi, please, stop," I begged of her. "This is the first time since me da went to prison that I've felt excited about somethin'. It's the first time in me life that I'm doin' somethin' so darin'. I *know* what Ash is, and I *know* there's no long-term future with 'im, but I still want to go out with 'im. I'm so tired of bein' sad all the time, of being so closed-off all the time, and when I'm around 'im, I'm anythin' but."

My cousin listened as I spoke.

"This date could be the only one we go on," I continued. "It could be a bust, a complete waste of time, and ye' could be one hundred per cent right about everythin', but I want to find out for meself. I know a part of me wants this because I've never had a lad, a *man*, pay me any attention before, and the woman in me likes it. I'm sorry for how I feel, but I want to experience a first date with someone who I like, even if it spells disaster."

Eddi groaned, and some of the tension in her body slipped away.

"Don't apologise. Ye' can't help if you're attracted to the ginger-haired bastard. He *is* very handsome . . . in a rugged, dangerous kind of way."

Eddi's hair was only a few shades away from *her* being a ginger, but she didn't seem to care about that, so I held my tongue on teasing her about it.

"Well, well, well," I mused. "How did those words taste comin' out of your mouth?"

"Like vinegar."

I laughed, and Eddi's lips twitched.

"I'm just worried he's only after you for sex," she admitted. "I know I'm bein' judgemental because I don't personally know the fella, but all the rumours goin' around over the years are hard to ignore. He's seasoned in a dangerous world, and you're so sweet and innocent . . . I think I'd kill 'im if he hurt ye'."

My lips parted with shock. "A week ago, ye' couldn't stand me."

"And today, I stand with ye'." She shrugged. "Things change."

I stared at my cousin, who over the last few weeks had come to not reminding me of my mother every time I looked at her. She looked like herself – she looked like Eddi, the cousin who I was coming to love very dearly. It scared me half to death opening myself up to her, but I knew it would be worth it. She was my blood.

"People can change too," I said softly. "We're proof that people can better themselves from past behaviours."

Eddi glared at me. "Ye' need to stop makin' sense, and just agree with me about Ash. It would make me feel a whole lot better."

"Sorry." I grinned. "No can do."

Eddi sighed, long and hard.

"If I can't change your mind, then I want ye' to at least put mine at ease."

Finally, some reason.

"What would make ye' feel better?"

"*You* textin' me where ye' are, how ye' are, and a picture of Ash so if anythin' goes wrong, I have proof that he did it."

"Did *what*?" I asked in surprise, then laughed. "What's goin' through your mind right now?"

"I keep thinkin' he's goin' to cut you up and feed ye' to savage pit bulls or somethin'."

My mouth dropped open. "How does a thought like that enter someone's head?"

Eddi shrugged. "I watch a lot of thriller films."

I stared at my cousin. "You're freakin' me out."

She only grinned in response before her eyes dropped to my body. "I like your jeans."

I spun around. "Aren't they fab?"

"Where did ye' get them?"

"Kildare outlets."

Eddi froze. "That outlets place that just has designer shops in it?"

I nodded.

"If ye' tell me ye' paid five hundred euros for a pair of jeans, I'm *definitely* goin' to smack sense into ye'."

"Don't be stupid," I smirked. "They were only two fifty."

"*What?*"

I burst into laughter. "I'm jokin'."

Eddi placed a hand on her chest. "Don't do that."

I shook my head, grinning.

"They were about seventy quid," I admitted. "And I *know* that's still pricey, but they're the best jeans I've ever owned. I have them in different colours."

Eddi looked at them again. "They *do* fit ye' perfectly . . . What size are ye'?"

"A twelve," I answered.

Eddi punched the air. "I'm a twelve. I am *definitely* borrowin' them sometime."

Amused, I said, "I'll tell ye' what, since I'm committin' treason against ye' by goin' out with Ash, ye' can have full run at me wardrobe whenever ye' want . . . how does that sound?"

"Like a promisin' start to a shitty situation."

I chuckled and turned back to the full-length mirror, my eyes roaming over my reflection. My hair hung over my shoulders, covering my breasts in loose curls. I wore a grey, low-cut, long-sleeved bodysuit that I'd tucked into my black fitted jeans, black ankle boots and a fitted black blazer. I'd also put on a silver necklace and matching earrings. I didn't want to overdo it, so I figured I'd dress up a normally casual look, and that way I'd fit in wherever Ash brought me.

I turned to face my cousin.

"Do I look okay?"

"Okay?" she repeated. "Gorgeous, more like, which makes me hate ye' a little . . . it's like ye' don't even have to try."

My mouth hung open with shock.

"Is that a joke?" I demanded. "I look like this after two hours of gettin' ready. *You're* the one with the perfect complexion and hair colour, *and* ye' actually possess boobs."

My breasts had always been an issue for me; they were on the small side, and Eddi didn't have that problem.

"What ye' lack in boobs," she said, smirking, "ye' make up for in your arse."

I felt heat burn my cheeks. My behind *was* fuller – and my hips and thighs a little thicker – than Eddi's, but I had never been embarrassed over it like I had been with my breasts. I turned back to the mirror and gave myself a nod.

"I think I look nice."

"Ye' look gorgeous," Eddi corrected. "Now, come on. The sooner ye' leave, the quicker ye'll come home."

It was insane to me that I was already thinking of this place as exactly that. *Home*. I knew it had nothing to do with the location, because I would move back to Kildangan in a heartbeat if I had the chance. No, it was the company I kept. Our once-broken family was on the mend, and I, for one, was delighted about it.

When Eddi and I headed downstairs, I checked to make sure my phone was fully charged, that I had money, then I checked the time. It was five to seven, and Ash had said he'd come and pick me up at seven. Butterflies invaded my stomach, and I began to feel a little sick with nerves.

"Look at you," my auntie praised. "As beautiful as your ma."

I looked up and smiled, "Thanks, Andrea."

"I don't want to ruin your happy mood," she said tentatively, "but I want ye' to be very cautious tonight. I'll be honest about it, I had to talk meself out of stoppin' ye' from doin' this, but I know that's not me place."

Not her too.

"You and Eddi sound very alike right now."

"I could hear ye' both when you were talkin' on the landin'," Andrea said. "Both of ye' make good points, but in the end, it's your decision, Ryan."

"I wouldn't go anywhere near Ash if I thought he would hurt me."

Andrea accepted that. "Then I trust your judgement."

"Thank you."

"Have a great night," she said. "And I know it's your birthday soon, and that ye'll be nineteen, but please don't be out too late. I'll worry, I can't help it."

"I'll do me best to be home by twelve."

It was at that moment that the doorbell rang.

Eddi sighed from behind me. "Of course he'd be bloody punctual."

"Me stomach is killin' me," I whispered. "I feel like I could be sick."

"It's your nerves." Andrea smiled warmly. "Ye'll be grand."

I took a deep breath, put on my blazer, grabbed my bag and walked towards the front door. I opened it, and the second I saw Ash standing outside in a plain blue buttoned-up shirt with the sleeves rolled up to the elbow, and a pair of nicely fitted jeans, I shook my head.

"Aren't ye' cold?"

He nodded. "Feckin' freezin'."

I laughed, waved at my auntie and cousin, then closed the front door behind me.

"Where's your jacket?"

"In me house," he said as he reached for my hand.

I was surprised, but threaded my fingers through his. I could feel slight callouses on his skin that tickled mine, but it didn't bother me. In fact, I kind of liked that his hands weren't supple and soft. They were rough and big . . . just like Ash.

"Let's go and get it before ye' freeze, then."

Ash tugged me into a walk, and we left my auntie's garden and walked along the path towards his house.

"Ye' look beautiful."

I looked down. "Thanks. Ye' look nice too."

"Nice?" he teased. "You get beautiful, and I get nice. Thanks a lot."

I could have squeezed him for his banter. I'd been nervous all day about our date, and I'd prayed that conversation wouldn't be awkward between us, and so far, Ash had put me completely at ease.

"Fine," I joked. "You're beautiful."

"Don't say it if ye' don't mean it. I don't want any fake compliments."

I chuckled as we turned into his garden and walked up to his front door. I was going to wait outside for him while he got his jacket, but when he gestured me into the house, I followed him.

"Can I take your blazer?" he asked.

I hesitated. "Okay."

I wondered why he would want me to take it off, then I realised we must be staying in his house for a while.

I cleared my throat. "Where's your brother?"

Eddi had pointed Sean out to me once before when he was on the road, and I had seen him around a few times since, but I'd never spoken to him or officially met him.

"He's up in his room," Ash answered as he took my blazer and hung it up on a coat rack. "He's grounded."

"Uh-oh." I winced. "What'd he do?"

"Where to begin?" Ash shook his head. "He led me to believe that he was doin' well in school, but when I spoke to his year head yesterday, I found out he'd failed four of his Christmas exams. I know they aren't state exams or anythin', but they're a review for what's been learned so far this year in school. Me brother's been slackin', and I'm not havin' that."

My heart thumped. He seemed genuinely upset, and it became obvious to me that he was concerned for his brother's education because he wanted him to have the best future possible. When you couldn't have something you wanted, you wanted it for the person you loved most.

"You're a wonderful big brother," I praised. "He'll thank ye' for it in the long run."

Ash grunted. "I hope so."

I had gone to hang my bag up on the coat rank too, when I remembered Eddi's request.

"I have to text Eddi where I am, and send 'er a picture of ye' so if ye' kill me, she has proof ye' did it."

I felt a blush grace my cheeks the seconds the words left my mouth, but Ash only chuckled.

"I'm not even surprised to hear that."

I texted Eddi that I was at Ash's house, then I turned the phone in his direction and said, "Smile."

"Take a selfie, it'll be better evidence at the murder trial that you're in the picture with me. I won't be able to talk me way out of it that way."

I nodded. "Good idea."

I flipped the camera on my phone, and when Ash bent his knees and leaned his head against mine and smiled, I didn't have to force a smile of my own. I took the picture, and the schoolgirl in me was jumping up and down because it was *cute*.

I focused on sending the picture to Eddi with the caption: *I'm still alive. For now.*

"Come with me," Ash announced. "I've been preparin' this all day for ye'."

What's he talking about?

"Ye' said we were goin' on a date," I stated quietly.

"We're *on* the date." Ash smiled down at me. "I cooked for ye'."

I paused mid-stride and looked up at him, completely taken aback.

"Ye' *cooked* for me?" I marvelled, hearing the awe in my tone.

From Ash's grin, he heard it too.

"Does that earn me points?"

I could barely contain my smile. "Only if the food is good."

"O ye of little faith."

I couldn't help but laugh. "Ye' really *are* a Disciple, quotin' the good book and everythin'."

"Hush," Ash chuckled, the sound a soft rumble in his throat.

He slipped his arm around my waist, and he might as well have set me on fire considering the way my skin heated at his touch. Then we were in front of a closed door, and he pushed it open, revealing the kitchen.

I sucked in a breath. "Ash . . . it's gorgeous."

CHAPTER FIFTEEN
RYAN

I placed a hand over my mouth when a sea of lit candles came into view, and the delicious scent of cooked meat made its way up my nostrils. The entire room was welcoming, and I felt like I'd walked into a fancy restaurant instead of a regular kitchen.

"This is a *first* date!" I exclaimed breathlessly. "I can't believe ye've gone to all this trouble for me."

My entire body began to tremble. The room was beautifully set up, and I knew this would have taken time, energy and planning to pull off. That fact that Ash did this for me, that he thought I was worth all this effort, made my stomach flip in the best way possible. My heart warmed, and in that moment, a tiny piece of it belonged to Ash.

He had placed candles around the room, and lit each one . . . for me. He did it all for me. It was so pretty, and instantly made the date feel that much more intimate.

"It's no trouble at all," Ash assured me as he led me to the beautifully set table. "I like cookin'."

"I feel so overdressed though," I said with embarrassment. "I thought we were goin' out somewhere."

Ash took my hand, stepped back away from me, and let his eyes roam over every inch of my body. I swallowed as his tongue slid over his lower lip.

"I think," he said, bringing his eyes back to mine, "ye' look perfect."

"It's hot in 'ere," I announced, using my hand to fan myself. "D'ye have the heatin' on?"

"It's winter, babe." Ash blinked. "The heatin' is always on."

At that, I laughed. Then I sat down on the seat that Ash pulled out for me.

"Such a gentleman." He placed his warm hands on my shoulders, leaned down until his mouth was by my ear and whispered, "That's me."

I shivered, and I could practically feel his smile as he straightened up and moved over towards the oven.

"Now," he said, rubbing his hands together, "when I was walkin' down to your auntie's house, I realised that I don't know if you're allergic to anythin'. I had a mini heart attack, so please, put me mind at ease and tell me if ye' are or not?"

I grinned. "No allergies for me."

Ash sighed dramatically and put a hand on his chest. "Thank God for that."

I shook my head, then when he began to take the lids off plates of food, I made a move to stand up and help. He cut me a look that halted me mid-rise, and with a smile I eased myself back down to my seat.

"No," Ash told me, "*you* stay right where ye' are."

"I feel like I should help though. Ye've gone through so much trouble for me."

"*I* asked *you* out on this date, so I get to wait on ye'. Deal with it, nightmare."

I wasn't sure when the change had happened, but now when he called me nightmare, it amused me more than anything, because I knew he didn't mean it as an endearment, and a big part of me loved that.

"Okay, okay," I acquiesced. "I'll do as ye' ask."

"Thank you." Ash bowed his head. "I appreciate it."

"So," I chirped as he turned his back to me, "what're we havin'?"

"You're so little, I figured goin' straight to a main course would be best, so I made chicken risotto. I wanted to play it safe, and make somethin' I've done a hundred times before. I also made chips for either a side or somethin' to pick at later."

"Colour me impressed, sir."

Ash looked over his shoulder and shot me a look that stopped my breath.

"What?" I asked, pushing my hair over my shoulder.

He shrugged. "I just liked hearin' ye' call me sir."

Either he was trying to purposefully embarrass me or he was simply teasing me. Either way, the comment made me blush.

"Well, I wouldn't get used to it if I were you."

That made him smile and turn back to the food.

"What would ye' like to drink?" he asked me. "Are ye' a wine girl?"

"Nah, I don't drink alcohol. Any fizzy drink ye' have is fine with me."

Ash got some Coke from the fridge, poured it into two large glasses and sat them on the table. Minutes later, everything was ready to eat, and Ash placed a plate of food in front of me. I couldn't help but inhale the aroma deeply.

"That smells heavenly."

Ash took the seat across from me and nodded in agreement.

"It's one of me favourite dishes."

I waited for him to reach for his knife and fork before I reached for my own. I was aware of his eyes as I took my first bite of the meal, and he smiled instantly when I groaned in delight as flavours burst over my taste buds.

"Ash, this is delicious," I gushed. "Ye' really *can* cook."

"I don't know whether to be happy with your praise, or insulted at your lack of faith in me."

"The former," I groaned, swallowing another bite. "*Definitely* the former."

He smiled as he ate his food. For a few moments, we ate in silence, then I took a momentary break to glance around the room.

"This is really pretty," I said, looking from the candles to Ash, who was staring at me. "I can't believe ye' did this for me."

"It was no trouble. Just a few candles."

"A few?" I questioned.

"Okay. Twenty-five."

I laughed with delight. "It's so cute."

"Cute?" Ash said. "Did ye' just associate the word 'cute' with somethin' I did?"

"'Fraid so, tough guy," I teased. "This is disgustingly cute."

"Don't ever tell Anto that," he pleaded jokingly. "He'll never let me live it down."

I winked. "It'll be my little secret."

Ash gave me a teasing glance before he returned to eating his food. I focused on my plate too, and during twenty-five minutes of talking, and laughing, I had eaten most of it.

"I'm so full," I said with a groan. "I think me eyes were bigger than me stomach, because I was sure I could eat it all."

Ash, who'd finished his entire plate a few minutes ahead of me, watched me with a smile. He got up and cleared our dishes before putting them and the used cutlery into the dishwasher.

"Thank you," I said when he sat back down. "I enjoyed that so much. And not just the food – the fact that ye've set me at ease so quickly."

"Were ye' nervous?"

"Nervous?" I repeated. "Ash, this is the first date I've ever been on. I was terrified."

He blinked. "How is that possible?"

"I live out in the sticks." I shrugged. "Our closest neighbour is ten minutes away. Socialisin' isn't somethin' I'm good at, but since I moved here I've been tryin' to be more outgoin'. I can appear shy, but I'm quiet mainly because I'm not really used to bein' around people. This place has been life-changin' for me."

"Wow!" Ash said with a shake of his head. "I guess growin' up 'ere, I never had that problem. Everywhere ye' look, someone is there. Privacy isn't granted often in estates like this."

"I'm learnin' that," I joked. "Trust me."

"I'm glad you're havin' fun. Bein' honest with ye', this is the first date I've ever been on too. I've been with girls, but dates just never happened, then you came along and shut me down at every turn but I wore ye' down, just like I said I would."

I felt my cheeks burn with pleasure at his words.

"I guess ye' did."

We were silent then as we stared at one another.

"Did Eddi have a problem with ye' bein' with me tonight? I'm guessin' she did, otherwise she wouldn't have wanted ye' to text 'er with picture evidence that ye' were with me."

I considered whether or not to answer truthfully, then I decided I had no reason to lie; he knew how she felt about him. I decided to give him the option.

"D'ye want me to be honest?"

Without missing a beat, Ash said, "Always."

"I had a devil of a time tryin' to convince 'er that this date wasn't a big deal," I admitted. "She isn't sold on ye', not in the slightest."

"And *you* are?"

I tried to keep cool by casually shrugging.

"I like ye'. I wouldn't have said yes to this date if I didn't."

Ash considered this. "I don't understand why someone like *you* could like someone like me though," he said. "I'm countin' me lucky stars, but I don't get it."

"What do ye' mean, 'someone like me'?"

"Someone as perfect as you," Ash answered with a tilt of his head. "You're a good girl, and I don't deserve one of those."

I frowned. "Why not?"

"Because of the life I lead," he said, the muscles in his jaw tightening. "I told meself it was pointless askin' ye' out because I was just teasin' meself, since I knew ye'd say no. I knew ye' liked me, at least a little, but I never thought ye'd actually say yeah to a date. Ye' surprised the hell out of me last night."

I'd surprised myself and my cousin too.

"I think you're a good man who's just misunderstood by a lot of people."

"Ryan," he said with a frown. "I am what everyone says, for the most part. I sell drugs, there's no gettin' around that."

"D'ye *like* sellin' drugs?"

He almost laughed.

"Christ, no." He grimaced. "I fuckin' hate it, but I don't have a choice."

"Exactly," I stated softly. "Exactly."

"But I still do it."

"Havin' your choice taken away from ye' changes things though."

I didn't want to relate this to my da's situation because that was something I couldn't talk about with him, so I focused on me ma.

"I don't want me ma to be dead, but that isn't me decision, and I just have to live with it. *You* do what ye' do because it isn't your decision either. I don't know why ye' have no choice because that's your business, but ye' still have no say. Both situations are different, but they're also the same. Once your choice is taken away, there's nothin' ye' can do about it. Ye' just have to accept it and get on with your life."

I tried to apply my own words to my da's situation, but I couldn't because I believed he was innocent. Accepting that he was stuck in jail for God only knew how much longer was too much to ask of myself.

Ash stared at me. "I don't know what to do with ye', Ryan."

"What d'ye mean?"

"I don't talk to girls . . . not like this."

Hearing that made my stomach flutter. This conversation wasn't staged or planned, it was real, and that's why the honesty flowed. That told me that even though we were just getting to know one another, his subconscious trusted me enough to allow him to be open with me. I realised then that I was doing the exact same thing with him.

"Well, tonight is a first for both of us then."

He said nothing, just watched me, his grey eyes shining.

"Why d'ye like me?" I asked before I lost my nerve. "Eddi says ye' just want to have sex with me. Is that it?"

Ash exhaled a deep breath.

"Please don't take this the wrong way, but I can have sex with plenty of other women, and to do that, I wouldn't have to go to any effort . . . I especially wouldn't have to cook them dinner or light candles for them." He reached across the table and took my hand in his, his thumbs brushing over my knuckles. "Is it so hard to believe that I like ye' just because I do?"

I didn't answer; my tongue was stuck to the roof of my mouth.

"Look," Ash continued, "I'm goin' to be completely honest with ye'. When I realised ye' made an impression on me, and that I liked bein' around ye', I told meself I was bein' stupid, because I've never been interested in a woman before unless it *was* for sex."

"Oh," I whispered.

I had never been more aware of the fact that I was still a virgin. The man in front of me was anything but a virgin. I didn't have to ask him if he was experienced, I knew he was, and I didn't know what to do if things between us ever escalated to sex, because that was entirely new ground for me. What if he was disappointed that I didn't know what to do if sex was on the table? Would he even want me then?

I was hurting my head thinking about it.

"I don't pretend to be a saint, Ryan, but I pride meself on bein' honest, at least. And I genuinely like ye'. You're interestin', ye' make me smile, and ye' give as good as ye' get in an argument even though I can tell bein' confrontational isn't your thing. Not to mention you're fuckin' gorgeous . . . I think you're a hell of a catch, nightmare."

I felt heat creep up my neck.

"This is a heavy conversation for a first date."

"I don't like bullshit or games," Ash said with a one-shoulder shrug. "It's why I want to be very clear before anythin' else happens with us. I am who I am and I can't change that, not even if I wanted to."

I had to take that into consideration. He was who he was, and I was who I was. I came from a law-abiding family . . . Could I just ignore that and see what could happen with Ash? Was that even possible? Did I want it to be?

"I wouldn't try to change ye'," I eventually said. "I'm not thrilled that ye' have the job ye' do, but I like ye' for the person ye' are."

I didn't like his "job" in the slightest, but there wasn't a lot I could do about that. The only thing I could do was decide if I wanted to bring someone who engaged in criminal activity into my life. My mind switched to my da, and I knew in my heart he'd never let me look twice at Ash. He wouldn't be able to see past his record . . . but I could. I wanted to, and I knew how dangerous that want could prove to be. Or, at least, I thought I did.

"Does that mean there'll be more dates and spendin' time together?" he said.

Heaven help me, but I wanted that. And that scared me, because I wasn't exactly sure what I was setting myself up for. I couldn't see a long-term future with Ash, but was that what I wanted with him anyway? I had no idea; all I knew was that I liked him and I wanted to get to know him better.

"*D'you* want that?"

"Yes," Ash answered instantly. "It's a bad idea, but I want it."

"Why is it a bad idea?"

"For all the reasons Eddi most likely gave ye'. I'm not a good match for ye', I know that, and I sure as hell don't want to hurt ye'."

I observed him silently, then I said, "Somethin' is tellin' me I can take a leap of faith and believe in ye' not to do that. I don't want to be full on and overinvest trust or emotions in anythin', but I want to get to know ye'. And I know there can be no future with us, I'm well aware of that, but I still want to get to know ye' in spite of that, so make of that what ye' will."

"Jaysus, Ry," he sighed. "You're supposed to be the level-headed one 'ere. You're supposed to tell me this date is a once-off and ye'll not look me way ever again."

"You're tellin' me." I smiled. "I've always been by the book, doin' what I'm told like a good girl. One date with you has me questionin' everythin', Ash. What are ye' doin' to me?"

His cheeks flushed and his eyes filled with desire . . . for me. His lips parted, and his pink tongue darted over his lower lip before he swallowed.

"Fuck," he groaned, his eyes locking onto mine. "I really want to kiss ye' now."

The declaration caught me off guard.

"Ye' do?"

"Yes," he growled. "But I don't want to scare ye' away."

A surge of boldness jolted through me.

"I seem to remember that *I* was the one who kissed *you* in the supermarket."

"True." He smirked. "But ye' were terrified then."

I was terrified now, but in a completely different context.

"Also true," I countered. "But I still did it."

"Care to do it again?"

My pulse spiked.

"When the moment's right . . . maybe."

Ash stood up. "I better create that moment then."

He walked over to the phone lying on the counter and tapped on the screen a few times, then music floated from the speakers. It wasn't exactly blaring, but it was loud enough.

"Me ma loved this song," he said as he turned and held out his hand to me. "Will ye' dance with me?"

I recognised the tune of "Wonderful Tonight" by Eric Clapton, and I felt my body turn beet red as I took Ash's hand. Then I tightened my grip on him, because it suddenly felt like the world had fallen away from beneath my feet. He pulled my body to his, and his strong arm slid around my waist. He held me close and I had never experienced a more intimate moment with someone in my life.

"Ashley, this is so—"

"Don't say cute," he rumbled, gently giving my waist a squeeze. "Don't ye' dare say that word."

I giggled as I put my arm around his waist and took his free hand.

"I'm too short to put me arms around your neck," I said as the lyrics of the song flowed around the room. "So this will have to do."

Ash chuckled as we swayed from side to side, but it didn't take long for his laughter to cease and his hold on me to tighten. I wondered if he could feel my heart slamming into my chest, because I could. His hard body was perfectly moulded against mine, and for a moment it felt like we were made to fit together. His scent was masculine, and when I sneakily inhaled a deep breath, a tingle ran the length of my spine. Butterflies exploded in my stomach, and goosebumps broke out all over my body as we danced. I couldn't believe we were dancing.

I had never danced with any man other than my da, and this was different. This was romantic, intimate. This was special.

Softy, Ash sung the chorus of the song in my ear, and my heart warmed. The moment was one I knew would imprint on my memory forever. I felt desired, respected . . . wanted. I felt special, and when I looked up at Ash, I worried that I might lose my heart to this man even though everyone – including him – was warning me against being with him.

"Ashley," I whispered, the need to be close to him overwhelming me.

He looked down at me, his grey eyes burning with desire.

"Ye' created the moment," I breathed, my body trembling. "Kiss me."

He didn't say a word, he just lowered his head to mine and caught my lips with his. I lifted my hands to his chest and fisted his shirt, pulling him closer to me. One of his hands slid up to my face and cupped my cheek, while the other held tight around my waist. He took control of the kiss, but wasn't demanding or rough. He kissed me with such tenderness that it melted me. I moved my tongue with his, and when my teeth grazed his lower lip and he groaned, a jolt of desire pulsed between my thighs, and that was enough to make me gasp and break the kiss.

With our lips inches apart, Ash leaned his forehead against mine and said, "Ye' shouldn't let me do this. You're too good to get involved with me, babe. You're fuckin' perfect."

I licked my swollen lips, tasting him on them. How could he stand there and put himself down, when in that very moment I thought the entire world of him?

"Let me decide what I want to do, okay?"

Ash swallowed. "Okay."

We both jumped when the doorbell rang and broke through the haze of our moment. I looked towards the closed kitchen door, and so did Ash. He pulled away from me, and already I missed his touch – which was insane.

"I'll be right back."

He left the room and I followed him, pausing at the kitchen door when I heard voices arguing. I strained to hear what was being said, and then decided I wanted to see what was happening too. I gently opened the door, peeked around it, and spotted Ash and Anto practically nose to nose with one another.

"I fuckin' *told* ye' that I was busy tonight."

Ash was forcefully trying to remove Anto from his house, but his friend was having none of it. He had a big smile on his face, and he didn't appear all that bothered that Ash was annoyed with him.

"Yeah, but I didn't think she'd actually go through with goin' out with ye'."

Ash grunted as he gave up struggling with Anto, and he placed his hands on his hips. "Well, she did, and ye' aren't ruinin' this for me, so *leave*."

"What d'ye mean?" Anto questioned, leaning his shoulder against the hallway wall like he had all the time in the world to talk. "Ruin what?"

Ash lowered his voice. "Whatever I've got startin' with Ryan."

Anto's jaw dropped open. "Are ye' fuckin' tellin' me you're gettin' *together*?"

I held my breath as I awaited Ash's response.

"Anto," Ash growled. "You're too much of a lad to be interested in me love life. Get out."

"*Love life*," Anto repeated, howling with laughter. "Jesus Christ. One date and ye' have a love life. Does country girl have your bollocks in 'er bag too?"

That made me laugh, and got both Ash and Anto's attention. Ash swung around to face me, his eyes wide with alarm. He looked worried that I'd overheard the conversation.

"His bollocks are still attached to 'im." I winked at Anto. "Don't worry."

Ash grinned at me, looking relieved that I found humour in his friend's antics, while Anto laughed joyfully.

"I like 'er, bud."

"I do too," Ash replied, his eyes locked on mine as he spoke to his friend. "So leave us *alone*."

Anto didn't move a muscle; he stood in the hallway, grinning like a fool.

"I'm goin' to use the toilet," I said, excusing myself so Ash could deal with Anto.

When I finished in the bathroom, I washed my hands, then took a moment to gather my scattered thoughts. I looked in the mirror and exhaled. This was turning out to be a hell of a first date. There was so much honesty between me and Ash; it felt like I'd known him a lot longer than I actually had. There was no confusion, just straight-up real talk about what we both wanted when it came to the other. And so far, we seemed to be on the same page. We liked each other.

I left the bathroom, and jumped with fright when a bedroom opened on the left and Ash's little brother, Sean, appeared. He saw me, and froze.

I plastered a smile on my face. "Ye' must be Sean."

Sean nodded slowly. "Who're *you*?"

"I'm Ryan," I answered, and held out my hand. "Nice to meet ye'."

He shook my hand, his lips twitching.

"Nice to meet you too. Um," he mumbled. "What're ye' doin' in me house?"

"Oh," I chuckled, embarrassed. "I'm 'ere with your brother. We're on a date."

Sean's eyes widened. "A *date*?"

I nodded, and he suddenly grinned and beckoned me towards him. "Come with me."

I hesitated but followed him into the room, and sat on his made bed when he gestured for me to do so.

"I want to mess with Ash."

For a moment, I wasn't sure how to react, but the devilish smile on Sean's face told me he was a typical little brother wanting to tease his older sibling for some laughs, and I was more than game to help him achieve that.

I smirked. "How?"

"Just go along with me," he whispered.

I nodded, and bumped fists with him when he held his hand out. It was a little awkward for me because I'd never done that with someone before, but it was cute. It was like Sean accepted me as his partner-in-crime . . . so to speak.

"You're on a date with me brother?" he asked loudly. "Let's talk."

"Okay," I said, raising my voice too, trying not to giggle. "Tell me everythin' I need to know about your brother. Be honest, is he worth me time?"

"Nah," Sean said with a wave of his hand. "You're *way* too good for 'im, I can already tell. Ash is *so* not on your level."

"Okay," Ash's voice suddenly shouted as footsteps pounded up the stairs, "that's enough of *that*."

When he entered the room and saw me sitting on Sean's bed looking up at him, he turned quickly to his brother.

"I've grafted for weeks tryin' to get this date with Ryan," Ash said sternly. "And *you* go and ruin it with one sentence."

"I'm talented." Sean grinned, making me laugh.

Ash looked at me, then at Sean, and blinked. I loved the dynamic between them. Ash was the older brother, the man of the house, and he was being firm but kind towards Sean. He didn't curse, shout or show any anger. He seemed like a young man who was irritated with his kid brother, and Sean happily knew it – and I loved it.

"What did I walk in on?" he mused. "I feel like I'm missin' somethin'."

"A set-up to mess with ye'," I answered, getting to my feet. "I like your brother."

"And I like *you*," Sean retorted, waggling his eyebrows and making me laugh again. "You're sound, Ryan."

Ash playfully shoved him onto his bed, but he had a massive grin on his face. "You're still grounded."

"Yeah, yeah," Sean sighed as he lay flat on his back. "Tell me somethin' I don't know, big brother."

I chuckled as we walked down the stairs.

"He's adorable."

"Don't let 'im hear ye' say that," Ash said as he led me into the sitting room. "He hates that word."

"Like *you* hate the word 'cute'," I mused.

"Precisely."

"Where's Anto?"

"He's not 'ere anymore. That's all I care about."

My lips twitched as I glanced around, admiring the room.

"This is beautiful," I said, looking at the family pictures in the frames hung on the walls. It felt homey, and somewhere that I could be at ease. There was lots of love that was shared in this house, I could almost feel it.

My eyes landed on a woman in her mid-forties – a smiling, beautiful woman. She had shoulder-length dark brown hair and stunning grey eyes, and the top of her head only came to Ash's shoulder as she stood next to him, looking happy and full of life.

"Is this your ma?"

"Yeah," Ash answered, his voice was soft. "She was beautiful, huh?"

I lifted my hand and ran my finger over her face, feeling my mouth transform into a smile.

"Incredibly beautiful. Ye' have 'er eyes. Sean is 'er double, though."

Ash didn't speak, so I turned to face him and found him staring down at me intently.

"What's wrong?"

"I want to see ye' again," he answered. "Often."

My heart jumped. "How often?"

"Is every day okay with ye'?"

After the words left his mouth, I saw the worry in his eyes that I might say no, and that comforted me because it meant he was as nervous as I was. A warm sensation spread out through my chest from knowing we were in the same boat.

However, doubt quickly flooded my mind as I thought of my da. I'd sworn that I was going to do something, anything, to help him. Find something to prove his innocence, and I had to start taking that seriously, which meant I had a lot of digging and research to do about his case and everything connected to it. That would require my full attention, and I worried that if I continued to see Ash, it would put my focus on him and not my da.

"Ye' look scared," Ash said.

I nodded. "I am . . . I don't want to rush anythin' with ye' . . . but I do also want to see ye' more."

My brain felt like it was on fire. Could I work, help my da and see Ash at the same time? Was I capable of that? I was going through so much change in my life in such a short period of time, I was afraid of breaking down.

"What are ye' thinkin', nightmare?"

I looked up at him, and my heart just about skipped a beat. *Screw it*, I thought. Moving here had been a huge change for me. But people all over the world had multiple things to focus and work on in their lives, so why couldn't I?

"I'll have to work ye' in around me job."

"I'll have to do that with you too. I work construction, so I'm gone all day most days," Ash said, a ghost of a smile tugging at his lips. "But I'm willin'."

"Yeah," I said, returning his smile. "Me too."

He blew out a shaky breath.

"I wasn't expectin' this date to happen in the first place, so I'm out of me depth 'ere. I have a lot of stuff rattlin' around in me brain. I want to say a lot of things to ye', but at the same time I want things to just be chill. I want . . . I want . . ."

"*What* d'ye want?"

His eyes locked on mine. "You."

My breath caught in my throat, and for a moment my body was frozen. My eyes were on his, and things were so silent I could hear my heart beat in my ears.

"Just you," he continued.

Just me.

"No bullshit," I said, remembering he'd said earlier he didn't want to deal with anything other than honesty. "What do ye' want between us?"

"No bullshit." He nodded. "I won't have anythin' to do with other birds, and I want *you* to steer clear of other blokes."

Like he had that to worry about; I hardly spoke to other people unless it was at work.

"That's a relationship, Ash," I pointed out. "Boyfriend-and-girlfriend kind of deal."

"We don't have to label it, it's too early for that. Hell, it's too early for a conversation like this, but 'ere we are." He shook his head. "I just need ye' to tell me what the story is so I know what's goin' on with us. I don't like not knowin' where I stand on things, so ye' have to tell me."

My mind was so torn about him because of all his gang ties, but my heart was focused on the person who he was when he was with me . . . and my heart was winning.

"I don't want to date other people. Just you."

There, I'd said it.

"Right," Ash acknowledged. "That's that then. We'll date each other."

"I repeat, that's boyfriend and girlfriend."

"No labels," he echoed. "Labels freak people out, and I don't want ye' to be freaked out."

"Do I look freaked out to you?"

"Ye' look like you're shittin' yourself, Ryan."

Nervous laughter escaped me. "I'm pretty calm. *You* seem to be the one freakin' out."

"You're right," he agreed. "How do I stop that?"

I snickered, which caused him to grab me and tickle me. I screamed as we fell onto the settee, and we laughed until we were lying side by side, with Ash's arm around me and my upper body leaning over his.

"I'm afraid if I kiss ye' right now, I won't be able to stop."

His honesty earned him my respect tenfold. I had been raised by a man who'd taught me that being honest was always the best policy. I knew it wasn't a trait that many men possessed, so it really touched me that Ash had that quality. But it scared me how naturally this honesty flowed between us. It was almost like it was too good to be true.

"Don't kiss me," he almost pleaded when he looked into my eyes, most likely seeing how badly I wanted to press my lips to his. "I don't want to fuck this up."

We sat up on the settee, not touching. I was so aware of his presence that the hairs on the nape of my neck stood to attention. I was back to being terrified, because I wanted to kiss him, to run my hands over him, to feel and experience a man just like I'd read about in my beloved books a million times over. The unknown was a scary but oh-so-tempting place.

"Should I leave?" I asked, my hands burning to touch him. "I will if ye' want me to."

Ash bobbed his head up and down, almost relieved I'd asked him.

"I don't want to push ye', but I want to kiss ye' somethin' fierce, and that leads to other things."

I licked my lips. "Things I've never done before."

Ash closed his eyes at my admission. "Definitely a good girl."

"Is that a bad thing?"

"No, babe," he answered. "It's really not. You're untouched in more ways than one. You're pure. I *love* that no other man has had your body."

No man had had my heart either.

He stood up, got my blazer and bag, shouted up to Sean that he'd be back in a minute, then we left the house. He held my hand as he walked me home, and we didn't speak a word the whole way. The warmth of his hand against mine sent a flutter through my heart. I really, really liked holding his hand.

When we got to my auntie's front door, he leaned down and kissed my cheek.

"Can I have your phone?" he asked. "I want to pop me number in it."

I got my phone from my bag and handed it to him. He tapped on the screen, entering his information, then he clicked into my message to Eddi and sent the picture I took of us to his phone. My lips parted in surprise when he did that, but pleasure flowed through my veins.

"There." He handed it back to me. "Now I have your number."

"And our picture."

"What can I say?" He grinned. "It's *cute*."

I snorted.

"Talk to ye' tomorrow, nightmare," he said, then with one last look, he turned and made his way out of the garden. I willed him to look back at me, but he didn't and it made me smile. He strode away with an aura of confidence, and it was so attractive I almost couldn't stand it. When he was out of sight, I entered the house and closed the door behind me.

"I'm back," I called out.

"Already?" Andrea called from the kitchen. "But it's only half past eight."

"I know," I laughed.

"Did ye' have fun?" she asked as I jogged up the stairs.

"It was great, Andie. He was a true gentleman."

I came to a dead stop at the top of the stairs when I noticed Eddi was standing in the doorway of her room.

"Hi." I smiled, wiggling my fingers at her.

She looked me up and down. "Hey."

I walked by her and entered my bedroom. I sat down on my bed, then lay back and just remained still. My brain couldn't fully absorb everything that had happened. I'd had my first date with Ash, and somehow we'd agreed that we wouldn't date other people, but we didn't want a label because it really *was* too early for that. I wanted things to be simple for the moment, and they were . . . once I forced myself not to think about how much I liked him.

I *really* liked him.

"What's wrong, Ry?" Eddi quizzed. "Ye' look scared."

"Not scared," I corrected. "Terrified."

"What happened?" Eddi demanded. "Did he hurt ye'?"

She looked like she would go and murder Ash if I said yes.

"Not at all," I answered, then smiled dreamily. "He didn't hurt me in the slightest."

"They why are ye' terrified?"

"Because . . ." I swallowed. "I think I'm in big trouble."

"With Ash?"

I nodded. "He's perfect, Eddi."

"Perfect?" she repeated, and managed to look angry and disgusted at the same time. "Ash Dunne is perfect?"

"Perfect," I said again. "I just had the best and most romantic night of me life with 'im, and I'm terrified about it."

"'Cause he's a Disciple?"

I closed my eyes and nodded.

"He always goin' to *be* a Disciple, Ryan."

That was exactly what terrified me.

Being a Disciple was always going to be part of who Ash was. I knew that, and I knew that nothing could truly become of us . . . but I didn't want to throw away an experience with him, no matter how small that experience might be, just because I was scared.

"I really like 'im, Ed."

"This is goin' to end badly," Eddi said, her voice low and her eyes closed. "I know it is."

In that moment, I hoped to God that for my and Ash's sakes, she was wrong.

CHAPTER SIXTEEN

ASHLEY

I was pretty sure that before this night was up, I was going to be profoundly sick.

"What did ye' tell Ryan to get out of your date?"

I looked at Anto when he spoke and said, "I didn't have to tell 'er anythin'. I got your text just after I walked 'er home."

My friend looked confused. "Did somethin' happen for 'er to go home so early? Ye' both seemed to be gettin' on like a house on fire when I stopped by."

I shook my head. "Things went great, it was just gettin' a little hot and heavy. She's a virgin, so I have to take things slow with 'er. I don't wanna fuck it up."

"A virgin," Anto echoed. "I've never been with one of those before."

I blew out a breath. "Me either, man."

I tried not to think of Ryan. She was so perfect, and so pure, and what I was about to do was neither of those things. I didn't want to mix her up with the dark side of my life, not even in my mind.

Anto looked down at his feet. "How are we gonna do this, Ashley?"

I had no idea how to answer him, so I didn't. After I'd walked Ryan home, Anto had sent me a text message saying he had the names of the two runners who'd stolen from Mr Nobody, as well as their current location. We didn't ask questions, and we didn't talk about it, we just met up at Anto's apartment and walked twenty minutes to Tallaght Village, where the kids were located in the bowling alley.

They were both fourteen, and from the information given to us, they were best friends and spent a lot of time together. They did runs together, and most likely came up with the plan to steal Nobody's money together too. They were a year younger than my little brother, and I had to help my best friend hurt them.

I had never hated being a Disciple more than I did in that moment, and I knew Anto felt the same way.

"Don't tell me their names," I said to Anto as we approached the bowling alley. "I don't wanna know either of them."

Anto's answer came out in the form of a grunt.

I waited outside the building in the laneway out back while Anto went inside to lure both boys out to me. There were no cameras in sight, so we didn't have to worry about someone recording what we were about to do.

I heard voices and some laughter as Anto rounded the corner with two skinny kids. The taller one had brown hair, and the shorter one had light blond hair with neon-blue ends. Both of them slowed down and lost their smiles when they saw me. But they listened to Anto when he told them to stand against the wall in front of him.

I watched as fear crept into their eyes, and their demeanour changed as they realised they were in a very bad situation.

"I don't wanna hear a word from either of ye'," Anto said, his voice gruff. "I know ye' both stole a grand each from me last shipment."

Wild terror filled both boys' eyes.

"Mr Nobody says both of ye' have to be punished," Anto sighed. "After this, ye' both are no longer Disciples. Ye' don't talk about this to anyone, and ye' don't hint that it was a Disciple who hurt ye'. We clear?"

Both lads looked at Anto and me, then at each other, and I saw the moment they decided to bail. I jumped forward and hooked my arm around the neck of the taller one, while Anto darted after the shorter one. I shoved the boy up against the wall and fisted the collar of his shirt.

"We *have* to do this," I said to the kid in front of me. "Ye' know that, right?"

He bobbed his head but he still tried to get away. I had to put him out of his misery, so I punched him in the face and got the beating underway. I lost count of how many times I punched him, kicked and stomped on his defenceless body as he fell to the ground. I hit him a couple times in the face, hard enough to make gashes and draw blood, but other than that I tried to steer clear of his head. I didn't want to cause permanent damage, just something cosmetic that would satisfy Mr Nobody.

"I'm sorry," he cried, and for a moment it made me hesitate. "I'm *so* sorry."

I gritted my teeth as his words caused a lump to form in my throat.

"Man up," I told him, kicking him in the stomach. "D'ye think we want to do shite like this? D'ye think we enjoy it? We have no choice, because of a stupid fuckin' decision ye' *both* made. If ye' steal from Nobody, you're gettin' decked."

I had no idea if Anto and I were being watched, but I felt like we were, so I had to put on a show that I was dishing out revenge for my friend. Nobody fucked with Disciples, not even other Disciples, and I had to prove that I was a ride or die. Or at least, I just had to make Mr Nobody believe I was.

Once I was confident that this kid had received a rough beating, I knew I had to do the part I dreaded most. I had to pick a limb and break it. Mr Nobody wouldn't want a finger or two snapped; he'd want something that would make a person suffer. Because of that, I picked the kid's ankle. I didn't think of it, I just raised my foot and slammed it down. I heard his ankle crunch under my boot, and for a moment I thought I was going to be ill.

The kid screamed, then he fell back onto the ground and went silent. My heart stopped for a moment, until I bent down and realised he was still breathing, still alive, just passed out from pain. I hoped he stayed unconscious until he reached the hospital.

I stood up, and looked to my left just as Anto walked towards me. The kid he'd battered was writhing around on the ground not far away. My friend's fists were bloody, just like mine, and as he approached me, he didn't look at the kid I'd had to hurt for him, he just kept on walking. I joined him, but felt unsteady on my feet as we walked.

I was silent as Anto took out a phone from his pocket, tapped on the screen and put it to his ear.

"The guards, please . . . Two kids have been attacked," he said moments later, his voice monotone. "They need an ambulance right away."

He rattled off the location, then wiped the burner phone clean and smashed it against a concrete wall. He glanced over his shoulder at the kids, then he turned his gaze forward and together we walked away. We didn't speak, we didn't look at each other, we just headed back to my house and didn't mention it.

Part of me knew that we'd never talk about it. It'd go to that dark place in our minds that was reserved for the truly appalling deeds we'd done as Disciples, and it would remain there. Never mentioned, never hinted at, but thought of frequently.

CHAPTER SEVENTEEN
ASHLEY

"I'm buyin' a car," I announced as I sat down on my settee, groaning as my limbs relaxed for the first time all day. "I know me last one was scrapped when I couldn't get it to pass the NCT test, but I don't care. I want another one. A new one. Nothing flashy, but somethin' reliable."

"What kind of car will ye' get?" Sean asked from the doorway.

"One with four wheels and an engine," I answered. "I'm sick of takin' the bus to work. I'm gonna start lookin' for one in January."

My brother entered the sitting room and sat down next to me.

"Why were ye' even in work?" Sean asked. "It's Christmas Eve, you're supposed to be on your holidays."

"Yesterday some of the other men on the site slacked on puttin' away all the gear and securin' the site until we go back to work in the new year, so the boss phoned me and I had to go in and help. It's only twelve o'clock, and I'm exhausted."

Work, as usual, was tough and physically demanding, and I wouldn't have had it any other way, as it took my mind off the horrors I'd committed the other night, but from the moment I'd got on the bus that morning, I couldn't wait to get home, and it had nothing to do with kicking back and relaxing.

I wanted to see Ryan again. I was a sap who had apparently turned into a fifteen-year-old girl where she was concerned, but I didn't care.

Our date had gone better than I could have imagined. After second-guessing myself all day about those stupid candles, I bit the bullet and put them around the kitchen and lit them. It was clear to me she was worth any insults my friends would throw my way the second I saw Ryan's face. She was blown away, and just by a few candles and a cooked meal.

She was pure . . . *really* pure, as I found out at the end of our date. I basically ran her home, because I was afraid I might push her too far with how physical we got. After learning she was a virgin, I knew I'd made the right decision. I wouldn't have touched her without her consent, but it was obvious to her that I wanted her, and I didn't want her to feel pressure in that department so I ended the date, and from her quick movements, she was glad of it.

It wasn't natural how quick I'd come to realise that I wanted to spend time with her and only her. And I didn't know why I'd pushed the issue with her, because long-term wasn't what I could give her. I knew that. She knew that. But label or no label, we were in some sort of relationship now, and while I was glad of it, I also hated it.

I had a person, a nutcase, who was purposely trying to harm my family. And after what happened with Kara, Ryan could easily become this loser's target, and I knew it was selfish of me to potentially put her in harm's way just because I wanted her so bad. I comforted myself by having lesser Disciples than myself take shifts of watching her around the clock. Whenever she wasn't with me, I wanted eyes on her. Getting involved with Ryan shouldn't have happened, and I should've called her up and told her that dating wasn't the right thing to do when I sat down and thought about it after our date. But I didn't, and I didn't plan on doing it either.

I was *really* fucking stupid.

"What's the story with you and that Ryan girl?"

I blinked and looked at my brother, noting he didn't seem to be teasing me, he was simply curious about her. I couldn't blame him. I'd never been in a relationship, and knowing a woman past having sex with her wasn't my usual style. I was most definitely a "wham, bam, thank you ma'am" kind of bloke.

"Why?" I quizzed. "D'ye not like 'er?"

I hadn't realised, but it struck me just how important Sean's opinion of Ryan was. He was my entire life, and if he didn't get on with Ryan, I didn't want to progress any further with her. I had to put him first, at least until he was old enough to understand grown-up relationships.

"Just askin'." He shrugged. "And yeah, I like 'er. She was nice."

I relaxed and scratched my neck. "I'm goin' to be spendin' some time with 'er."

"Like ye' spend time with other birds?"

"No," I said a little too harshly. "Not like that, she's different."

"Yeah, I figured as much, since ye' never brought a mot to the house on a date before."

"She's a good girl," I explained. "I'll be doin' things differently when it comes to 'er."

"Is she your girlfriend?"

"We agreed on no label because it felt too soon, but yeah, she is. We're only goin' to be seein' each other."

Sean nodded in understanding. "I got with Kerry after four days of knowin' 'er, and we're goin' out seven months now. When ye' know, ye' know."

I clapped him on the shoulder. "I'll have to take notes from you, since ye' somehow manage to keep your bird around."

Sean grinned. "I'm 'ere whenever ye' need advice."

At that, I laughed.

"How d'ye think Anto will take the news?"

I furrowed my brow in confusion.

"What d'ye mean?" I asked. "What news?"

"That Ryan will be around more." Sean mused. "Anto is like your second arm, so he'll have to get used to someone else takin' his spot."

I froze. "He'll probably kill 'er for takin' me away from 'im."

Sean and I shared a look, then laughed.

"He'll be grand," I chuckled. "Me only worry when it comes to 'im is that he'll probably irritate 'er."

"Anto, irritatin' someone?" Sean smirked. "When has that *ever* happened?"

I shook my head. "Smartarse."

"Am I allowed out today?"

"Yeah, but you're still studyin' over your Christmas break; that's non-negotiable. I'm furious about ye' failin' classes, so ye' have to get your marks up."

"I will, I promise."

Just as I opened my mouth to praise him, a loud bang sounded, followed by a ripple of crashing glass. It took me a second to realise that the bang was so loud because it was the sound of my sitting-room window being smashed. I jumped and dove on Sean, covering his body with mine. When I was sure nothing else was a threat to him, I jumped to my feet and ran out into the front garden, but there was no one in sight.

"Stay the fuck away from me family!" I shouted, hoping whoever had smashed my window heard me loud and clear. "I'll fuckin' kill ye' otherwise!"

"Ash?" Sean called from inside the house. "Ashley!"

I sprinted back inside, alarmed by his tone.

"What?" I demanded, grabbing his shoulders. "What's wrong?"

"What's this mean?"

I looked down to his hands, and saw a brick in one hand and a piece of paper in the other. The note was unfolded, and it was clear from my brother's expression that whatever he'd read had terrified him. I stared at him, and knew that I couldn't continue to lie to him, not anymore.

"It was tied to the brick with an elastic," Sean continued, his voice shaky.

"Listen to me," I said, placing my hands on his shoulders. "Some nutter out there is tryin' to mess with me, and he's tryin' to hurt me through *you*, but I'm not gonna let anythin' happen to ye', okay?"

Sean swallowed. "Okay, Ashley."

I took the paper from his hand and said, "Ring Anto from your phone. Tell 'im to get 'ere now."

Sean fumbled as he got his phone out of his pocket and did as I asked. I, however, focused on the piece of paper, and with a sensation of dread in the pit of my stomach, I unfolded the note and read words that made my blood run cold.

Enjoy Christmas. It'll be his last.

CHAPTER EIGHTEEN
RYAN

An unexpected day off from work was what I had to look forward to. I had headed to work at nine with Eddi this morning to start our Christmas Eve shifts, but when I got there, one of the girls begged me to give her my shift so she could take St Stephen's Day off to go to the last dress fitting for her sister's wedding. She was the maid of honour.

Of course, I swapped shifts with her. It didn't bother me, working during the holidays, because my da wasn't around and I didn't feel like celebrating much without him. Before Ash, I never would have thought of making plans, but after our date on Saturday I was looking forward to spending time with him.

I was so giddy when I thought about him and the date overall. It had been magical. That was such an eye-roll-inducing word, but it was the perfect word to describe it. My first assessment of Ash had proven to be *so* wrong. I'd thought he was this terrifying criminal who was going to swallow me whole. Comparing that to the Ash I'd spent time with the other night was a complete one-eighty spin.

Everyone saw him as a scary Disciple because that was what he was. But they never considered the possibility that there was more to him. I got to see a glimpse of the man who cared for his younger brother, and how he put Sean and his best interests above all else. I saw him as a best friend in his interactions with Anto, and from my experience with him so far, I got the impression he would be a great boyfriend too. I still had to get to know him, but I believed that he was a good man.

My heart believed he was.

At the thought of him, I picked up my phone and searched for the picture of us. I smiled when it appeared on my screen. Christ, he was a good-looking man, scarred lip and all. His grey eyes reminded me of liquid silver, something I could get lost in. His ever-there stubble made me wonder what he'd look like with a full beard. Even more gorgeous than he already looked, I suspected.

I opened a new message, selected his name, and thumbed out a message and hit send before I overthought it.

What's up, big head?

He had called me that once before, and after consulting Eddi, she'd confirmed it was just a playful endearment of sorts lads would say to girls. I didn't get it, I probably never would, but I used it anyway.

I had just made a cup of tea when my phone vibrated, and I practically dove for it on the counter. I smiled; it was Ash.

Who the fuck is this?

I furrowed my brow at his harsh response.

It's Ryan.

I added the wide-eyed emoji just so he knew I was taken aback by his reply. He must have stopped whatever he was doing to text me, because he replied quickly.

I'm sry. I didn't realise it was u, babe. 4got to save your name with your number. U on a break at work?

I blew on my tea, then sipped it, humming in satisfaction.

I'm at home. I swapped shifts so I'm working on Stephen's Day instead. We're only open until the afternoon that day, so it doesn't bother me.

I went into the holiday-decorated sitting room, curled up on the sofa and turned on the telly. I switched on one of the music channels, which was playing a constant loop of Christmas songs. I looked down at my phone when it vibrated. It was Ash calling, so I quickly put my cup of tea on the coffee table, lowered the volume of the telly and answered.

"Hello?"

"Why d'ye sound breathless?" he probed. "Were ye' runnin'?"

I blinked. "No."

"Ye' were just excited to talk to me then?"

God, his voice was sexy. Just hearing it sent ripples of delight throughout my body. My excitement over this was embarrassing. Even I could admit that to myself.

"Yeah," I mused. "I saw ye' were callin', and boom, instant breathlessness."

I sounded like I was joking, but Ash didn't need to know how true that statement was. His deep chuckle brought a smile to my face.

"What're ye' doin'?" I queried. "At work?"

"No," he answered. "I'm off until the new year. The fourth, to be exact."

"That must be nice," I said. "I just have tomorrow, and now today, off."

"Are ye' workin' on New Year's Eve?"

"Most likely, the shop is only open until two that day," I answered. "I never do anythin' for me birthday, so it doesn't—"

"Wait," Ash interrupted. "Your birthday is *on* New Year's Eve?"

"Yeah."

"How old are ye'?" he quizzed. "Twenty?"

"Nineteen."

"Jaysus, I've been kissin' a baby."

I rolled my eyes. "Give over, aul' lad."

Ash chuckled. "I want to see ye' later."

"Another date?" I grinned.

"Are we goin' to call it a date every time we're together?"

"Nah. Only when we do somethin' nice."

"I had a great time the other night, Ryan. I mean that. Did you?"

I was glad he wasn't there to see heat climb up my cheeks.

"Of course I did; ye' know I did."

"I wasn't sure," Ash said. "Ye' didn't text me yesterday."

"I was workin' all day, and when I got home I ate dinner and went straight to bed. Trust me, I had a great time with ye'," I said softly. "Who knew that ye' were a nice man?"

"Ye' can't tell anyone," he said, and I heard the laughter in his voice. "Hell, they probably wouldn't believe ye' anyway if ye' did."

The doorbell of the house rang and got my attention.

"One second," I said. "Someone's at the door."

I walked out of the sitting room into the hallway, and opened the front door. The person who stood before me was the last person I expected to see. The shock almost caused me to drop my phone.

"*Ciara?*" I spluttered.

Ciara Kelly was in front of me, in the flesh. For a split second, I almost didn't recognise her. For as long as I'd known her, she's always worn fitted skirts and business suits, and on her down time she wore pretty dresses and high heels. In fact she always wore high heels, no matter the occasion. But the woman before me was wearing blue jeans, a black jumper and black Nike runners. Her hair was tied on the top of her head in a messy bun too.

I couldn't believe what I was witnessing – this was a version of Ciara I'd never seen before. She had no make-up on her face, and her usual chin-up confidence was gone. She actually looked pretty vulnerable.

"Hello, Ry." She nodded curtly.

She had never called me "Ry". Ever.

I balled my hands into fists. "Ye' have some fuckin' nerve showin' up 'ere, Ciara."

"Please," she said, holding her hands in the air. "I'm not here to fight with you."

I was angry with her, but the shock of seeing her outweighed that at the moment.

"How did ye' know I was 'ere?" I demanded. "Who told ye'?"

Ciara shrugged. "Johanna."

"Ye' hassled Johanna when she's ill?"

"I didn't hassle her," Ciara stated. "I dropped by her daughter's house, and she told me you were here. She's very sick."

My lips thinned to a line.

"I *know* she's sick," I growled. "I call 'er every day to check in on 'er."

I had gone from living with Johanna, and seeing her all the time, to speaking to her for a few minutes a day over the phone. I wasn't entirely sure what was wrong with her, she wouldn't tell me, but I knew it was bad because she wouldn't let me to go and visit her. Her pride wouldn't allow me to see her when she was so poorly. Being cared for was a lot for her to accept; she much preferred being the caregiver. So I'd abided by her wishes and stayed away.

It didn't mean I was happy about it, though.

"Can I come in?" Ciara sounded so tired. "We need to discuss your father."

My heart stopped.

"Why d'ye want to talk about me da?"

"Ryan?" I looked to my left, and when I saw Ash jogging into the garden, I looked down at the phone in my hand and realised I'd forgotten about our phone call. "Are ye' okay?"

"I'm sorry," I said as he approached me and Ciara. "I forgot ye' were still on the phone."

"I heard ye' shoutin' at someone, and since I knew it wasn't me, I figured I'd come and see if ye' were okay."

I swallowed. "I'm fine."

"Babe," was all he said, indicating he knew that I was lying.

Ciara looked between Ash and me, and I didn't like the sneering look she shot his way. She looked at him like she'd already made up her mind about what kind of man he was, and that pissed me off.

"This is Ashley," I said firmly. "Me boyfriend."

Ash stared at me but he didn't correct me; he seemed to know that I was making a statement to Ciara that he was mine, and he was perfectly okay with that.

"I'm Ciara Kelly," she said to Ash. "I'm Ryan's stepmother."

"Oh my God," I gasped. "Ye' did *not* just say that! You and me da are *not* married, Ciara! Why would ye' say that when you haven't even bothered to visit 'im? I'll tell ye' why, because you're a selfish fuckin' bitch! He's stuck in prison, and you're out 'ere doin' God only knows what!"

My chest was rising and falling rapidly after I spoke. Ciara didn't respond, but what I'd just said must have struck something in her. I saw her lower lip wobble ever so slightly before she schooled her features. I couldn't decipher her reaction, but when my eyes flicked to Ash, I could read his. I widened my eyes when I realised what I'd just said in front of him.

"Your da is locked up?"

I couldn't speak, I only nodded.

"For what?"

"None of your business," Ciara answered him.

Ash shifted his eyes to her, and narrowed them. "I wasn't talkin' to *you*."

If Ciara was intimidated by Ash, she didn't show it. She ignored him completely and focused on me.

"We *need* to talk."

I hated to admit it, but she was right – we did need to talk.

"Fine," I answered. "Go into the sittin' room."

She breezed by me without another word, and Ash stepped closer.

"What's goin' on?" he asked, lifting his hand to my cheek and rubbing his thumb over my skin. "Ye' look shaken."

"I'm always like this around Ciara," I said. "We aren't on the best terms right now."

"Ye' said your da was in prison."

My legs felt a little weak. "Yes, I did."

"Ye' want to tell me about it?"

I had promised Eddi, and my auntie, that I would keep my da and where I was from to myself, but I couldn't see how I could do that now that he'd overheard me saying Da was in prison. I decided I would tell him everything, because I knew he wouldn't go around spreading my business to every Tom, Dick and Harry.

"Not now." I paused. "But I will later. I have to deal with Ciara first."

"Okay," he said, leaning down and pressing his lips gently to mine.

When we parted, he said, "Calm down and deal with that woman. Don't stress yourself out over 'er."

I blew out a breath. "Easier said than done."

Ash kissed me once more, then he turned and walked out the garden. I closed the door, and went into the sitting room, where Ciara was sitting down on the settee facing me.

"Does your father know you're with a boy like that?"

"Ash is twenty-three, he isn't a boy," I said with a sneer. "And no, me da doesn't know, because me relationship with Ash is new. I also don't need me da's permission to date someone, Ciara. I'm about to turn nineteen."

Ciara said nothing, but her expression spoke a million words. She didn't approve of Ash, but I didn't give a rat's arse whether she approved or not. The last thing I needed was her blessing.

"Why are ye' 'ere? Ye've dropped off the face of the Earth these last few months, and now suddenly ye' show up and want to talk? Ye' haven't even bothered to visit me da."

Ciara flinched as if my words wounded her.

"I can explain everythin', if you'd just calm down and let me speak," she said as she brushed a stray piece of hair out of her face. "It's important, so for once in your life, shut up and listen to me."

My gut reaction was to tell her to clear off, but I'd be damned if I didn't want to hear what she had to say.

"Fine," I relented. "Talk."

Ciara took a breath, and said something that shook my entire world.

"You were right all along," she said, her expression tight. "Your father is innocent."

For the last year I'd been made to feel crazy by the Gardaí, and for a time, even my own cousin. I knew my da was innocent. I knew he hadn't fought his case for a reason, but no one else believed he could be innocent. No one but me. Hearing Ciara say out loud what no one would believe made me want to cry.

"*What*?" I gasped. "What did ye' just say?"

"Your father didn't do what he admitted to."

"I knew it," I whispered to myself. Then to Ciara, I repeated it louder. "I knew he was innocent, but how *d'you* know that?"

"I've spent months combing through every piece of paper, every note, in your father's files that was connected to the Hopkins homicide case." Ciara intertwined her fingers. "What do you know about the case?"

I knew everything about it. John McCarty had been on trial for murdering a man in cold blood. He shot him, execution style, in the middle of the night on the docks of Dublin port. No one knew the reason why this senseless act took place; many speculated it was a drug deal gone wrong or maybe something more sinister, as Arthur Hopkins, the victim, was a known gangland criminal, just like John McCarty. My father had been the barrister to fight against John McCarty in court, with the intention of putting him away for life for first-degree murder . . . but he ended up going to prison as well as McCarty.

I swallowed down bile. "I know everythin' about it."

"Everything about that poxy case was textbook, up until the end when a new piece of evidence was discovered in your father's possession. It was a CCTV video of the homicide itself taking place. Originally it was thought that no footage could be recovered from CCTV cameras in the area, but that wasn't true. Your father concealed the video's existence, though I've no idea how he came to have it in the first place. This piece of evidence would have put John McCarty behind bars instantly. It shows him clearly committing the murder. It was your father's ticket to winning the case, but he withheld it."

"No," I whispered, horrified. "I know he admitted to that, but my da would never actually *do* that, Ciara."

"He *did* conceal the evidence, but not out of his own free will."

My head was spinning as I leaned forward and asked, "What d'ye mean?"

"Your father was forced," she stressed. "The day after he was assigned the case, he received a visit from two men at the office. Around that time he started to act distracted and worried, but after he was arrested I forgot about that behaviour. It wasn't until I started doing some digging that I decided to check the surveillance footage from the office, just to see if there was anything out of the ordinary. Those two men entered your father's office, and when they left twenty minutes later, your father was visibly distressed."

"What d'ye think happened?" I asked, my stomach churning.

"I think they threatened your father, and the threat was enough for him to try to ruin a case so a murderer could walk free. The only good thing to come out of this was that he was caught, and John McCarty *did* go to prison thanks to the CCTV footage that was retrieved. I honestly don't know if your father planned it that way, but that's how it happened."

A new barrister had taken over the case after my da was arrested, and he'd put John McCarty behind bars for first-degree murder thanks to the CCTV tape.

"Do you remember," Ciara continued, "when we went to visit your father at the start of his sentence, and we tried to talk to him about the case, but other than mumbling, 'I had to protect my family,' he wouldn't speak any more of it?"

I nodded. I had never understood what he'd meant by that.

"I think he was referring to *you*," Ciara explained. "I think that the men that approached your father threatened to harm you unless he did their bidding."

I felt my jaw drop. To think that I could have been the reason my father did what he did was almost unbearable.

"But if all that's true, Da failed in destroyin' the case and nothin' has happened to me. Shouldn't he have been punished in some way by the men who threatened him?"

"I think the punishment *is* your father being in prison. He could have easily admitted the truth, that he was being forced to do what he did, and he would have possibly been acquitted or received a much lighter sentence. But he didn't. And I think that was to protect you," Ciara said, her fingers tightly clasped together. "But we won't know the truth until we confront your father with this. I stopped going to visit him because it broke my heart to see him in that state. He wouldn't let me help him, he wouldn't tell me what actually happened, so I stepped back and focused on finding out what had happened myself."

I stared, wide-eyed. "I thought ye' didn't care about 'im."

"Didn't care about him?" Ciara repeated, her lips parted with shock, and her voice cracked as she spoke. "Ryan, I am in *love* with your father."

I leaned back into the settee. "Really?"

"What do you mean, 'really'?" she demanded. "Of *course* I love him. I wouldn't be marrying him if I didn't love him!"

I sat in silence, because I honestly didn't know what to say.

"You don't know a thing about our relationship," Ciara said firmly. "So don't pretend otherwise. You've always hated me, so you came up with your own conclusions as to why I'm with him."

"I haven't always hated ye'," I said defensively. "I tried me best with ye' at the start, but ye' were hell-bent on tryin' to be a mother figure when all I needed was a friend! Then when me da went to prison ye' just left 'im . . . ye' left *me* without a word. I *had* to hate ye'. I couldn't let meself be upset with ye' because it *hurt*."

It was at that moment that I realised, as much as Ciara got on my nerves, she had become part of my life, and I'd unknowingly accepted her into it even though I thought I'd convinced myself that she wouldn't be long-term. Deep down, I knew that she and my father were in love; he wouldn't have been with her otherwise. He wasn't stupid, he could read people very well, and he'd have known if Ciara wasn't genuine. My childish ways had blinded me from seeing that.

Ciara's mouth opened for a moment, then when nothing came out, she closed it.

"Ryan," she began, her hands suddenly trembling as her eyes shone with unshed tears. "I'm sorry for cutting you and your father off while I focused on his case. At the time, it seemed like the best option, but now I see how foolish that was of me. And . . . and I'm sorry I haven't been more patient with you in the past. I've always wanted children . . . to have a daughter of my own . . . but that never happened for me, and when I met your father, and met you, I thought I would finally have that. I'm so sorry for pushing myself on you. It went horribly wrong and when we started clashing, I didn't know how to backtrack and make things better."

My heart stopped, and it felt like a stone had clogged in my throat. Then I felt tears splash onto my cheeks, and that was when the sobbing started.

"Sweetheart, don't cry."

When Ciara quickly moved to sit beside me, she didn't hesitate, she hugged me tightly and held my body to hers while she rocked me from side to side. Remorse and sorrow filled me as I wrapped my arms around her. My pig-headed ways had kept me from seeing that she didn't only want my da . . . she wanted me too.

"I'm sorry," I choked out. "I'm sorry for bein' so horrible to ye'. I wish I could take it all back. I've been so wrong about ye', Ciara. Please forgive me."

"Hey," she pulled back, tears sliding down her cheeks too. "You're forgiven only if I am. Deal?"

I bobbed my head and hugged her once more. When we parted, we both laughed as we wiped our faces clear of tears. I took a few deep breaths before I said, "What are we goin' to do about me da?"

"When is the next visiting day at the prison?"

"The second of January."

With a nod, Ciara stood up. "I'll meet you at the prison. Hopefully we can finally get your father to tell us the truth, and we can try to help him."

"Try?" I frowned, getting to my feet too.

"He committed the crime," Ciara said, her shoulders slumping. "He has to be punished for that, but if I prepare a new case in his defence, and I can prove he wasn't acting willingly, I might be able to get the rest of the sentence overturned and have his licence to practise law restored. But we need your father to help make that possible."

"Okay, okay," I agreed. "I'll see ye' there . . . And Ciara?"

She brushed the stray hairs away from my face.

"Yes?"

"Thank you," I said, my lower lip wobbling. "Thank you so much."

She hugged me once more and kissed my temple.

"Thank me when we get your father home."

She left then, and I stood still, staring after her, not quite believing what had just taken place. An emotion surged through me that I hadn't felt in a long time.

Hope.

For the first time in fifteen months, since my da was arrested and this nightmare began, I had hope.

CHAPTER NINETEEN
ASHLEY

"Are ye' *sure* she said that? That 'er da is in *prison*?"

I grunted, "I'm sure."

Anto mulled over what I'd told him about Ryan, the lady called Ciara who clearly bothered her, and the mention of her da being in prison.

"What d'ye reckon he did to get locked up?" Anto wondered out loud. "D'ye think it's somethin' serious?"

I shrugged. "I don't know, and I don't really care."

"Why not?" he pressed. "I'd wanna know what he did."

"'Cause 'er da's choices are not Ryan's choices," I answered. "If I judged 'er for whatever 'er da has done I'd be a hypocrite, considerin' the piece of shite mine turned out to be."

"Don't think about 'im," Anto instructed. "He could be dead for all ye' know."

"I doubt it," I grunted. "Ye' can't kill a bad thing."

I gritted my teeth at the thought of the man who'd fathered me. My memories of him had been all bad. From him beating my mother, to kicking the shite out of me and drinking every minute of every day. I'd hated that man before I even knew what hate truly was.

"It's kind of funny," Anto said with a huff of laughter. "Ryan was so scared of ye' for bein' a Disciple, like ye' were the baddest criminal out there, and all the while 'er da is the one locked up!"

"I don't know the whole story," I said. "So I'm not assumin' anythin' until she talks to me about it."

Anto didn't say a word in response, he just looked at me.

"What?" I questioned. "Why're ye' lookin' at me like that?"

"You're serious about 'er, aren't ye'?" he asked. "About Ryan."

"Can anyone really be serious after one date?"

"Yeah." Anto nodded. "I see couples' stories all the time on Facebook about how they met one day, fell in love the next, got married a week later and were still married sixty years on. I'm not sayin' it's happenin' to *you*, but it happens."

"I can't believe ye' just said somethin' so . . . so sweet."

"I can be sweet when I want to be," Anto teased. "I'd be real sweet if Eddi gave me the time of day."

"Eddi?" I repeated. "Ye' have it bad for *Eddi*?"

"Just because I've never *told* ye' I fancy 'er doesn't mean me likin' 'er is *that* surprisin'."

I raised my hands. "I'm actually pleased for ye'. Ye' never usually like a girl for more than a shag . . . unless that *is* what this is?"

"It's not," he answered. "I don't know for sure, because I don't know 'er, but I think she's a good, hard-workin' girl. She's beautiful. I've never seen someone who fits that description, but she does. I sometimes go to SuperValu and buy shite I don't need just so I can see 'er."

"Anto . . ." I blinked. "I had no clue, man."

"It's cool, bud. She won't give me the time of day. She's scared of me and always will be." He smiled sadly. "Bein' a Disciple keeps all the good ones away . . . except in your case."

I leaned my head back on the settee and said, "Don't take the piss outta me when I tell ye' this, okay?"

"Ash," Anto said, sincerity in his voice, "I take the piss all the time, but if you're feelin' somethin' for this girl, I'm not goin' to bust your bollocks for it."

I looked at my friend. "I know, man."

"So, where's your head at with 'er?"

I snorted. "All over the place."

"A standard response where women are concerned."

My lips twitched. "I think she's pretty fuckin' perfect. She's funny, utterly stunnin', has a backbone, and she makes my stomach have those stupid butterflies girls always talk about," I said, not embarrassed to admit it. "I can't explain it, but I feel a pull towards 'er. And trust me, I know it's crazy since I don't know 'er all that well, but I'm not scared to be meself around 'er. She knows I'm a Disciple, and she knows what me life is like, and ye' know what? She doesn't blame me for it. She understands me. She treats me like a person, not like a scumbag who sells drugs. She's a hell of a woman, mate."

Anto whistled, his eyes wide. "It sounds like this is the real deal to me, so why're ye' tied up in knots over it?"

"Because, man." I sighed. "What if she comes to 'er senses that I'm not the kind of person anyone in their right mind would want a future with?"

"Hold on," Anto said, sitting upright. "Are ye' tellin' me that you're afraid of havin' a real relationship with this girl because it could go south?"

Reluctantly, I nodded.

"Ye've never been a fanny, so don't start that wimp shite now," Anto warned gruffly. "Ye' can't worry about things that may or may not happen. That's no way to live your life."

I widened my eyes. "But—"

"But nothin'." My friend cut me off. "If your ma's death has taught ye' anythin', it's to grab life by the bollocks with both hands, because ye'll never know when it's about to end."

I stared at Anto, shocked.

"What?" He shifted in his seat. "I joke around a lot, but I'm not blind, or stupid."

"I know," I agreed. "You're spittin' straight wisdom right now."

"Are ye' goin' to listen to me?"

I swallowed. "I'm goin' to try."

"Good." He nodded. "Stop worryin' about what Ryan might decide, because ye' can't control that any more than ye' can control the weather. She's decided she wants to explore a relationship with ye', and she decided that with everyone who's close to 'er tellin' 'er not to. Your bird has faith in the two of ye' . . . maybe *you* should too."

A smile stretched across my face.

"Ye've really made me feel better. Thanks, man."

"Good," Anto said, satisfied.

He glanced up and looked through the new window in my sitting room that he'd arranged to be fixed just thirty minutes after it was broken. I never questioned Anto's contacts, I just appreciated how quickly he could get shite done. When he jumped to his feet, it startled me.

"Ryan is walkin' into the garden," he said. "I'll go and make meself scarce so ye' can both talk."

I didn't have a chance to reply, as Anto practically bolted from the house, shouting a greeting and a farewell to Ryan as he left. I got up and walked out to the hallway. Ryan was standing on the porch, looking down at the floor.

"Ry?"

She looked up as if surprised to see me, even though she was standing on my doorstep.

"Sorry," she spluttered. "I was in me own world."

"Don't be sorry, come in."

She did as asked and closed the front door behind her. I guided her into the sitting room, where we sat down. I didn't speak, I simply watched her. She looked like she was deep in thought.

"Me head is all over the place," she said, and from her tone she sounded a bit lost. "I'm sorry if I'm a little off."

"Ye' don't have to tell me anythin' that ye' aren't comfortable with," I assured her. "Don't feel like ye' have to."

"No," she sighed, "I want to. We want to have a relationship with each other, so ye' have the right to know who I am and where I come from. We agreed on no bullshit, and this falls into that category."

I reached over and took her hand in mine, giving it a reassuring squeeze.

"I've grown up in a life of privilege. I had everythin', or at least every materialistic thing I ever wanted. Me life was pretty standard after me ma died, and nothin' life-changin' happened until me da met Ciara a few months before I turned fifteen. We got off to a really rocky start, and for a long time our relationship was hostile, but we actually just had a heart-to-heart and I realised how much she truly loves me da."

Ryan scooted closer to me until our sides were pressed together. I put one arm around her shoulders and then moved the other so she could hold on to my hand, which she did.

"Me da is a barrister," she said after clearing her throat. "Fifteen months ago he was arrested and admitted to concealin' evidence in a homicide case. He was sentenced to prison for seven years." She swallowed. "Me world turned upside down, Ashley. He's me best friend, and he was just plucked from me life."

Every one of my instincts wanted to rip apart anything that would ever hurt her. I leaned my head on hers, and held on to her as she bared her soul to me.

"I never believed he did what he was charged with, never mind that he admitted to it." She took a deep breath. "I thought I'd just have to stay strong and wait out his sentence, and then today Ciara showed up and said that me da is innocent and she thinks she can prove it."

"Ryan," I exclaimed, hugging her tightly. "That's amazin', babe."

"I had to keep all that from ye'," she continued. "Me auntie and Eddi didn't want anyone to know me business."

"I'm glad ye' told me, Ry," I replied, leaning back so I could look at her. "You're the strongest person I've ever met. Ye've had to endure a lot. Your da goin' to prison, you believin' his innocence then havin' to move 'ere and in with family ye' hardly knew. I'm sorry your da is goin' through what he is, but I'm so grateful that our paths crossed. I can't imagine not ever knowin' ye'."

She started crying then, and I held her tightly again, hoping my presence was easing some of the emotion she felt.

"I'm happy," she said, her face against my chest. "These are tears of joy, in case ye' were wonderin'."

"Good. Ye' deserve to be happy."

"I'm happy 'ere with *you*."

We pulled apart to look at one another, and for the umpteenth time, I couldn't believe my luck that she wanted to be with me.

"Ye' know I think ye' deserve better than me, right?"

"And *you* know that I don't care about anythin' but the person ye' are when you're with me."

My chest swelled. "I'm goin' to try me best not to ruin this."

Ryan rested her forehead against mine. "Ye' couldn't if you tried."

We stayed like that for a few minutes, basking in each other's presence, but then I felt like I needed to let her know about my past. She had just told me her story, and it was only right that she heard mine.

I had never talked to another person about it before, but with Ryan, everything felt so easy. So natural.

"When I was twelve," I began, "me ma kicked me da out, and we haven't seen 'im since."

Ryan snuggled into me as I spoke.

"The only memories I have of 'im were of 'im bein' drunk off his arse, and beatin' on me ma and me every chance he got. The day he left our lives was the happiest day of me life, but it changed things and added weight onto me shoulders.

"Sean was only four – he hadn't a clue what was goin' on or where Daddy had gone – so I knew I had to grow up fast to help me ma. I stepped up and started doin' more for me brother, and for her."

Ryan placed her hand on my stomach, and stroked her thumb back and forth.

"I took this new role very seriously. I wasn't perfect, far from it – it took shiteloads of ruined dinners until I caved and asked me ma to teach me how to cook properly. There was no stoppin' me after that, I learned how to work the washin' machine *and* dishwasher."

Ryan chuckled lightly, her thumb still stroking my stomach.

"I did everythin' a father should do for me brother, while still bein' a kid myself, but I wouldn't change it for the world. I love Sean to death. He acknowledges me as both his da and his brother, and that makes everythin' feel worth it. He knows who was there for 'im. I've had a good life, I just wish I hadn't gotten involved with the Disciples."

I paused for a moment, and thought about what I was going to say so I didn't name drop anyone I shouldn't be talking about. Not because I didn't trust Ryan – I did – but because I wanted to keep as much of that dark part of my life to myself as I could.

"I was thirteen when I became one of them," I continued. "And I'll be one for the rest of me life. Me ma sobbed over it – she hated that I was in a gang, and I did too. I still do. I did everythin' I could to help 'er, but in the end I couldn't help what happened to 'er. I was eighteen when she got sick. After 'er diagnosis, things went downhill fast. For three years she fought long and hard, but the day after me twenty-first birthday, she died in 'er sleep at the hospital. Her body couldn't fight anymore and she slipped away."

I blew out a breath when my voice cracked, and my eyes stung with tears. I looked up at the ceiling and willed them away. This was why I didn't talk about her, didn't think about her. It broke me down.

"Talkin' about 'er, it hurts."

"Ashley," Ryan said, and tugged on my shirt until I looked at her. "Don't hide from me. I want all of ye'."

I thought she might regret asking me that, because all of me came with a whole lot of bad. I closed my eyes briefly, and tears splashed onto my cheeks. Ryan leaned in and kissed them away, and my spine straightened at the contact. A sensation close to pain lingered in my stomach, and I felt so connected to her in that moment that I knew Anto was right when he said she was the real deal.

"You're so special to me," I told her. "The connection I feel with you doesn't happen to people often."

"I know what ye' mean," she said softly. "I'm aware how fast this is, but it doesn't feel fast. It feels easy, it feels . . ."

"Natural," I finished. "We feel natural."

Ryan leaned up and pressed her lips to mine softly before she pulled back and said, "Ye' know me now, and I know you."

When she kissed me again, it felt different, like she'd made a decision with that kiss. My breathing increased when she turned her body, lifted her leg and straddled me. I forced my hands to remain on her waist; I didn't want to direct this, I wanted her to go as far as she wanted to, without any nudges from me. I opened my mouth and kissed her with a hunger that I knew would never go away. I would always want this woman in the way I wanted her in this moment.

When she broke our kiss and rid herself of her cardigan, I placed my hands on hers as she reached for the hem of her shirt. I knew where this was about to go, and I had to be certain that *she* wanted this.

"Are ye' sure?" I asked, searching her eyes for doubt, but I saw none, only determination. "We don't have to do anythin' other than kiss if ye' don't want to."

She leaned in and pressed her forehead to mine.

"I've never been more sure of anythin' in me life, Ashley."

With her hands guiding mine, we lifted her shirt over her head, and I groaned when the top of her breasts became visible. Her bra still hid them from me fully, so when Ryan reached her arms behind her back and undid the clasp, letting the material fall down her arms, I hummed in delight. Her breasts were small but perfectly supple, with hardened pink nipples. I flicked my gaze up to her face, and found her eyes on me, her cheeks flushed.

"You're so beautiful, babe."

She smiled at me, and it just about knocked the breath out of me. She looked down at my shirt then back up to me. I grinned, knowing what she wanted me to do. I reached behind my neck, gripped my shirt and pulled it over my head. I looked at Ryan's face as her eyes scanned my torso. She reached out and ran her fingers over scars that were the result of stupid mistakes in my runner days.

She looked up at my lip then, and asked, "How?"

"A broken bottle was thrown at me," I answered.

She didn't need to hear any more; she leaned in and kissed the scar. It was a simple act, but it touched me more than she would ever know. She shifted above me, and grazed my rock-hard cock. I bit down on my lower lip to stop myself from rolling her under me. This was her show, she was in charge of what happened, and I'd call on every bit of willpower I had to keep from moving.

Ryan's breathing came out in pants as she covered my mouth with hers and kissed me hungrily.

"Help me," she whispered against my lips. "I have no idea what I'm doin', Ashley."

Those words were all I needed to hear. I wrapped my arms around her, and turned our bodies until she was on her back and I was in between her thighs, hovering over her. I broke our kiss so I could taste one of her nipples. The moment my tongue flicked over the hardened point, her back arched off the settee and she moaned.

Loudly.

I sent a silent thank you up to God that my brother would be out with his girlfriend all day and wouldn't be home until the evening. Then I pushed Sean from my mind and focused on Ryan. I licked and sucked at her nipple, released it and moved over to the other one, showing it the same love and attention. I didn't move from her breasts until she was unable to remain still underneath me. I kissed down her stomach, and when I came to the band of her jeans, I paused and looked up at her for permission.

Ryan, her face beautifully flushed, caught my gaze and said, "Yes."

I undid the button, pulled on the zip, and carefully pulled her jeans down until they were free of her ankles. I dropped them on the floor, and stared at the prize between her thighs. I bent down, and noticed her legs were trembling. I kissed the insides of her thighs, and it drew sweet music from her lips. Her scent was driving me wild, her thong was wet with desire, and I licked my lips in anticipation of tasting her.

I brought my mouth down to her pussy and licked over her clit. Even though a thin strip of fabric guarded her, she could feel the heat of my tongue on her.

My cock throbbed painfully; her scent and taste was driving me, and my body, crazy.

"Ye' taste fuckin' incredible."

I reached up and pushed her thong aside, and my cock jumped at sight of her pussy. She was deliciously pink and wet, with a small patch of dark curls. She was so aroused that I could see her swollen clit without having to push back the hood that protected it. I leaned in, and with a long swipe of my tongue from her entrance up to her clit, I got my first real taste. My cock screamed for attention as I feasted on her, and her initial gasp at the first touch of my tongue gave way to lustful cries.

It wasn't until that moment that I realised how fucking terrified I was. This was her very first sexual experience. No man had done to her what I was doing to her, or what I was *going* to do to her. This was more than sex. I didn't want to ruin this for Ryan, because I knew it would be something she'd always remember.

Ignoring my own need, I put my whole being into pleasuring her. I explored her with my tongue, and sucked on her clit and folds until her thighs quivered. I paid close attention to her when her body jerked or a cry left her parted lips, and when I learned what she liked the most, I focused on that.

"Ash-Ashley," she panted. "Fuck. Don't stop."

She had no idea how much I didn't want to stop, and she had no idea how much I loved hearing my name coming from her mouth in a breathless moan.

It didn't take very long for Ryan to reach the edge of bliss. Once I applied direct pressure to her clit, and swirled my tongue around and around it before I sucked it between my lips, she was done for. I shook my head from side to side, and with one final scream, she arched her back and became deathly silent. I felt the second she fell apart. Her clit pulsed under my tongue as her orgasm surged through her. When she came back down to Earth, I placed a chaste kiss on each of her thighs, then one on her clit before I moved up her body until I was hovering over her. Her eyes were closed, and she looked to be in such a state of satisfaction that I envied her.

I reached into my back pocket and thanked God when I felt the foil packet of a condom. I put the packet between my teeth and ripped it open, undid my jeans, and pushed them down to my knees. I rolled the condom onto my cock, then I kneeled between Ryan's legs.

"Are ye' still sure?" I asked her, leaning down so I could run my tongue over her lower lip. "It's okay if ye' aren't."

Please say yes.

She opened her emerald-green eyes, looked deep into mine and whispered, "I'm sure, Ashley."

I reached down, gripped my cock and stroked it once before I lined the head up with Ryan's entrance. I looked back up at her face and said, "Relax."

"I am *so* relaxed," she hummed. "I've never felt this good."

My chest swelled, knowing I'd put that drunken look of bliss on her face. I sucked my lower lip into my mouth, and bit down on it as I placed my elbows on either side of her head and slowly pushed my hips forward.

"Christ," I rasped as I pushed inch by inch into her.

Ryan's breathing was steady, and she didn't look uncomfortable, so I kept moving painstakingly slowly to keep it that way. When I was about halfway in, the muscles of her pussy contracted around me, squeezing me like a vice. I felt myself go cross-eyed as pleasure shot through me.

"Ryan," I whispered. "Christ."

Her eyes were now closed, and I realised why when pushing in slowly gained no results.

"If ye' want me to stop," I said, trembling. "Tell me and I will."

"No," she cried out, her eyes opening. "No, don't stop."

I didn't need any more encouragement. I pulled my hips back, then pushed forward with more force, and just like that I was buried in her to the hilt. She sucked in a sharp breath, so I stilled over her, and waited even though every muscle in my body screamed at me not to. It took only a few seconds for her eyes to find mine and for her to say, "It was just a pinch."

"You're okay? Ye' swear?"

She didn't answer, she simply ordered: "Move."

I slowly pulled out, and gently thrust back in.

"Yes," she hummed as her hands went to my shoulders. "Keep goin'."

I moved just like that, slow and steady, until I couldn't stand it anymore. My hips involuntarily bucked forward, sending my cock deep within Ryan's pussy. She didn't complain, she didn't ask me to stop, instead she moaned loudly, which was a green light for me to get moving again. I hissed when she slid her hands down my body and gripped my bare arse, digging her fingers into my flesh and roughly pulling my hips forward. A groan started in the back of my throat as I picked up my pace and did my best to think of everything other than how good my cock felt as I pounded into her.

With each thrust, the urge to come became greater and greater. Nothing was stopping me from fucking her as hard as I wanted to, so I took advantage of that and went balls deep each time. My heart was slamming in my chest, and I felt sweat bead on my forehead as heat consumed my body. I focused on Ryan's face, and the expression of pleasure she wore caused an emotion to run through my chest.

I'm doing that, I'm making her feel that good.

I was normally never mentally present with a woman during sex – I only focused on my own pleasure – but it wasn't like that with Ryan. I cared how about how she felt, and my own pleasure came second to hers. I wanted to experience every second of it with her.

"Ryan," I said, groaning her name. "Baby."

"Please," she panted. "Don't stop."

"Never."

My breath came out in rough gasps, and my heart beat uncontrollably as pressure began to build in my lower stomach. Sharp tingles spread out from my balls, adding to the building pressure and increasing the bliss I felt. I hissed as bolts of what felt like electricity shot up and down my legs. Without warning, my balls drew up tight, and the contractions started and my hips began to jerk.

"*Yes*," I moaned as the pressure drained and released itself. "Fu-*uck*!"

My hips moved of their own accord, pushing my cock deep into Ryan to milk the remaining pressure. I almost collapsed on top of her when all my energy fled, but I managed to hold myself up long enough to see her lazily smile up at me. I leaned down and kissed her. Hard.

"That," I panted against her lips, "was like nothin' else I've ever experienced."

Ryan hummed. "Because I was a virgin?"

"No," I answered, placing my forehead against hers. "Because it was with you."

CHAPTER TWENTY
RYAN

It was New Year's Eve, and also my nineteenth birthday.

Since Ash and I had bared ourselves to one another on Christmas Eve, we hadn't spent a day apart. When I went back to work after Christmas, he'd be outside after my late shifts, waiting to walk me home. We usually went to his house and hung out, doing nothing but talking, laughing, eating, watching telly, and when the moment was right, sex too.

He was a great distraction from the anticipation of seeing my da on the next visiting day. Ciara and I had spoken on the phone frequently since her visit. Being in contact with her was the only thing keeping me from losing my mind where my da was concerned.

I focused almost all my energy on Ash. Every moment I had free, I spent with him. I spent a lot of time with Sean and Anto too. Especially Anto, because he and Ash seemed to be joined at the hip. Ash had joked that he was worried Anto's over-the-top antics would drive me away, but I assured him that Anto in all his craziness was pretty perfect. Anto and Ash's bond was almost brotherly, and it was obvious that they loved one another, even if it seemed like they wanted to kill each other half of the time.

I loved their friendship . . . but there was someone who didn't.

"Why does Ash's best friend *have* to be Anto?" Eddi asked me, linking her arm through mine as we walked to Ash's house. "He drives me mad."

It had taken me all day to convince her to ring in the new year with me at Ash's place since Andrea had been asked out on a special date by Eddi's father. She'd refused at first because she knew that Anto would most likely be there. A few weeks ago, she would have been reluctant because of Ash, but she'd since seemed to accept that he was part of my life now. She saw how happy I was with him, and that none of the bad stuff she'd predicted had come to pass. I didn't want to push my luck, but she wasn't tense or on edge anymore around Ash . . . I wondered if maybe she was starting to think of him as a friend.

"What's your problem with 'im?" I probed her. "Why d'ye hate 'im? He's lovely, Eddi."

She brought us to a stop.

"I don't hate 'im," she said clearly. "I'm just annoyed by 'im."

"Because he's always happy?"

"No," she said with a huff. "Because he always says somethin' stupid that embarrasses me."

"Like what?" I asked, moving from foot to foot to keep warm. "Give me an example."

"Easy," she said. "In the chipper, back when ye' agreed to go on a date with Ash. He called me beautiful."

I stared at my cousin in disbelief.

"How can ye' be mad over someone callin' ye' beautiful?"

"Because he *only* said it to embarrass me."

"And ye' know that how?"

"Because I just do, okay?"

"That's very judgemental of ye', Ed."

My cousin's lips parted, but before she could speak, I held my hand up. I had wanted to get this off my chest for the last few days.

"Just hear me out," I pleaded. "Ever since ye've been hangin' around Ash with me, you're constantly on guard with Anto. He's done nothin' but be nice to ye', Eddi. He compliments ye', and yeah, even though he takes the piss out of ye', he still gives ye' so much attention. Did ye' ever stop and ask yourself why? It's not to tease and embarrass ye' like *you* think."

She huffed. "They *why* does he give me so much attention?"

"I think it's because he likes ye'. Before ye' deny that, and make out like he's the worst person ever, think of one time where he's truly done somethin' awful to warrant your attitude towards 'im. Give me one example, and I'll kept me mouth shut."

Eddi glared at me for a moment, then her shoulders sagged and her gaze lowered.

"I can't think of one."

"Exactly." I smiled, nudging her elbow. "When he compliments ye', say thank you. Ye' *are* beautiful, and fair play to 'im for seein' that beauty and sayin' it like it is."

Eddi's cheeks burned. "D'ye really think he likes me?"

I tilted my head. "Would ye' like 'im too?"

She looked thoughtful for a moment, but that look was only fleeting.

"He's a Disciple, Ryan."

"So is Ash, and he makes me happy."

She thought about that as we began to walk again.

"By the way, since when are *you* Anto's fan-club president?"

"Since I've been spendin' time with 'im and gettin' to know 'im," I countered with a grin. "He's brilliant. He'd make even the most miserable person smile . . . which is why I brought *you* 'ere tonight so he could loosen ye' up."

Eddi playfully smacked at me, which made me laugh as I jumped onto Ash's porch and rang the doorbell. The door opened seconds later, revealing Sean.

"Ry," he said, beaming, when he saw me.

He stepped out into the cold, put his arms around my waist and lifted me into the air, making me howl with laughter.

"Happy birthday!"

When he put me down, I pulled him in for a hug and squeezed him tight. It was insane to me that I suddenly had so many new people in my life who I cared for. I never thought I'd have anything like what I had right now, and I loved it.

"Thank you, Sean."

He moved aside and gestured us inside. He went into the sitting room as I took off my coat and hung up it and my bag on the coat rack. I entered the room to laughter. As per usual, Ash and Sean were on the settee doubled up over something Anto most likely said. I didn't announce myself, I simply dropped onto Ash's lap, making him wince before he snaked his arms around me and pressed a kiss to my neck.

"Did ye' miss me?"

His lips curved upwards. "Of course, dear."

Anto shook his head, but his eyes showed the amusement he felt. "And so it begins. Ye' may as well take me lad's bollocks now, they're useless."

Before I could stop myself, I said, "I wouldn't say *useless*."

I widened my eyes and clapped my hand over my mouth. Anto glanced to Ash, then on cue, the entire room erupted with laughter. I laughed too, but it was more out of embarrassment. Saying something crude, even in the form of a joke, was not something I'd usually do, but this was yet another part of me that had come out since the move to Dublin. It was freeing, fun and made me feel so . . . normal.

Ash poked a finger into my side, making me jump as I leaned back against him. I looked for my cousin, but there was no sign of her. I called out, "Eddi?"

"I'm hangin' me coat up," she answered.

Yeah, right. Stalling, more like.

When she entered the room, she sat on the settee opposite us. Sean, like Anto, stared at her, and I wondered why he was suddenly so interested in my cousin. Eddi glanced at Sean, then to me, then back to Sean.

"Hi, Sean."

"Hi," he replied, leaning in closer to her. "Have ye' *always* been this pretty?"

Ash almost choked, and Anto cracked up with laughter. My poor cousin's face turned red as a tomato. She opened her lips to speak, but seemed to decide against it. She was embarrassed, and when she looked at Anto, who was still laughing like a hyena, she seemed to think he was laughing at her and got annoyed.

"Did ye' tell 'im to say that?" she practically growled at him. "*Well?*"

Anto wiped his eyes. "No, but I'm bettin' he picked it up from me somewhere along the way."

Eddi folded her arms, pushing her already big boobs further up her chest. Sean's gaze was attached to them, and I didn't know what had got into him. He was suddenly acting like he'd just noticed boobs, and women, in general.

"Where's your *girlfriend*?" I asked, gaining his attention.

He glowered at me. "We broke up."

"On New Year's Eve?" I frowned. "Why?"

"I kissed 'er friend . . . by mistake."

My mouth dropped open. "Get out."

"Literally?" he asked, making his older brother chuckle.

"No, not literally." I shook my head. "Why did ye' kiss 'er friend?"

"Kerry and Sammy look a *lot* alike from behind," he said, throwing his hands up in the air. "I walked up behind who I *thought* was Kerry, then rounded on 'er and kissed 'er. She kissed me back. I had me eyes shut, so I was none the wiser until I felt a whack across the back of me head and heard Kerry cursin' me to hell and back."

I winced.

"It was a misunderstandin'," he stated with a huff. "I'll get 'er back."

"The man knows what he wants," Anto announced. "Good job, bud."

We all chuckled, except Eddi.

"Red," Anto called her when he noticed her silence. "Hello? Red?"

He'd taken to calling her "Red" as a nickname, and at first she'd refused to answer to it, but now whenever he called her it, she answered without a fuss. Eddi looked at Anto and raised an eyebrow in question.

"It won't kill ye' to smile," he teased. "I promise."

She tensed. "I'm fine. I just wasn't payin' attention."

Ash moved his mouth to my ear. "I wonder where she gets *that* from."

I chuckled, and nestled back into him. "It's in our genes to zone out now and then, we can't help it."

"Red," Anto said again.

Eddi looked him. "Yeah?"

"Are ye' gonna be me New Year's kiss?"

She flushed once more. "No."

I kicked at Anto and said, "Leave 'er alone."

He held up his hands in surrender, then jerked his head as he locked eyes with Ash.

"Come help me get the drink out of the fridge."

I slid off Ash's lap, and settled on the settee as both he and Anto left the room. I focused on my cousin, who was glaring at me.

"D'ye *see* what he's doin'?" she hissed. "Why does he keep teasin' me? I didn't even do anythin' to 'im."

"Eddi, he asked ye' to be his New Year's kiss. I don't think he was teasin' ye'."

"I can't tell when he's jokin' or when he's serious." She frowned. "He's always bloody smilin', so it makes it *hard*."

I chuckled and got to my feet. "I'll go ask 'im what his problem is, since it means that much to ye'."

I left Sean and Eddi alone, and walked into the kitchen. Anto and Ash had their backs to me as they got bottles of beer from the fridge.

"D'ye think that stalker will try anythin' tonight?" Anto asked Ash. "New Year's is as good a night as any to make a statement."

I froze at Anto's words.

Stalker? Ash has a stalker?

"I hope not," Ash sighed. "I don't want anythin' to mess the night up."

I shifted my stance. "What are ye' talkin' about?"

Both of them jumped about a foot in the air as they spun to face me.

"Holy Mary mother of God!" Anto snapped, and placed his hand on his chest. "I nearly *died*, Ryan!"

I ignored Anto and focused on Ash, whose eyes were locked on mine.

"Ashley, what were ye' both talkin' about?"

"Oh, shit." Anto froze, glancing at his friend. "She used your full name."

"I heard 'er," Ash growled. "I'm standin' right here."

I looked at Anto. "You. Go into the sittin' room, and *please* stop tormentin' Eddi. You're upsettin' 'er."

"Upsettin' 'er?" Anto widened his eyes. "I only ever joke with 'er, for God's sake."

"She thinks when you're callin' her beautiful and so on that you're really just slaggin' her."

"What?" he gaped. "I'd never slag 'er for real, I think she's the bomb diggity."

I managed a smile. "Ye' do?"

"Uh, yeah. She's stunnin'."

I placed my hands on my hips. "Are ye' tellin' me ye' *like* 'er?"

I had a feeling he did, but I wanted to hear him admit it out loud.

Anto looked at Ash. "Didn't I just say that?"

"Not in English ye' didn't."

Anto scoffed and looked back at me. "Yes, I like 'er."

"She won't have sex with ye'," I said firmly. "She's not like—"

"I know she's not like the women I'm used to, and trust me, I've known it for years."

Years.

He spoke no further. Instead, he walked out of the room, two beers in hand. I stared after him for a moment, before I turned back to Ash.

"I'm so confused."

"He's into Eddi, like I'm into you."

"I *knew* it," I said. "I bloody knew it."

"He's liked 'er for years, she just never gave 'im the time of day because he's a Disciple, so he never pressed the issue with 'er."

"I understand. Eddi's clueless though."

"Anto's good at coverin' up things he doesn't want other people to notice."

I folded my arms across my chest. "Like the stalker he mentioned."

Ash remained mute.

"Ashley," I pressed. "You're scarin' me. What's goin' on?"

He put down the beers in his hands, closed the fridge door, then said, "I didn't want to upset ye'."

Too late.

"Well, I'm upset now."

He blew out a breath. "I can see that."

"What did Anto mean when he said 'stalker'?"

Ash cleared his throat. "These past few weeks, someone has been troublin' me."

"How so?"

"Before I met ye', whoever he is, he broke into the house and ransacked the sittin' room. He's left sick messages, and he's had me a bit on edge."

"What were the messages?"

Ash's hands flexed. "Threats to hurt me brother."

I placed my hand over my mouth.

"Why?" I asked, dropping my hand back to my side. "Why would someone do that?"

"I have no idea." He looked lost in that moment, and I had an overwhelming urge to protect him. "In one of the messages, he said I took someone he loves, so he's takin' someone I love."

"Ashley!" I said, panicked.

"No, no," he said, crossing the room. "Please, just relax. Panickin' won't help the situation."

"Why didn't ye' tell me?" I gripped his arms and shook him. "When we talked on Christmas Eve, why didn't ye' tell me? We shared so much of ourselves, so why didn't somethin' as serious as this make the cut for that conversation?"

"Ye' were so happy about the prospect of good news about your da." Ash frowned, his hands covering mine. "I didn't want to worry ye'."

I felt myself tremble. "Ye' should have told me, Ash."

"I'm sorry, Ryan."

I released him, then placed my hands on my hips. "Can we go to the guards?"

"Nooooo," he said and even laughed, as if my suggesting that was somehow funny. "Disciples don't work well with the guards."

"Then how the hell are we goin' to know who's tryin' to hurt your brother?"

Ash moved his hands to my shoulders "I don't know. I've reached out to everyone who could possibly help me, and I've heard nothin' back. It's like this son of a bitch is a ghost."

Knowing someone was threatening people I cared about made me feel sick.

"Ye' can too call the guards," I stressed. "Ye' can't just sit 'ere unprotected waitin' for some arsehole with a chip on his shoulder to show up and hurt you or Sean."

"Ye' don't understand," he said, annoyance contorting his features as he dropped his hands from my shoulders. "The guards won't take me seriously until somethin' happens."

I turned away from him, angry that the world he lived in as a Disciple limited him so much.

"Please," he said as he pressed his front against my back and brought his hands to my waist. "I'm sorry for keepin' this from ye', but ye' have to understand, I thought I was doin' what was best."

I tried to see it from his point of view. He was a Disciple, a known criminal to the law. He couldn't ask the law for help; it was part of some unspoken code. It was hard to accept that, but I understood it.

"Try to put this out of your mind," he pleaded as he turned me to face him. "It's almost twelve, let's not start the New Year worryin' or arguin'."

"How can ye' ask me that, Ashley?" I demanded softly. "This is serious, this is *dangerous*."

"I know, baby, but I'm doin' everythin' I can to handle it," he stressed. "This arsehole has been on me case for weeks . . . I just want tonight with you, and our families. I want to start a new year with only *you* on me mind, Ryan."

My knees felt weak at his words, and with a nod, I agreed to not speak anymore . . . for the rest of the night at least.

"Quick!" Sean shouted from the sitting room. "The countdown is startin'!"

I squeezed Ash's hand when he grabbed hold of mine. He led me out of the kitchen and into the front garden, where Anto, Eddi and Sean stood. I glanced around and saw many other neighbours were in their gardens as well.

"Ten," Sean shouted, his chant echoed by the neighbours. "Nine, eight, seven, six, five, four, three, two, one . . . HAPPY NEW YEAR!"

I turned in time to see Anto snake his arm around Eddi's waist before he pulled her against him and kissed her something fierce. What was even more surprising was that she willingly *returned* his kiss. Her hands went to his shoulders, then her fingers tangled themselves in Anto's hair. He kissed her as if to prove that his interest in her didn't come close to him joking around. All the ill will towards him she'd previously harboured must have disappeared, because in that moment there was only the two of them.

I stared at them in disbelief.

"What the fuck?" I laughed and looked up at Ash, who leaned down and captured my lips in a kiss as fireworks and cheers sounded around us. I wrapped my arms around him, and he slid his around me. I kissed him, and felt an emotion wrap around us both so tightly it brought tears to my eyes.

"Happy New Year," I hummed against his lips.

He rubbed the tip of his nose against mine. "Happy New Year, nightmare."

I smiled, then looked at Sean when he appeared beside us. Before he could ask Ash whatever he was going to ask him, I reached over, pulled him against me and gave him a kiss on the lips, before I hugged him like a boa constrictor.

"Happy New Year, Sean!"

He returned my hug and said, "Best New Year's *ever*."

I laughed when we separated because Ash playfully swung for his brother, but he was smiling, and when he looked at me I felt as if he was thanking me for not leaving his brother out of a special celebration.

"Can I have *one* bottle of Bud, Ash?" Sean asked his brother. "Please."

Ash looked down at me, and I shrugged. "I've no idea why you're lookin' at me, I'm not that much older than 'im. I'm only legal a year, remember."

"I remember," he murmured before he lowered his head back to mine. "Did I wish ye' a happy birthday yet?"

"Me birthday is technically over by about a minute."

Ash smiled. "I guess I'll just have to make it up to ye' on your next birthday."

"D'ye plan on bein' around for it?"

His grey eyes held a promise as he said, "Definitely."

"Uh, Ash, can I have a bottle or not?"

Ash straightened up, rolled his eyes, and to his brother he said, "Okay, but *only* one."

Sean whooped and ran into the house. Ash hugged my body to his, and we looked up as more fireworks went off and lit up the sky in an array of colours. The chill of the night sent a shiver up my spine, and as I leaned against Ash, I knew what contentment felt like – until a scream from the house made my blood run cold.

"Ashley!" Sean cried. "Help!"

"Yeah, Ashley . . . Help," a strange voice said, mimicking Sean's cry.

Anto and Ash sprinted into the house. Eddi and I automatically ran after them, and came to a stop when Ash and Anto thrust us behind their bodies. I gripped Ash's waist and peeked around him, only to freeze when I realised the barrel of a gun was pointed at us.

CHAPTER TWENTY-ONE
ASHLEY

I stared at the kid in my kitchen. He couldn't have been older than seventeen. But it was stupid of me to focus on his age rather than the gun he had pointed at me, so I quickly snapped out of it. First, I made sure Ryan was safe. Reaching behind my back, I gripped her arm, holding her still. Her fingers dug into my sides as she held on to me.

The kid had his arm hooked around Sean's neck, and my brother was paralysed with fear as tears ran down his cheeks.

"You'll be okay, Sean," I promised. "Everythin' will be okay."

"It's not really goin' to be okay, Ash, is it?"

My gaze hardened as I turned it on the prick who'd sneered those words. His haunted brown eyes danced from person to person like he couldn't get them to focus.

"Why?" I demanded. "Why are ye' doin' this to me and me family?"

"Oh, I don't know," he hissed sarcastically, the muscles in his face twitching. "Maybe because *your* family has ruined me entire fuckin' life!" I wondered if he was on drugs, because he was acting like a lunatic. "Don't fuckin' look like ye' don't know what I'm talkin' about!"

"Tell me," I demanded. "Tell me what I've done."

"Ye' fuckin' *know*," he snapped. "He took everythin' from me!"

"I don't even know who ye' are."

"Ye' don't know who *I* am?" he laughed. "That's fuckin' *funny*! Ye' *should* know me."

I resisted the urge to place my hands on either side of my head and scream. This little bastard was making absolutely no sense.

"Arthur Hopkins is my da."

I furrowed my brows, not recognising the name. I looked at Anto, wondering if it clicked for him, but he didn't look at me, he only stared at the kid.

"Oh my God," Ryan whispered from behind me. "Oh my fuckin' God."

I didn't turn to her or draw attention to her in any way. I squeezed her tightly, hoping she understood that I wanted her to be quiet. This kid holding Sean was bad enough; I didn't want him focusing on Ryan too.

"And what's *your* name?" I asked the kid. "Can ye' tell me that?"

"Max," he answered. "Max Hopkins."

"Max?" I repeated. "Okay, Max. Listen to me. I don't know who your da is."

"No, but *he* does."

He didn't look at anyone when he spoke, so I had no idea who he was talking to.

"*Who?*" I demanded. "Who the fuck are ye' talkin' about?"

"Your father!" Max screamed as he brought the gun to my brother's temple. "Your fuckin' piece-of-shite *father*!"

Fear made me take a step forward.

"We don't kn-know our da," Sean sobbed. "He left wh-when we we-were kids."

"No," Max shook his head. "I've seen 'im around this house."

What the fuck?

"No ye' haven't."

"Don't fuckin' lie to me!" Max roared. "I've seen 'im in 'ere!"

"Just calm down, okay?" I relented, raising my hands. "We're just talkin'."

Max bobbed his head up and down fast.

"Just talkin'," he agreed. "Until the killin'. I'm takin' one back. A life for a life. A life for a life. A life for a life."

One of the girls released a muffled cry.

"Why don't ye' tell me what all this is about, okay?" I suggested. "We can figure this out together once we know what the problem is."

"The problem?" Max repeated manically. "I don't have a problem; *d'you* have a problem?"

This little cunt was something else.

"Max," I said firmly. "Can ye' let me brother go? And we can talk one on one, just you and me." Ryan's grip on me tightened. "What d'ye say?"

"No!" Max bellowed. "No! NO! NOOOOOOO!"

Sean cried out in fear as Max pressed the barrel of the gun harder against his temple. My stomach was rolling, and terror raced through me like a drug.

"Ye' look just like 'im! Just like 'im, *just like 'im.*"

I tensed when he hurled the words my way.

"I look like who?"

"Your da!"

"I can't help if I resemble the man, Max," I explained calmly. "But since ye' see how much I look like 'im, can't ye' see that *I* was the person who ye' mistook for me da?"

The only feature I got from my mother was her grey eyes – everything else I'd inherited from my father. My ma had always said I looked like his double, and it seemed this had confused Max.

"Shut up!" Max shouted as he shook his head from side to side. "Just shut *up*!"

"Okay," I acquiesced. "Okay."

Max blinked his eyes about twenty times as he stared at me, then flicked down to my right.

"You're tied up in this too, pretty girl," Max said to Ryan, and she gasped from behind me as he bounced on his feet. "Aren't ye'? I figured it allllll out. I saw your picture in the paper when your da was in court for sentencin'. Didn't know where ye' lived though, then *bammmm* . . . ye' showed up 'ere. It was fate. Fate. Fate. Fate. Fate."

Max laughed then, and from the sound, and what I'd seen of his behaviour, there was no doubt in my mind that he was crazy.

"She has nothin' to do with it," I said roughly. "Leave 'er alone."

"Of course she does. 'Er da too. Yep. Yep. Yep. The circle is complete, I know it."

Ryan's da too?

"I don't understand any of this," I said.

"I do," Ryan whispered. "I understand it."

"Come 'ere," Max said to Ryan excitedly. "Come 'ere and explain it alllll, pretty girl."

I stood firm. "No."

Max hissed, "Give 'er to me, or he's dead. *Dead*."

"I'll come," Ryan shouted. "I'll come. Just leave Sean *alone*."

She slapped at my hand until I released my hold on her. She quickly moved forward and out of my reach, and stopped a metre away from Max, who began to laugh. He looked elated, while I felt sick.

"I *knew* ye'd know me da's name. I knewwww it."

Why would she know Max's da?

Ryan was shaking. "I do, and I'm so sorry about your—"

"Don't!" Max shouted, cutting Ryan off. "Don't say sorry when you're not. Your da tried to cover it up, didn't he? And I bet *you* knew about it. Ash too. Did ye' plan it? Did ye' *laugh* thinkin' me da wouldn't get justice?"

"No," Ryan whimpered. "Your da *did* get justice. The man who killed him is in prison, remember?"

"Not good enough!" Max screamed, his voice cracking with the strain. "He should suffer like me da did."

Ryan reached out and gripped the countertop as her body shook.

"Ye' have it all wrong, Max. Me da was forced into hidin' evidence. He wouldn't have done it otherwise. I swear. He's a good man, Max. He is."

"Good man?" Max repeated, then cackled. "Your da did a *bad* thing to help the man who killed me da. He *helped* 'im."

I couldn't begin to try to figure out what was going on. Too much was happening for me to focus. I kept looking at the gun pressed to my brother's head, and had to force myself to remain still.

"What's he talkin' about?" I demanded of Ryan. "Babe, what's goin' on?"

"'Member I told you me da concealed evidence in a homicide case?"

At my nod she said, "The man who was killed was Arthur Hopkins."

I looked at Max. "How does that relate to me?"

"Your da," Max growled, and I noted even his voice sounded different. "Your *poxy* da killed mine. John McCarty killed him."

My mouth dropped open. "What?"

"Your da killed mine," Max repeated. "Killed, killed, *killed* him."

I felt every word he spoke as if it were a kick in the teeth. I hadn't seen my father since he walked out on my family all those years ago, but to hear the man who'd fathered me had killed another person made me sick to my stomach. I had no idea if this kid was telling the truth, but I couldn't say that he was lying either.

"I don't know what ye' want me to say." I swallowed. "I didn't know. I haven't seen John since I was twelve. We don't even use his surname, we use our ma's and have done since we were little. I'm Ashley Dunne, not Ashley McCarty."

"I don't believe ye'," Max snapped. "Lies. All lies."

I held up my hands. "I have no reason to lie to ye'."

"It was all over the papers and the news when it happened!"

"I don't watch the news, or read the papers. I don't let me brother, either."

I looked at Anto when he said my name, and when I found him looking at me with worried eyes, I tensed.

"What?"

Anto swallowed. "I knew your da went to prison," he began. "We all knew within the set, but none of us told ye' because we knew ye' wanted nothin' to do with 'im."

My lips parted with shock. "Anto."

"I'm sorry, man," he said. "I was tryin' to shield ye' from 'im 'cause I know ye' hate 'im. I knew it'd kill ye' to know he murdered someone."

"Shut up!" Max snapped, regaining our attention. "I don't fuckin' care. Ye' look exactly like your da, and I can't get to 'im so you're the next best thing."

I blanched. "You're goin' to kill me because of somethin' me estranged da did?"

"No," Max said, smiling sinisterly. "I'm goin' to kill someone ye' *love* because of what your da did."

My eyes flew to my brother, and my heart nearly burst with terror.

I froze. "Please, don't hurt 'im."

Max looked at my brother as if he'd forgotten he was there.

"I'm not *completely* heartless," he snickered. "I'm not about to kill a kid. A little wittle kid."

Didn't he realise that he was a kid too? He couldn't have been much older than Sean.

"Ye' said ye'd take someone I love," I said, panicking. "Ye' wrote that in your note, remember?"

"You're right." He grinned sadistically. "But not your brother. Oh no, oh no."

Ryan moved towards me and I instantly grabbed hold of her. I felt a huge sense of relief when Max pushed Sean forward, and both Anto and I grabbed hold of him and forced him behind our bodies along with the girls. We made a wall as we stood shoulder to shoulder.

"Then who?" I demanded. "Who do I love that ye' want to take from me?"

"*Him.*"

Max trained the gun to my right, and without hesitation he pulled the trigger.

A bang echoed throughout the room. The second Max lowered the gun, I shot forward and knocked it out of his hand. I punched him so hard, the stream of piss fell to the floor, unconscious.

"No!" Ryan screamed. "Oh, Jesus. *No!*"

I spun around, and saw the girls and Sean leaning over . . . Anto.

"Fuck! No!" I shouted. "Someone call an ambulance!"

"I will!" Ryan screeched as she ran from the room. "Oh, please God."

"Anto?" I shouted as I dropped to my knees next to him, smacking the sides of his face. "Look at me, mate."

"Ambulance!" Ryan cried from the hallway. "Ambulance. Me friend has been shot! Send help, please."

I ripped Anto's jumper and T-shirt, which revealed the wound, blood spilling from it. I applied heavy pressure and he groaned in pain. I wanted him to keep making noise so I knew he was still alive. I didn't want him to go silent.

"He's goin' to be okay," Sean said from somewhere in the room. "Isn't he, Ashley?"

"Definitely, bud."

Anto groaned, and focused his eyes on me.

"This is goin' to fuck up me week big time, mate."

Anto was laughing as he spoke, but blood somehow continued to spill from his shoulder, all over the floor under him, despite me pressing on the wound as hard as I could.

"Was he shot twice?" I asked Eddi, unsure if I'd heard one bang or two.

"Once," she stated.

She moved next to me and pushed Anto until he was slightly on his side, then shouted, "Fuck!"

She pulled off her jumper and held it firmly against a bloody spot on the back of Anto's shoulder. "There's an exit wound," she said through her tears. "We have to keep pressure on both of them."

Jesus Christ!

Anto moaned when Eddi touched him.

"I'm so sorry," she whimpered. "I have to keep pressure on it so it stops bleedin'."

He thrashed about, and I had to release his shoulder and hold him down so Eddi could keep pressure on his wound. There was blood everywhere, and I knew he couldn't afford to lose any more.

"Ambulance is two minutes away, the woman said!" Ryan announced.

My heart was pumping a mile a minute as adrenaline rushed through my veins. This was my fault. Anto was dying because of me. I wanted to scream, cry, punch something, but I couldn't move. I couldn't leave my friend when he needed me the most.

"I can't believe he shot me," Anto suddenly said. "The skinny little bastard actually shot me."

He was looking really, really pale.

"I love ye'," I told him, my voice cracking. "You're me best friend, me brother, and ye' make me shitty life better by bein' there. D'ye hear me, mate? I love ye'."

Anto tried to focus on me, but when he couldn't, he just chuckled. His eyes kept opening and closing, and his head rolled from side to side. "Am I goin' to die?" he asked, his body involuntarily shaking.

"No!" was my automatic answer. "No, you're not. You're gonna be okay."

"Then why are you tellin' me ye' love me?"

His voice had started to sound like it did when he was stoned out of his face.

"Because I *do* love ye'," I swore to him. "I just wanted ye' to know."

He smiled again, as tears spilled from his eyes and down his temples.

"I love ye' too, Ash . . . just not as much as I love Ryan."

When he wiggled his eyebrows, I laughed at the same time as tears rolled down my cheeks.

"She wouldn't have ye'," I choked. "I'm a much better choice."

"Nah," he groaned. "She just hasn't . . . come to 'er senses yet." He was fighting the sleep that wanted to take him. "I'm sorry I didn't tell ye' about what your da did."

I shook my head. "It doesn't matter. Ye' were right, I wouldn't have wanted to know that. Ye' did the right thing, mate."

He smiled, and it looked like staying awake was becoming harder for him. Eddi had broken down completely and was sobbing.

"I'm so sorry," she cried, leaning over Anto. "I take back every moment that I was ever mean to ye', Anto! Every single one of them."

Anto winced as he lifted up a hand and rubbed his index finger over Eddi's cheek. "You're so pretty."

Eddi was shaking.

"Ye' can't die, Anthony," she told him, leaning down and pressing her lips to his. "We have to see if we can be together like Ash and Ryan, okay? Isn't that what ye' told me before ye' kissed me when the fireworks went off?"

"Definitely," Anto hummed, licking his lips. "I knew ye' liked me, Red."

Eddi frantically bobbed her head up and down. "I do like ye', so stay awake, okay?"

Anto began to fade.

"Anto?" Eddi cried, using one hand to slap him across the face before pressing it back on his shoulder. "Anto?"

Ryan suddenly screamed, "I hear the ambulance. I hear it!"

I looked over my shoulder as she ran out of the house and out the garden. Sean was hot on her heels, waving his arms and screaming to get the ambulance's attention.

"Here!" I heard them yell. "Over *here*!"

Blue flashing lights filled the garden, and for once in my life I was glad to hear sirens blaring. I turned back to Anto, who was still awake but barely, and said, "The ambulance is 'ere, you're goin' to be okay. D'ye hear me, Anthony?"

Even as I spoke the words, I knew I didn't believe them.

Once the paramedics took over, neither myself nor Eddi and Ryan moved away as they began to work on my friend. They were talking to him and asking him all kinds of questions. They put an oxygen mask on him, and like Eddi, one of the paramedics put pressure on Anto's gunshot wound while two others lifted him onto a stretcher and covered him with blankets.

I jumped when I felt a hand on my shoulder. I turned and came face to face with a guard.

"What happened?" the man asked.

I turned and looked down at Max, who was still unconscious.

"*Him.*" I pointed at the kid. "He shot me friend. He's been stalkin' me for weeks and leavin' all kinds of threats."

Two guards checked on the kid, and when they confirmed he was okay, just out cold, I itched to get my hands on him. My best friend was dying because of him, and I wanted to make him pay for it. I froze when I realised the revenge I sought was exactly what had driven Max to do what he did. He wanted revenge for his father dying, and he didn't care who he hurt to get that.

I refused to be like him. I wouldn't let revenge consume me, I had too many people in my life that I cared about for that to happen.

"Tell me everythin'," the guard said. "And leave nothin' out."

I gave my statement while other guards took statements from the girls and my brother. Things were a blur of activity – guards flooded my house and people gathered outside, their curiosity getting the better of them.

I answered question after question, but I wanted one of my own answered . . .

Was Anto still alive?

CHAPTER TWENTY-TWO
ASHLEY

When we were finally allowed to leave the house, the four of us got into Eddi's car and drove to the hospital. The drive there was the longest of my life.

"I can't believe this is happenin'," Ryan said as she sat next to me in the back seat. "This doesn't feel real."

She was in shock . . . I think we all were.

I reached over and tugged her against me. She wasted no time in embracing me as she promptly burst into tears. I squeezed her tightly, realising how close I'd come to losing her tonight. Max could have chosen to shoot her instead of Anto at any time during our confrontation.

"Tell me he's gonna be okay," she cried against my shoulder. "Tell me."

I placed my hands on her face and said, "He *will* be okay."

I wasn't sure if she believed my words, because I didn't believe them. When we pulled up in front of the hospital, I jumped out and headed straight towards the reception desk in Accident and Emergency.

"I need help."

The woman behind the counter gasped when she saw me, so I looked down and remembered I was covered in Anto's blood.

"It's not mine," I blurted out. "It's me friend's, he was brought in about half an hour ago. He was shot. His name is Anthony Lynch."

The lady blinked, then tapped her computer keyboard and said, "Are ye' family?"

"No, but—"

"I'm sorry, sir, but only family are permitted to know a patient's information."

I smacked my hands on the desk, making the woman jump.

"He's like a brother to me," I growled. "I need to know if he's okay."

The woman swallowed and glanced at the screen. "Mr Anthony Lynch, who was brought in with a gunshot wound to the shoulder, is currently in surgery. There are no updates from theatre at this time. We have a waitin' room that family members will be sent to if and when they arrive. You're welcome to wait there if you wish."

Feeling defeated, I mumbled, "Thank you."

I walked down the hallway to the room she directed me to. I hadn't seen Ryan, Sean or Eddi yet, so I assumed they were still parking the car. I entered the room, and was surprised to see Mr Lynch, Anto's uncle. An uncle who wasn't very involved in his life. I had no idea how he even knew that Anto had been shot.

"Mr Lynch," I said.

He looked up from his phone, and widened his eyes when he saw me.

"Christ, Ash."

I looked down at my T-shirt and arms. "Sorry, I forgot to wash the blood off."

Mr Lynch walked over to the connecting bathroom and wet some paper towels, which he passed to me. I thanked him, and cleaned as much blood as I could off my hands and arms. There was nothing I could do about my T-shirt, so I didn't worry about it. I then fell into a seat a few spaces away, clasped my hands together and looked down at the floor.

"Ash?" Mr Lynch said.

I looked up at him. "Yeah?"

"I said are ye' okay?"

"What the fuck d'*you* think?" I snapped. "Me best friend was shot."

Mr Lynch didn't respond, he simply raised an eyebrow, and regret filled me.

"Sorry, sir," I said with a shake of my head. "I'm all over the place. Pay me no mind."

"It's okay, kid." He patted my shoulder as he took the seat next to me. "How are ye' holdin' up?"

"I honestly don't know," I admitted. "I just can't believe Anto's been shot, over me."

"It wasn't over *you*," he said. "I talked to the guards, and from the statements given, this kid wanted revenge for your da killin' his da."

That baffled me. I had no idea how he'd had time to find out Anto was shot, speak to the guards and get to the hospital.

"That changes nothin'. This kid wanted to hurt me by killin' someone I love because of who me da is. That makes this *my* fault. Anto could die because of me."

Mr Lynch said nothing in response.

"That's just fuckin' insane," I said, placing my head in my hands. "I haven't seen me da in years. I had no idea he killed someone."

"He's locked up in Portlaoise over it."

I looked up. "How d'ye know?"

He shrugged. "Followed the case on the news as it happened."

I could only nod in response.

"He'll be okay, that nephew of mine," he said. "Anto's tough."

"Tough or not, he took a bullet over somethin' that had nothin' to do with 'im. I don't even fully understand it all."

After a few moments, Anto's uncle said, "I did as promised. I kept me ear to the ground, but this Max kid didn't let on to anyone that he planned a hit on ye'. I couldn't give ye' information if none was available, kid. I'm sorry I couldn't help more. I'm even more sorry me nephew had to pay for it."

For moment, I had no idea what Mr Lynch was talking about. Then, recalling who I'd asked to get me that information, my blood ran cold. I looked up at Mr Lynch, and when I looked into blue eyes, instead of green, my brow furrowed in confusion.

"Mr Lynch?" I whispered, staring at Anto's uncle in shock. "You're . . . you're Mr Nobody?"

He nodded.

"Ye' can't be, I've met with—"

"The person ye' met with is paid very well to present himself as me when he has to meet people face to face. The risk on me life is very high, as ye' can imagine, so ye' understand the lengths I must go to keep me identity a secret?"

I couldn't form a coherent sentence so I nodded.

"Does Anto know?" I asked after a minute.

"No," he answered. "Only Bobby."

"Who's Bobby?"

"The man I pay to act as me durin' sit-downs."

I nodded. Again.

"It's just one thing after the other tonight," I said in disbelief. "I don't think I can take any more surprises right now."

Mr Lynch – or Nobody, whatever his fucking name was – chuckled. I wanted to snap at him, and ask how he could laugh when Anto was lying on an operating table after being shot. I didn't, though, I knew better than to run my mouth, so I kept it shut. This man . . . he was very powerful.

"Ye' look like you're thinkin' hard."

"I am," I admitted. "I definitely am."

I'd been fed up with being a Disciple since the moment I became one, but I'd never wished for another life as much as I did then in the hospital waiting room. Anto was probably dying; he could already be dead for all I knew. Sean had had a gun put to his head, Ryan came face to face with a maniac. I'd sold drugs nearly half of my life and probably had a hand in dozens of people dying through taking them. I'd battered a kid bloody and broken his ankle. I was a Disciple, and I was fucking miserable.

I didn't want to be miserable anymore.

I wanted out.

"Anything' ye' want to share?"

"Yeah," I said, taking a tentative breath. "I'm thinkin' that I don't want to be a Disciple anymore." When Mr Lynch didn't respond, I added, "Neither does Anto. We want out, sir."

Mr Lynch leaned back in his chair. "D'ye know how many people have wanted out of this life once they realised it wasn't all sex, money and drugs, Ash?"

"I can imagine." I swallowed. "I've been loyal to you and me fellow Disciples since I was thirteen. I've done everythin' asked of me. If I didn't have people I love, people I need to take care of, I probably wouldn't give a shite, but that's not the case. Me and Anto want out, and we'll do what we have to in order to make it happen. If ye'll give us the chance, sir."

Mr Lynch regarded me for a moment before he said, "For me nephew . . . okay."

I almost choked on air. "What?"

"I said okay," he repeated. "You're out, you're no longer a Disciple. Anto too. I'm allowin' this *because* of me nephew. I've had to keep out of his life because of the life I live, but if he doesn't want to live that same life, he doesn't have to."

My heart started pounding, and my palms were sticky with sweat.

"Thank you, sir," I said. "Thank you."

"If Anto wasn't in your set and so close to ye', I'd have your throat slit for even askin' me this, but I'm feelin' particularly kind today." His eyes darkened. "Don't mistake my act of kindness for weakness, Ash," he said as he watched me. "If you *ever* reveal who I am, Sean, Ryan, her cousin Eddi, even your mate Deco . . . ye'll never see them again. I promise ye'."

Fear filled me.

"I won't," I swore. "After I leave this room, I'll never think of ye' again."

That was a lie, but I would never reveal who he was. Not even to Anto. I'd take it to my grave.

"Ye' know what, kid?" His lips twitched. "I believe ye'."

I remained silent as my heart continued to pound.

"Ye'll have to leave the area," he said. "I don't care if ye' stay in Dublin, but ye' can't show your face around Tallaght again. Anyone who knows ye' were a Disciple will think I've gone soft if I let ye' roam around free. Everyone in your set will be told that you're bein' . . . relocated. Deco, Doyler, Beanie, even that pretty little thing Kara that ye've been keepin' an eye on. You're never to contact them again. D'ye understand me?"

"Not a problem," I said, swallowing. "I won't come back to Dublin."

"Anto too?"

"Anto too." I nodded. "We'll disappear."

He stood up.

"To Anto, I'm still only his uncle. He's not to know who I am. Ye' can make up a story of your own to tell him how ye' met Mr Nobody and struck a deal. We clear on that?"

"Crystal."

"Not a soul," he said. "I'll know if ye' do. I know everythin', remember that."

"I promise, sir," I swallowed. "It'll . . . it'll be my little secret."

"Good," he said, then turned and left the room, me staring after him in disbelief.

I could hardly believe it. Had that really happened? Mr Nobody was Mr Lynch?

"What the fuck," I said.

I didn't know whether to laugh or cry. I stared at the door, wondering if Mr Nobody would come back and laugh at me for thinking he was serious, but he never did. The only people who came into the room were Ryan, Sean and Eddi. Not long after, Eddi's ma showed up, and she comforted the girls and Sean as best she could. Ryan asked me multiple times if I was okay, and I simply nodded, not able to form words to speak.

My mind hadn't comprehended everything I'd been through tonight. It all felt too wild to be real, but it was real. This was my life . . . my life was finally my own again, and I couldn't fucking believe it.

I hoped and prayed to God that Anto would walk out of here healthy, because when we left this hospital . . . we would be free.

CHAPTER TWENTY-THREE
RYAN

"Let me do the talking, okay?"

I looked at Ciara. She hadn't stopped fidgeting and fixing herself since we entered the visitors' room. She had, however, reverted to pretty dresses and high heels, which made me smile. Looking sharp and put together was Ciara's trademark, but I knew how nervous she was to see my da today.

It was mind-blowing to think of everything that had happened just two days ago. I was nineteen now, and in the few weeks leading up to that I had changed and grown as a person, and learned how to be a friend, a cousin and a girlfriend. I wasn't the quiet, lost girl who'd moved to Dublin anymore. There was a hardness to me now. I'd had a gun pointed at me and I'd seen a person get shot, a person I cared about.

"I heard ye', Ciara."

She clicked her tongue. "Grouchy."

"Not grouchy," I answered. "Just emotionally scarred over recent events."

"Your friend getting shot would do that to you."

My jaw dropped open. "Ciara!"

She looked at me and widened her eyes.

"I'm sorry, that sounded better in my head. What I mean is, going through something as traumatising as that would leave anyone feeling the way you do, so it's no surprise. However, I'm so happy your friend is going to be okay, sweetheart."

And thank God for that. Anto was one of the luckiest people on planet Earth. If the bullet had hit him one millimetre to the right, it would have severed an artery, and he wouldn't have survived the trip to the hospital, let alone made it onto an operating table.

"Yeah, but he almost died." I frowned. "His heart *stopped* durin' his surgery, for God's sake."

"And I *am* glad that he's okay," she repeated. "The last thing the world needs is another senseless murder, especially when the person is as lovely as you say Anto is."

My lips curved upwards. "He'll get a kick out of talkin' to ye' since you're so proper."

She turned to me. "From the look in your eyes, I don't know if I'll enjoy that."

She probably wouldn't, but Anto sure as hell would.

I laughed. "I can't believe I thought ye' didn't have a sense of humour."

Ciara's jaw dropped. "I'll have you know that I'm hilarious when I want to be."

I snickered, then full-on laughed when Ciara looked offended. She placed her hands on her hips and shook her head as she smiled. Then she put her arms around me and hugged me tightly. She had hugged me five times since we met up for this visit with my da, and I liked it. It was like she was catching up on all the hugs we'd missed out on over the years during our ridiculous feud.

We separated just as we heard a commotion from outside the visiting room. Both of our gazes snapped to the right when the door to the room opened. My da's normal beaming smile was on his face, but when he saw Ciara, he lost it. He stared at her, and she stared right back. He didn't even notice that the guard had removed his cuffs and that he could move freely if he wanted to.

"Hi, Da," I said, gaining his attention.

His smile instantly returned, and we shared a long hug. When we separated, I stepped back and looked between both Ciara and him as they had some sort of showdown.

"You're back," he said, stating the obvious to her.

"Yes. No thanks to you."

My da blinked, looked at me, and when I shrugged, he looked at Ciara again.

"Excuse me?"

"You heard me, Joe."

"I did. But I don't understand what ye' mean."

"Well," she said, taking a seat. "Let me inform you."

My da slowly sat down, but he looked extremely wary as he did so.

"You'll have noticed my absence these last few months, I assume?"

Da jerked his head in a nod, and sadness crept into his eyes. I eyed him as he watched Ciara. It was obvious that he had missed her dearly, and my chest hurt wondering just how much his heart had ached during the time she wasn't around.

"Would you like to know why?"

"Yes, Ciara." He swallowed. "I would like to know why."

"I stopped coming to see you because seeing you in here killed me as much as it did Ryan. I couldn't bear it, and I couldn't bear that you wouldn't tell the damn truth about this case."

"Ciara," he began with a sigh, "we've been over this, I don't know what—"

"That's where *I'm* goin' to step in and shut ye' down, Da."

My da's attention turned to me. "Excuse me?"

"I've come to realise that nothin' good comes from keepin' secrets from the people ye' love most, and I can't deal with it anymore. This case has haunted me since the moment ye' got arrested, and two days ago I had a gun pointed at me, and then a friend of mine got shot, all because of this case."

My da paled. "Jesus, what happened?"

"Arthur Hopkins," I said flatly. "His lunatic of a teenage son is what happened."

"Maxwell?" he questioned.

"Yes. He blamed the man who killed his father, obviously, and he also blamed *you* because ye' tried to ruin the case by messin' with the evidence."

My da covered his mouth with his hands and listened to me as I spoke.

"Since he couldn't get to ye' in 'ere, he went after the killer's children, who happen to live in Tallaght and are close friends of mine."

"Christ in Heaven," Da choked, reaching out and squeezing my hand tightly. "Are ye' okay?"

"Physically I'm fine, but that could have easily been different, Da. The only reason I'm alive was because Max wasn't as interested in hurtin' me as he was in hurtin' someone else. I want the truth about how ye' got involved in all of this," I demanded. "Please, don't keep it from me anymore. I know ye' didn't do this out of your own free will. The past few days have been hell on me, and me friends, and it's all connected to this case."

He glanced at the guard in the room, who as usual was reading a paper and didn't look like he was paying attention to what we were discussing.

"Okay, okay," he relented, scrubbing his face with his hands as he lowered his voice. "Not long after I took on the case, two brutes who worked for John McCarty came into me office at the firm. He'd paid people to get rid of the CCTV footage, but an anonymous Good Samaritan posted it to my office, and McCarty somehow found out and arranged for his men to visit me before I could present it at court. He threatened bodily harm to you if I didn't interfere with the evidence so he could get a lesser sentence or have the case thrown out completely. I knew I had to keep ye' safe, but I also knew I couldn't let McCarty get away with murder, so I ratted on meself so I'd get arrested as well as McCarty."

"Ye' did what ye' did to protect me?"

"Sweetheart" – he leaned forward – "I'd do *anythin'* to protect ye'."

I swallowed. "Is that why ye' never voiced what happened?"

Da nodded. "I knew that John McCarty had connections to the gangland that poisons this country, but I wasn't about to test how powerful those connections were."

"Da," I whispered, squeezing his hand tightly. "All this time, and you're in 'ere, an innocent man."

"Not innocent," he corrected. "I committed the crime."

"Because ye' were *forced* to commit the crime with the threat of harm to another." Ciara scowled. "I could have helped you had you just told me, Joe."

"I couldn't," he stressed. "I couldn't risk the men who paid me a visit payin' one to Ryan if I talked."

"I understand," I said to him. "I do. Ye' were protectin' me."

Da nodded. "I had to."

"Well, ye' don't have to anymore. We're all movin' to the house – Eddi and Andrea I mean. They want out of Tallaght. They'll be staying in Kildangan with me and Ciara . . . and a few others."

"A few others?" Da questioned. "Who?"

"Me boyfriend, his little brother, and me friend who was shot . . . all were targeted because of this case."

Da blinked. "Since when do ye' have a boyfriend?"

"Joe, focus."

Da looked at Ciara before returning his attention to me. "How were they involved?"

"Ash Dunne is me boyfriend, and Sean Dunne is his little brother. They're John McCarty's sons, but use their mother's maiden name," I said, watching my da's eyes widen. "They haven't seen 'im since they were kids, but Max targeted them."

Da shook his head. "They want out of Dublin too?"

I didn't mention anything about Ash and Anto being Disciples, because according to Ash, they weren't anymore. Once we'd found out that Anto was going to live, Ash took me aside and gave me the incredible news. His boss had contacted him, and when Ash had demanded that he and Anto be allowed to leave the Disciples after what they'd just suffered, he was granted the request. I didn't care how or why it happened, all I cared was that Ash and Anto were free from a life they both hated.

Their lives were their own, and they would never belong to anyone else in that horrid way ever again.

"Well," Da began, "the house is big enough until everyone gets on their feet."

I smiled. "I knew ye'd understand."

He nodded, then looked at Ciara. "*You* seem like ye' have more to say to me."

"I do," she answered. "I'm goin' to put a case together to get your conviction reduced."

"Ciara—"

"No," she said. "I'm gettin' you out as soon as possible."

"Love," he began as he reached for her hand, "it's too risky. I've survived one year in here, I'll survive the rest until I'm released."

"No," Ciara repeated. "That's not how this is happenin', Joe."

"Da, ye'll never be able to go back to your job if ye' don't fight this."

"Me credibility was ruined from the moment I was arrested, Ryan," he said with a sad smile. "I've accepted that me days as a barrister are over, but that doesn't mean I can't continue to help people. I'm sure Ciara will need help a time or two on some cases. I may even find somethin' else that I love to do. Who knows?"

I frowned and looked at Ciara, who didn't look happy in the slightest, but when she looked at me, the tension left her body and she seemed to accept my da's decision – because, like him, she wanted to protect me too. I leaned over and rested my head against her shoulder, and my da's eyes widened.

"When did . . . this happen?"

"Recently," I answered. "I realised how amazin' she is, and she realised that while I'm a pain in the arse, she'll love me and want to mother me anyway."

Ciara laughed, but I didn't miss the tears that filled her eyes. I gestured for my da to comfort her, and he did so without hesitation. They hugged and kissed, and when I heard soft cries coming from Ciara, my heart fluttered. She loved my da. They held on to each other like they were the other's world.

After we left the prison, Ciara and I made plans to meet the following day so we could get her moved back into our house. Ash was waiting for me in the car park, leaning against his new truck. Sean was in the back seat, tapping on the screen of his phone. He was still shaken up over the encounter with Max, but he was hanging in there. We all were.

Eddi was in the hospital in Dublin with Anto, and had been from the moment he came out of surgery. She hadn't left his side, and didn't plan on it either.

"How'd it go?"

"Surprisingly well," I said. "We went through everythin' and he admitted to committin' the crime because me life was threatened."

"Ye' don't look happy about it," Ash commented. "What else happened?"

"We didn't get him to agree on appealin' his case because he's worried it could come back to haunt 'im if your da's men take action. None of us can say for sure that it won't happen, so he decided that there'll be no appeal and he'll finish out the remainder of his sentence."

Ash pulled me into his arms and said, "I'll never let anyone hurt ye', Ryan."

I relaxed against him. "I know ye' won't."

He hugged me tightly.

"Any word from Eddi on how Anto is doin' today?"

"She said he was still loopy from the morphine, but he understood that we're no longer Disciples and he's celebratin' by raising his good arm up and down. Eddi swears that he's tryin' his hardest to cop a feel and to chat her up, so he must be okay if he's doin' that."

Laughter bubbled up my throat. "I can't wait till he gets out of hospital and everyone can get out of Dublin once and for all."

Ash brushed my hair out of my face. "We're in your neck of the woods now, babe. Ye'll have to teach me the ways of your people."

"Well, well, well," I mused as we walked hand in hand towards his truck. "Look who's gone country."

"It'll take some time for us Dublin folk to get used to the farmland life. D'ye think I'll manage?"

I looked up at him and smiled. "I think that together, we'll manage anythin'."

Ash leaned down and pressed his lips to mine. "You're the best thing to have ever happened to me, Ryan. I still can't believe ye' want me, knowin' how far from perfect I am."

"You're *my* version of perfect, Ashley Dunne, and I think I knew that from the get-go."

Ash smiled, placed his hands on my cheeks and stroked his thumbs over them.

"We're gonna be a family," I said to him. "Ye' know that, right?"

"I do, and I wouldn't have it any other way, nightmare."

It had taken Ash's charming, cocky self to pull me out of my shell, and one night to put into perspective how quickly a life could be ended. I'd always thought that since I had my da, I had everything I needed, but now I knew the heart-warming fullness of having an entire family of people to love.

I didn't know what the future held for us, but with Ash by my side, I'd look it dead in the eye and welcome it with a smile.

EPILOGUE

ASHLEY

Six and a half years later . . .

"Ye' look like you're about to cry, princess."

I looked at my soon-to-be cousin-in-law, and grinned as she addressed my fiancée, who was indeed about to sob her little heart out. I slid my arms around Ryan's heavily pregnant stomach, leaned down and kissed her temple.

"Leave me missus alone, ye' bully."

Anto, who was next to me, punched me in the shoulder and said, "And *you* leave *my* missus alone, ye' little bitch."

"*Both* of ye' shut up," Ryan sniffled. "Look at how happy me ma and da are!"

My heart warmed when I looked at the newly wedded Mr and Mrs Mahony. They'd become a married couple mere hours before, and getting to know them over the years – and waiting for this day to come right along with them – made me happy. Mr Mahony had been released from prison six months ago, having fully completed his sentence. He didn't receive any time off for good behaviour like we thought he would, but he didn't let it get him down.

Since Mr Mahony left prison, he'd lived life to the fullest. He didn't dwell on no longer having a licence to practise law. Instead, he self-published the first book of a thriller trilogy he wrote in prison that drew the attention of a publishing house a few weeks after its release. The publisher bought the rights to the trilogy and had plans to release the second and third books in due course. The first book, after only being out a couple of months, had recently exploded and made the *New York Times* bestseller list, amongst many others.

My future father-in-law had found an escape with his writing during a very dark time in his life, and he'd turned it into something he loved and was passionate about, just like when he'd practised law. I was delighted for him and Ciara, who'd taken over as the head of Mr Mahony's firm and become a very successful barrister herself.

But they weren't the only people thriving in life.

I looked at my best friend Anto, and his wife of three years, Eddi. Their pairing was just as wild and unexpected as mine and Ryan's, but their love for one another could never be denied. It had taken my friend's near-death to bring them together, but love is what kept them that way.

After we were released from what we thought was a lifelong commitment to the Disciples, we'd left Dublin and never returned. Our lives had changed, but it wasn't as drastic as we'd thought it would be. For the first two years, we all lived in the Mahonys' huge house, then Andrea and Ian, Eddi's father, officially rekindled their relationship and moved into an apartment a town over from Kildangan. Not long after that, Anto proposed to Eddi, and they were married in the local church – surrounded by our tightknit group – and moved into a house in the same town as Andrea and Ian.

Sean remained in the house with Ryan, Ciara and me, until his long-term girlfriend Kerry Andrews moved to town and they got an apartment together. She and Sean, who both recently turned twenty-one, planned to attend the same college.

I had proposed to Ryan three months after meeting her, and we still lived in her childhood home. We planned to buy a home of our own, but we weren't rushing it. Ryan was enjoying every moment of being with her father after years of only fleeting prison visits. Our long-term engagement may have drawn raised eyebrows from strangers, but everyone who loved us knew that Ryan wanted her father to walk her down the aisle and give her away – and I wanted that too.

We'd kept busy over the years, so much so that we didn't even notice we weren't married. We already thought of one another as husband and wife, so to us it didn't matter very much. Ryan received her nursing degree, which she obtained after four years of hard work. She now had one year of work experience under her belt, and would start her first job as a fully qualified registered nurse at the local hospital come the new year, when our baby was nine months old.

There were no words to describe how proud I was of her. Every day, my love and admiration for her grew . . . right along with her ever-expanding belly. I nuzzled my face against hers as my hands slid over the swollen stomach that harboured our first child, a daughter who we'd decided to call Shane, in order to keep with the tradition of calling a girl by a name that was more commonly male.

"I'm goin' to miss ye' when ye' start your new project next week at work," Ryan said as she leaned her head back against my chest, her eyes still on her parents, who were having their first dance as husband and wife in the middle of their back garden, with the sun setting over the horizon.

I had continued to work in construction. Heading into work every day was something I looked forward to. I loved creating new things and helping build structures that would make people stop and stare. The new project Ryan spoke of was a sixty-house private community that my company would be starting on the following week. Dunne Construction was a small company and this was my first big project, and as much as I looked forward to it, I knew it would be time-consuming – and my love knew it too.

"What did I promise ye'?" I asked Ryan, my thumbs stroking her belly.

She sighed. "That ye' would always be on time for dinner."

"That's right," I chuckled. "There'll be long days for a little while, but we'll get through it together. We always do."

"I love ye', big head."

I smiled. "I love ye' too, nightmare."

She hummed. "Your child will be born, and I'll be stuck with Anto tellin' me to push while you're at work, I bloody know it."

I laughed and hugged her tightly.

"I wouldn't miss 'er comin' into the world for anythin'," I assured her. "Ye' know that."

"I won't miss it either," Anto said as he wrapped his arms around Eddi, who was cradling their six-week-old daughter against her chest. "I was the *best* support system for Eddi when she had Charli. I'll be there for ye', Ry, don't worry. We'll laugh that kid right out of ye'."

We all laughed so hard we almost cried.

That had been a constant thing in my life since we left Dublin – laughter . . . and the joy that I shared with the people I loved most. I thought of my mother and smiled. There was a time when thoughts of her brought an ache to my chest, but while I still missed her dearly, I could think and talk of her now with love and fondness, keeping the memory of what a beautiful person she was alive.

Everything had worked out for my little family. After living a life of darkness, and doing things that still gave me the odd nightmare every now and again, I had finally found peace. I didn't have to look over my shoulder, wondering if someone was going to stab me in the back. I could smile at strangers in greeting and not watch them turn away because they feared me. I was a regular man with a regular life, and I loved every second of it.

I had everything I'd ever wanted, and it was all because of a promise I'd made to one man.

Mr Nobody, the Disciples, and every bad thing from Max Hopkins to the man who fathered me, were in my past where they belonged. I'd kept my word to Mr Nobody and never revealed his true identity to anyone, not even to the woman I loved most. It was a piece of information that I would always keep to myself, to ensure my family's safety. I hardly ever thought of him, but his threat always lingered, a silent warning for me to keep my mouth shut. And I would.

For as long as I lived, it would always be my little secret.

ACKNOWLEDGMENTS

Annnnddd another one bites the dust. I never know what to write when I get to this section of writing a book. I always worry my words won't convey how much I appreciate the crew of people it took for *My Little Secret* to happen.

Sending an abundance of love to my family, daughter and friends. From day one of my career, you've shown me nothing but support, and it means the world to me. I love you all to the moon and back.

I want to thank Sammia – and everyone at Montlake Romance – immensely, for taking a chance on *My Little Secret*. Your hard work, and trust in me and my stories, is very much appreciated.

The ultimate high-five to Melody Guy. We've worked together on a few books now, and you're truly a credit to your profession. Developmental edits are the roughest part for me to get through in the publishing process, but when I know I'm going to be working with you, it takes the sting out of it. For your patience when I switch up our schedule, and your reading between the lines so my plot stays fresh, thank you.

A virtual hug to Gemma Wain, for your thorough copyedits and your wonderful insight. Thank you so much.

Thank you to Trevor Horwood for your in-depth proofread, I really appreciate it.

As always, a massive thank you to Mark Gottlieb. You're a fantastic agent, and always have my back. Thank you for all you do for me.

To you, my readers. I hope you enjoyed reading *My Little Secret* as much as I did writing it. I say this all the time, literally, but you all make my world spin.

ABOUT THE AUTHOR

L.A. Casey is a *New York Times* and *USA Today* bestselling author who juggles her time between her mini-me and writing. She was born, raised and currently resides in Dublin, Ireland. She enjoys chatting with her readers, who love her humour and Irish accent as much as her books. You can visit her website at www.lacaseyauthor.com, find her on Facebook at www.facebook.com/LACaseyAuthor and on Twitter at @authorlacasey.